英語 *Make Me High* 系列

英文作文

這樣寫，

就 OK!

張淑娭、應惠蕙　編著
車昀庭　審定

12個英文作文必備的寫作技巧

三民書局

國家圖書館出版品預行編目資料

英文作文這樣寫，就OK！／張淑娸,應惠蕙編著；車
昀庭審定.－－初版四刷.－－臺北市：三民，2022
　　面；　　公分.－－(英語Make Me High系列)

ISBN 978-957-14-6478-7　（平裝）
1. 英語 2. 作文 3. 寫作法

805.17　　　　　　　　　　　　　　107015695

英 Make Me High 系列
語

英文作文這樣寫，就 OK！

編 著 者	張淑娸　應惠蕙
審 定 者	車昀庭
發 行 人	劉振強
出 版 者	三民書局股份有限公司
地　　址	臺北市復興北路 386 號 (復北門市)
	臺北市重慶南路一段 61 號 (重南門市)
電　　話	(02)25006600
網　　址	三民網路書店 https://www.sanmin.com.tw
出版日期	初版一刷 2019 年 1 月
	初版四刷 2022 年 4 月
書籍編號	S800840
I S B N	978-957-14-6478-7

序

英語 Make Me High 系列的理想在於超越，在於創新。

這是時代的精神，也是我們出版的動力；

這是教育的目的，也是我們進步的執著。

針對英語的全球化與未來的升學趨勢，

我們設計了一系列適合普高、技高學生的英語學習書籍。

面對英語，不會徬徨不再迷惘，學習的心徹底沸騰，

心情好 High ！

實戰模擬，掌握先機知己知彼，百戰不殆決勝未來，

分數更 High ！

選擇優質的英語學習書籍，才能激發學習的強烈動機；

興趣盎然便不會畏懼艱難，自信心要自己大聲說出來。

本書如良師指引循循善誘，如益友相互鼓勵攜手成長。

展書輕閱，你將發現……

學習英語原來也可以這麼 High ！

給讀者的話

張淑媖

　　「寫」是語言學習的重要環節之一，不論寫作的目的是傳達訊息、解釋想法或溝通意見等。要達到目的，句子和內容是關鍵，因為句子必須文法正確且文意通順，而內容必須具說服力。本書從字彙 → 句子 → 段落 → 文章，逐步介紹每個寫作環節，讓讀者學習並培養寫作的興趣。

　　本書分為兩個部分，第一部分是修辭與寫作要素。不同於一般寫作書介紹許多文法規則，本書從中英文句子基本結構的差異開始，進入寫作的前置作業。引導讀者進行腦力激盪，把字彙組織成句子，再來增加句子的長度和句數，進而使句子的文意連貫，寫成一個段落。

　　第二部分為實用寫作文體。說明各種文體的寫作原則和技巧，提供範例(文)，引導思考、分析文章的組織架構，並提供相關的寫作練習。從簡單到複雜，容易到困難，逐步踏實地學習，讓讀者增進自己的寫作能力，學會從段落寫成一篇有條理的文章。

　　一本「對」的書可以讓學習事半功倍，本書對英文學習有整體提升之效，讀者在學會寫作外，可以熟悉每種英文文體的結構，進而有助於閱讀，讓讀和寫相輔相成。

　　本書適用於準備學測等大考的同學以及對英文寫作有興趣的人士。學無止境，讓我們一起努力，給自己一個 OK，一個讚！

應惠蕙

　　作者任教二十餘年來，有感於有極大比例的學生在寫英文作文時，腦中一片空白，不知從何下筆。更有許多老師抱怨學生的作文毫無章法，言之無物。因此，一直希望能寫一本既適用於課堂教學、同時又能提升寫作能力的英文寫作書。抱持著這個目標和信念，著手這本書的編寫。

　　本書從基本的寫作概念開始，教導讀者如何將句子加長，讓用字更精確，內容更豐富。接下來才教常見的英文文體：記敘文、描寫文、說明文以及議論文。另外，書中還介紹大考作文題型：書信寫作、看圖寫作和圖表寫作，讓讀者可以完整學習到各種類型的文體。

From the Teachers

在練習寫作前，每個章節先按部就班介紹該文體的寫作原則，透過腦力激盪來蒐集資料和組織架構，寫出大綱中的主題句、支持句與結論句，讓讀者學會如何寫出完整的段落和文章。

本書還有兩大特色：一、提供各文體常用的字句和轉折詞。二、每個寫作要點皆提供詳盡解說，讓讀者對英文寫作不再感到恐懼。

本書協助讀者學習各種英文文體的寫作，因此適用於準備學測、全民英檢、雅思等英文檢定。筆者深切希望本書能對讀者有所助益，也期盼各位前輩後進不吝指教。

車昀庭

英文老師最常在看學生的文章時說出：「這一句是中文！」這是因為學生總以中文的思考模式和句構來寫英文作文，所以寫出來的英文句子或文章，無論在架構、邏輯、甚至句子本身其實都是中文。想要擺脫寫出中式英文的困擾，這本英文寫作書就很實用。

這本書的第一部分就是從中文和英文句子本身的差異開始談起。從舉例到練習判斷，再到自己練習書寫，作者一步步教讀者如何從中文思考轉為英文思考，單元的發展則從句子結構的差異延伸到句子的豐富性、常見的錯誤以及如何透過簡單的腦力激盪，找出文章可以發揮的細節和主題。

學會這些扎實的基本功後，這本書的第二部份就完整介紹英文寫作常見的各種文體。同樣的，作者以帶領的方式從文體寫作原則、範例、剖析到引導寫作，一步步讓讀者掌握各種英文文體的寫作重點。

我喜歡這本書，不只是因為寫書的兩位老師們都有超過好幾十年的教學經驗，更因為這本書是從根本上探討讀者在寫英文文章時的困擾，並且提供實用的寫作教學。對於想學好英文寫作的人來說，只要跟著每一個單元確實地學習和練習，一定能夠看到十分正面的效果！

Contents

PART I

修辭與寫作要素

(Elements of Writing)

Unit 1　中英文句子基本結構的差異 (Sentence Structures)

1-1 比較中英文句子基本結構的差異

不論中文或英文的寫作，句子都是文章的基本單位。若能了解中英文句子結構的不同，就能避免許多寫作上的錯誤。以下以 106 年學測和指考翻譯題為例，從中英文對照比較就可以看出這兩種語言在句子基本結構上的不同。

(A) 玉山在冬天常覆蓋厚厚的積雪，使整個山頂閃耀如玉。

(B) 征服玉山一直是國內外登山者最困難的挑戰之一。(106 年學測)

例 Jade Mountain is often covered with thick snow in winter, which makes the entire mountain top sparkle like jade.

例 Conquering Jade Mountain has always been one of the most difficult challenges for both native and foreign mountain climbers.

(C) 世界大學運動會是一項國際體育與文化盛事，每兩年一次由不同城市舉辦。

(D) 在比賽中，來自全球大學的學生運動員建立友誼，並學習運動家精神的真諦。(106 年指考)

例 The Universiade is a great international sports and cultural event, (which is) held by different cities every two years.

例 In the games, student athletes from universities around the world form friendships and learn the true spirit of sportsmanship.

❶ 中文是「主題＋敘述的言談來表達結構」；英文是「主詞＋敘述，語法正確和文意完整的結構」

1. 中文句子提出要談的主題後，接著針對主題提出敘述。敘述包含事實、解釋、意見、說明、評論等，能夠表達出完整思想的就是對的句子，如 (A) 句主題談的是玉山，接著敘述玉山冬天的景色「常覆蓋厚厚的積雪，使整

個山頂閃耀如玉」；(B) 句主題談的是征服玉山，接著說明這「一直是國內外登山者最困難的挑戰之一」。

(C) 句主題是世界大學運動會，接著提出事實，說明它「是一項國際體育與文化盛事」、「每兩年一次」、「由不同城市舉辦」。(D) 句主題是學生運動員，接著提出事實和看法「建立友誼，並學習運動家精神的真諦」。

2. 跟中文句子在結構上不同的是，英文句子敘述的主要部分是動詞，動詞和主詞的關係是密切的，主詞必須是動詞的執行者或是存在的關係。如 (A) 句使整個山頂閃耀如玉的主詞是「玉山在冬天常覆蓋厚厚的積雪」，所以用非限制關係代名詞 which 來代替。如果依字面翻成英文："Jade Mountain is often covered with thick snow in winter makes the whole mountain top sparkle like jade."，就是錯的句子。

英文句子除了必須表達完整的意思外，也必須合乎語法，如主詞和受詞必須是名詞性質——名詞、不定詞 (to V)、動名詞 (V-ing)、名詞片語或名詞子句等。所以在 (B) 句主詞是「征服玉山」，就必須把動詞 (conquer) 改成動名詞 (conquering Jade Mountain) 才能當主詞。

選出正確的句子 (每題多選)。

_____ 1. 學英文必須天天練習。

(A) Studying English must practice every day.

(B) To study English, we must practice every day.

(C) Studying English requires everyday practice.

(D) English studying requires everyday practice.

(E) If we study English, we must practice every day.

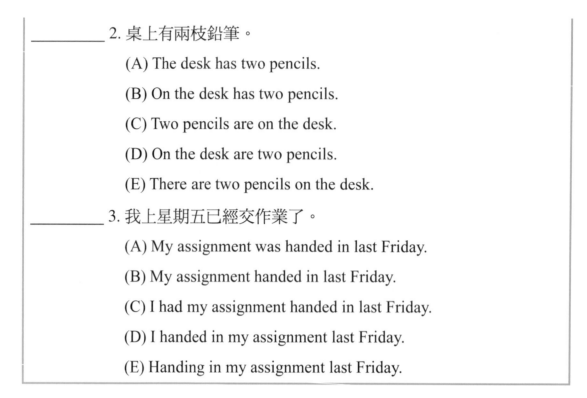

_____ 2. 桌上有兩枝鉛筆。

(A) The desk has two pencils.

(B) On the desk has two pencils.

(C) Two pencils are on the desk.

(D) On the desk are two pencils.

(E) There are two pencils on the desk.

_____ 3. 我上星期五已經交作業了。

(A) My assignment was handed in last Friday.

(B) My assignment handed in last Friday.

(C) I had my assignment handed in last Friday.

(D) I handed in my assignment last Friday.

(E) Handing in my assignment last Friday.

❷ 如何寫出句子

由於中英文句子結構的不同，從中文句子轉換成英文句子時，應該先確定主詞和動詞。

1. **確定主詞**：從上面的練習寫寫看 A 可以看出中英文句子結構的轉換，有時候中文句子的主詞是隱藏的，真正的主詞必須從文意和動詞的關係去推論、確定，然後在英文句子中寫出或補上真正的主詞。

例 You should be careful when doing everything. 做任何事情都要小心。

　(動詞「要小心」的主詞應該是「人」，所以補上主詞「you」。)

2. **確定動詞和主動 (active voice) / 被動 (passive voice) 語態和時態 (tense)**：中文句子的動詞並無時態之分，不管是在過去、現在或未來發生，都是用時間副詞來表達，動詞形式是不變的，如：「我昨晚去看電影。」和「我明天要去看電影。」，動詞「看」的形式是不變的，而是從時間副詞「昨晚」和「明天」來表示動詞發生的時間點。

注意，英文句子的動詞則必須根據發生的時間點，而有過去式、現在式和未來式之分，這是翻譯寫作時必須小心的細節。

例 I **watched** a movie last night.　我昨晚看電影。

例 I **am watching** a movie now.　我現在正在看電影。

例 I **will watch** a movie tonight.　我今晚要去看電影。

另外，中文句子的動詞除了沒有時態的區別外，主動／被動也不會在動詞上有所變化，如：「我的作業交了」、「花園的花已經澆水了」。中文的被動常用在負面的訊息，如：被處罰了、被騙等。

Tip
1. 在寫英文句子的時候，應該先確定主詞為何，以及該主詞所相對應的動詞與時態，就能寫出正確的英文句子。
2. 中文是以主題來思考，而英文則以主詞來思考。

練習寫寫看 B

I 寫出主詞並翻譯句子。

1. 我們暑假要去澳洲旅遊。

主詞：＿＿＿

＿＿＿＿＿＿＿＿＿

2. 你應該早一點睡。

主詞：＿＿＿

＿＿＿＿＿＿＿＿＿

3. 雨已經下一個星期了。

主詞：＿＿＿

＿＿＿＿＿＿＿＿＿

4. 搭火車從臺北到桃園大約半小時。

主詞：＿＿＿

＿＿＿＿＿＿＿＿＿＿＿＿＿＿＿＿＿＿＿＿＿＿＿＿＿＿

5. 很多國家講英文。

主詞：＿＿＿

＿＿＿＿＿＿＿＿＿＿＿＿＿＿＿＿＿＿＿＿＿＿＿＿＿＿

Ⅱ 填寫正確的動詞形式。

1. 這支手錶是我爸爸在十年前給我的。現在看起來還很新。

This watch ＿＿＿＿＿ to me by my father ten years ago. It still ＿＿＿＿＿

new now.

2. Amy 明天早上會去圖書館。

Amy ＿＿＿＿＿ to the library tomorrow morning.

3. Peter 的皮夾被偷了，他感到很傷心。

Peter's wallet ＿＿＿＿＿, and he ＿＿＿＿＿.

4. 我從出生就一直住在新竹。

I ＿＿＿＿＿ in Hsinchu since I ＿＿＿＿＿.

❸ 翻譯中文句子的「的」

在中文句子中，「的」使用得非常頻繁，如果能了解「的」的詮釋方法，對
於表達和英譯十分有幫助。中文的「的」幾乎都是名詞前修飾語，置於名詞
前，用來修飾、說明、限制名詞，如：美麗的風景、可以坐的椅子、在樹上
唱歌的鳥、我的書等。以下說明如何用英文譯出中文的「的」：

1. 所有格／形容詞＋名詞：英文的「的」視為所有格或形容詞(包括當形
   容詞的現在分詞或過去分詞)時，置於名詞前，如：my book (我的書)、
   beautiful scenery (美麗的風景)、trembling hands (顫抖的手)、fallen leaves (掉
   落的樹葉)。

> **Tip**
> 當兩個 (以上) 的單字形容詞來修飾同一個名詞時，前後順序如下：
> 冠詞 / 限詞 / 量詞 + 評價 / 觀點 / 大小 / 長度 / 形狀 / 顏色 / 材質 + 名詞 / 動名詞 / 分詞 (當形容詞) + 名詞
>
> 例 some tall and strong working men　一些又高又壯的工人們
>
> 例 the child's charming small pink face　這個孩子的迷人粉紅小臉

2. 名詞 + **of** + 名詞：前面的名詞是後接名詞的一部分或屬性，如：the price of vegetable (蔬菜的價格)、the cover of the book (書的封面)、the amounts of the material (材料的數量)。

3. 名詞 + **with** ~：with 表示有或附帶條件，如：a house with a front yard (有前院的房子)、a girl with long hair (一位長髮的女孩)。

4. 名詞 + 介系詞片語：介系詞片語可以用來表示「位置、地點」，如：the lamp on the desk (桌上的檯燈)、the fish in the river (河裡的魚)、tourists from Japan (來自日本的觀光客)。

5. 名詞 + 不定詞片語 **(to V)**：不定詞片語用來表示「可以…的，應…的」，如：someone to talk to (可以說話的人)、rules to follow (應該遵守的規則)。

6. 名詞 + 關係子句：關係子句用來說明名詞的特質或範圍，如：birds which are singing on the top of the tree (樹上唱歌的鳥)、an employee who was fired from his job (一位工作被解雇的員工)。

7. 名詞 + 分詞片語：子句能夠簡化成現在分詞片語或過去分詞片語，如：birds (which are) singing on the top of the tree (樹上唱歌的鳥)、an employee (who was) fired from his job (一位工作被解雇的員工)。

練習寫寫看 C

將下列中文翻譯成英文。

1. 好吃的食物　　　_____

2. 著名的旅遊景點　_____

3. 有車庫的房子　　_____

4. 一個留長鬍鬚的老人　_____

5. 穿著牛仔褲的女孩　_____

6. 說英文的能力　　_____

7. 一個無趣的人　　_____

8. 一位美麗動人的女孩　_____

1-2 片段的句子

完整英文句子的基本元素必須有主詞、動詞、補語或受詞等，且合乎語法、句意表達完整。當缺乏某些元素時，就成了片段的句子 (a fragment)，而非完整句子。片段的句子出現在口語 (conversation) 中，常常會被接受，但在寫作中，片段的句子即使表達出完整思想，也是錯誤的句子。修正方式是必須根據文意補充或修正句子缺乏的元素來使句子合乎語法並句意完整。

常見的片段句子及修正方法

❶ 名詞片段

只有名詞 (片語) 或名詞子句、句子不合語法或文意不完整。修正方法如下：

Tip

名詞 (片語) 和例子：

1. 限定詞 + 名詞：a girl, an apple, the man
2. 複數名詞：books, pens
3. 不可數名詞：money, milk
4. 形容詞 (修飾語) + 複數名詞：old people
5. 限定詞 + 形容詞 + 名詞：the charming lady, some small cakes
6. 限定詞 + 名詞 (修飾語) + 名詞：my picture books, a history teacher

1. 已經有名詞 (片語)，所以加上動詞或動詞敘述，使文意完整。

例 All the students. (✕)

→ All the students **are in the classroom**. (○)　所有學生都在教室裡。

(將名詞片語加上 are in the classroom 成為完整句子。)

2. 將名詞子句改為句子。

例 What the girl said. (✕)

→ What the girl said **was very impolite**. (○)　這個女生所說的話非常失禮。

(將名詞子句加上 was very impolite 成為完整句子。)

3. 加上主要子句成為複雜句 (complex sentence)。

例 The dish that is served as the last course of a meal. (✕)

→ The dish is served as the last course of a meal. (○)

這道菜是最後一道上桌。(去掉 that 成為完整句子。)

→ The dish that is served as the last course of a meal **is always fruit or dessert**. (○)

最後一道上桌的菜色總是水果或點心。(加上主要子句。)

❷ 動詞片段

出現沒有主詞的動詞、句子不合語法或文意不完整。以下說明修正的方法：

例 John went to a movie left his homework undone. (✕)

1. 將上述的錯誤例句加上對等連接詞來連接動詞。

例 John went to a movie **and** left his homework undone. (○)

John 去看電影，而且沒寫完作業。(加上對等連接詞 and。)

2. 將上述的錯誤例句加上主詞，成為兩個獨立句子。

例 John went to a movie. **He** left his homework undone. (○)

John 去看電影。他沒寫完作業。(加上主詞 he。)

3. 將上述的錯誤例句加上主詞和對等連接詞成為複合句 (compound sentence)。

例 John went to a movie, **and he** left his homework undone. (○)

John 去看電影，而且他沒寫完作業。(加上主詞 he 和對等連接詞 and。)

4. 將上述的錯誤例句改成分詞構句。

例 John went to a movie, **leaving** his homework undone. (○)

John 去看電影，沒寫完作業。(改為分詞構句。)

根據以上的修正方法，來修正只有動詞片段的例句。

例 Do nothing all day. (×)

→ **Hank** does nothing all day. (○)　　Hank 整天無所事事。(加上主詞。)

→ **Doing** nothing all day **is a waste of time**. (○)

整天無所事事是浪費時間。

(動詞改成動名詞後成為主詞，再加上動詞和補語使文意完整。)

❸ 從屬子句片段

句子缺乏主要子句、不合語法或文意不完整。以下說明修正的方法：

例 When polar bears are starving due to a lack of food. (×)

1. 將上述的錯誤例句刪掉從屬連接詞成為獨立句子。

例 Polar bears are starving due to a lack of food. (○)

北極熊因為缺乏食物而捱餓。(去掉連接詞 when 使句子完整。)

2. 將上述的錯誤例句加上主要子句成為複雜句 (complex sentence)。

例 When polar bears are starving due to a lack of food, **that means the climate all over the world is changing**. (○)

當北極熊因為缺乏食物而捱餓時，這表示全球的氣候正在改變。

(加上主要子句使句意完整。)

❹ 不定詞或分詞片語片段

一般說來，不定詞或分詞片語僅作副詞使用，句子不合語法且文意也不完整。

修正方法如下：

1. 加上主詞使其成為完整句子。

例 Having worked hard all her life. (×)

→ **Maggie** has worked hard all her life. (○)

Maggie 一生都很認真工作。(加上主詞。)

2. 加上主要子句使其成為完整句子。

例 In order to win the competition. (✕)

→ In order to win the competition, **Johnson practiced hard**. (○)

為了贏得比賽，Johnson 認真練習。(加上主要子句使句意完整。)

例 Having worked hard all her life. (✕)

→ Having worked hard all her life, **Maggie earns respect at work**. (○)

一生都很認真工作，Maggie 在職場上得到尊重。

(加上主要子句使句意完整。)

Tip

片段句子的錯誤修正方法不只一種，需要根據句子結構的概念以及要表達的意思，多加練習。

NOTE

11

I 以下句子如果是完整句子寫 C (a complete sentence)、片段句子寫 F (a fragment)，並將片段句子修正，使成為文意相同的完整句子。

_____ 1. Yuanbao which was a type of money.

_____

_____ 2. Yesterday, I ran into Miss Lee, my English teacher in junior high.

_____

_____ 3. If you have an opportunity to visit Tainan to taste a variety of local foods.

_____

_____ 4. Air is highly polluted especially in the southern part of Taiwan.

_____

_____ 5. Because a cellphone is so popular has become something necessary in our lives.

_____

II 下列每個段落都有一個片段句子，請指出並加以修正。

_____ 1. (A) "A white elephant" is used to describe something that is useless and a waste of money. (B) If you own a car that does not run and cannot be fixed.

_____

_____ 2. (A) Getting into the habit of taking notes. (B) Whether you are reading, studying, or listening to a speech, it is helpful to write down the information you may want to look up later. (C) In the process of writing down what is mentioned, you are actually organizing information at the same time.

_____

_____ 3. (A) As an old saying goes, "Necessity is the mother of invention." (B) Many times, people come up with ideas to meet their own needs. (C) Later, the solutions to their problems may become great inventions. (D) Change our way of life.

_____

_____ 4. (A) There are several reasons I need to find a roommate. (B) She can share the rent. (C) Having someone to talk to. (D) Most importantly, the room would be like "home" instead of a place to live.

_____

_____ 5. (A) There is a sharp contrast between the poor and the rich. (B) The poor may have to worry about their next meal the rich may spend tens of thousands on a handbag.

_____

1-3 連寫句和逗號誤用

比較下面兩個句子：

(A) 在中文裡，豬傳統上被視為笨拙的動物，狗代表忠心，狼意味著暴力和殘忍，老虎則是權威的象徵。(正確的中文句。)

(B) In the Chinese language, pigs are traditionally seen as clumsy animals, dogs represent loyalty, wolves indicate violence as well as cruelty, tigers are a

symbol of authority. (是錯誤英文連寫句，因為逗號誤用。)

(A) 句中文是一連串句子連接在一起，只用了逗號，沒有連接詞，以中文邏輯而言是對的句子。(B) 句英文沒有連接詞，只用逗號把多個獨立句子串在一起，這些句子會被稱為連寫句 (run-on sentences)，在英文句子結構中是錯誤的。逗號被當作連接詞是逗號誤用 (comma splices)，因為逗號雖然可以斷句，使文意清楚，但不能取代連接詞。如 (B) 句在最後兩句之間加上連接詞 (and)：“In the Chinese language, pigs are traditionally seen as clumsy animals, dogs represent loyalty, wolves indicate violence as well as cruelty, **and** tigers are a symbol of authority.”，就是語法結構正確的英文句子。

根據 1–1 的介紹，中文的句子結構為「主題 + 敘述」，敘述部分可能針對同一主題提出一連串的描述，所以連寫句可能頻繁出現。而英文的句子結構為「主詞 + 敘述」，並且要求語法正確和文意完整，所以連寫句必須改為語法正確的句子。

練習寫寫看 E

下面句子是連寫句寫上 R (a run-on sentence)，正確句子寫上 C。

_____ 1. No matter how successful you are, you must be humble.

_____ 2. Peter failed again, he felt discouraged.

_____ 3. Everybody was tired out, no one made complaints.

_____ 4. My mother felt much better, she said she would leave the hospital as soon as possible.

_____ 5. Helen is busy all day. She has to go to work, picks up her daughter after school, and does all the housework.

其他改正連寫句的方法

有許多方法可以改正連寫句，譬如加上連接詞使單句成為複雜句 (complex sentence) 或複合句 (compound sentence)，或是改變句子的基本結構 (如改成分詞結構等)。以下討論內容以比較簡單、不改變句子的基本結構為主。

❶ 用對等連接詞，如 and、but、or、nor、so 等，連接句子使文意更清楚

例 Because of global warming, a large amount of Arctic ice is melting away, the seal population is falling sharply. (✕)

→ Because of global warming, a large amount of Arctic ice is melting away, **and** the seal population is falling sharply. (○)

由於全球暖化，大量的北極圈冰層正在融化，

而且海豹的數量正急遽減少。

例 You had better read the road map, you may get lost. (✕)

→ You had better read the road map, **or** you may get lost. (○)

你最好看一下地圖，不然你可能會迷路。

> **Tip**
>
> 對等連接詞 nor 表示「也不」，前面應該有一個否定句子。若 nor 置於句首，句子必須倒裝。
>
> 例 Tim doesn't have a Ph.D., he hasn't been abroad.
>
> → Tim doesn't have a Ph.D., nor has he been abroad.
>
> Tim 沒有博士學位，也沒有出過國。

❷ 用句點 (.) 將句子分成兩個、甚至多個完整句子

例 John Harrison has an enviable job in most people's opinion, he is the official taster for Dreyer's Grand Ice Cream. (✕)

→ John Harrison has an enviable job in most people's opinion. **He** is the official taster for Dreyer's Grand Ice Cream. (○)

John Harrison 從事一份令大部分的人都稱羨的工作，他擔任醉爾斯冰淇淋公司的官方試味員。

❸ 用分號連接前後文意密切的句子，尤其是一連串的敘述、說明或比較

例 Presidents' Day is on Monday, Easter is on Sunday, Thanksgiving is on Thursday. (✕)

→ Presidents' Day is on Monday; Easter is on Sunday; Thanksgiving is on Thursday. (○)

總統日在星期一，復活節在星期天，感恩節在星期四。

(中文可以一直用逗號來連接句子。)

❹ 用從屬連接詞連接，使句子成為複雜句 (主要子句 + 從屬子句)

常用的從屬連接詞有：when、while (當；然而)、before、after、as、until、since (自從；因為)、because、unless (除非)、even if/though (即使)、 as long as (只要)、if (如果)、whereas (然而)、in order that (為了) 等。

例 Frank insisted on buying the ring for his girlfriend, its price was much higher than he had expected. (✕)

→ **Even though** the price of the ring was much higher than Frank had expected, he insisted on buying it for his girlfriend. (○)

即使這只戒指的價格遠比 Frank 預期高出許多，他還是堅持買給他的女朋友。

例 I won't agree with you, you prove that your idea will work. (✕)

→ I won't agree with you **unless** you prove that your idea will work. (○)

我不會同意你，除非你能證明你的想法行得通。

例 Knowledge can be acquired from books, skills must be learned through practice. (✕)

→ Knowledge can be acquired from books, **whereas** skills must be learned through practice. (○)　知識能從書本上汲取，然而技能必須從練習而來。

❺ 用轉折詞將連寫句分成獨立的句子

例 Allen failed, he didn't feel frustrated, he worked even harder. (✕)

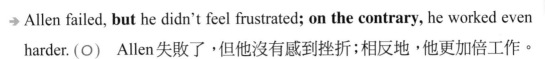

→ Allen failed, **but** he didn't feel frustrated**; on the contrary,** he worked even harder. (O)　　Allen 失敗了，但他沒有感到挫折；相反地，他更加倍工作。

例 Success belongs to those who work hard, fooling around will get a person nowhere. (X)

→ Success belongs to those who work hard**; in other words,** fooling around will get a person nowhere. (O)

成功是屬於那些努力工作的人，換句話說，遊手好閒會讓人一事無成。

Tip
在句子結構中，轉折詞很重要，有關轉折詞的用法及標點符號的使用，請見 Unit 4。

練習寫寫看 F

I 用從屬連接詞改正下列連寫句。

1. There is anything you don't understand, just let me know and I'll help you.

　→ _____

2. You keep working hard, you are sure to get somewhere.

　→ _____

3. Don't panic, you get a flat tire on the freeway.

　→ _____

4. Leo won't forgive you, you make a sincere apology.

　→ _____

5. Mary insisted on marrying Jack, her parents strongly objected.

　→ _____

6. The fool love wealth, the wise treasure truth.

　→ _____

II 用轉折詞改正下列連寫句。

1. It had been raining heavily for days, many low-lying areas were flooded.

   → _____

2. A man can stay alive for more than a week without food, a man without water can hardly live for more than three days.

   → _____

3. Robert works as a volunteer in the hospital. He donates money to the orphanage regularly.

   → _____

4. Jerry had a sore throat, he couldn't speak at the meeting.

   → _____

III 改正下列連寫句。

1. The press has a strong influence it can bring about significant changes to the lives of ordinary people.

   → _____

   _____

2. Turn to the last page, you will find the key to the questions.

   → _____

   _____

3. Small islands could soon be underwater, the residents of major cities are likely to have nowhere to live by the end of the 21st century.

   → _____

   _____

4. The ice-cream taster uses a gold spoon, regular spoons leave an aftertaste that can dull the taste buds.

→ _____

_____

5. William works two part-time jobs, he could save enough money to study abroad.

→ _____

_____

1-4 標點符號

標點符號 (punctuation) 的作用是將句子劃分成有意義的單位，使句子意思更加清楚。常用的英文標點符號和用法列舉於下：

❶ 句點 /period (.)

用於直述句 (declarative sentence) 和祈使句 (imperative sentence) 的句尾。

例 Stories about individual people tend to attract far more public attention than political events do.

關於個人的報導往往比政治事件更能吸引大眾的注意。

例 Wish everyone be healthy and happy.　希望每個人健康快樂。

❷ 問號 /question mark (？)

用於疑問句 (interrogative sentence) 或附加問句 (tag question) 的句尾。

例 What makes you change your mind?

是什麼讓你改變心意？

例 Bill has been abroad for years, hasn't he?

Bill 長年旅居國外，不是嗎？

❸ 驚嘆號 /exclamation mark (!)

用來強調語氣或是表達強烈的情感。

例 Amber was excited to have the chance to play the video game and said happily, "Sounds great!" 有機會玩新的電玩，Amber 開心地說：「聽起來很棒！」

例 Sue cried out, "Ouch! You are stepping on my toe." Sue 叫出聲來：「唉喲！你踩到我的腳了。」

❹ 逗號 /comma (,)

逗號是使用最頻繁的標點符號，有下列幾種用法：

1. 用來分隔三個 (以上) 相同結構的單字、片語或子句。

例 Professor Chen can speak French, German, English, and Japanese. 陳博士會說法文、德文、英文和日文。

例 When you read, you have to actively use your memory to recognize words and arrange them into phrases, then sentences, and then ideas.

閱讀時，你必須活用記憶來辨認單字、組成詞組和句子，並形成概念。

2. 在對等連接詞 (如：and、or、but、yet、so、nor 等) 前加上逗號，分隔獨立句子。後方子句若非完整的子句或內容很短，可以省略逗號。

例 Susan is a singer, and her sister is a dancer. Susan 是位歌手，而她妹妹是個舞者。(可省略 singer 後面的逗號。)

例 Freedom of the press is rightly protected in most democratic societies, but it is just this protection that sometimes allows this freedom to be made bad use of.

媒體自由在大部分的民主社會裡是獲得充分保障的，但正是這份保障，使得這自由有時受到不當的運用。

3. 加在句首的轉折詞、副詞、副詞片語、分詞片語或副詞子句後。

例 It began to rain heavily. Therefore, we canceled the picnic. 開始下起大雨。因此，我們取消野餐。

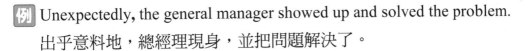

例 Unexpectedly, the general manager showed up and solved the problem.

出乎意料地，總經理現身，並把問題解決了。

例 By working hard, I had my job done in a few days.

透過認真工作，我在幾天內完成工作。

例 Having finished his homework, Lucas was allowed to watch TV.

在寫完作業後，Lucas 就能看電視了。

例 Though readers enjoy reading about the lives of other people, few of them would like themselves to be the topic of such reports.

雖然讀者們喜歡一窺別人的生活，但很少人願意自己成為報導的題材。

4. 在插入的同位語前後都加上逗號，使文意更明確。

例 Tommy, the spoiled child, always has his own way.

Tommy——被寵壞的孩子，總是為所欲為。

5. 在非限定關係子句前需加上逗號。

例 It was raining hard, which prevented us from going on a picnic.

當時正在下大雨，這讓我們無法去野餐。

❺ 分號 /semicolon（；）

除了常用在有轉折詞連接的句子外，分號也可以取代對等連接詞來連接獨立句子。

例 Friendship can't be bought; love can't be bought, either.

金錢買不到友誼，也買不到愛情。

> **Tip**
>
> 在英文句子中，轉折詞的標點符號 (逗號、分號) 會因為句子結構的不同，而有不一樣的表達方式，在 Unit 4 會有詳細說明。

❻ 冒號 /colon（：）

1. 用來介紹一連串的字、詞、子句、舉例、解釋或列舉細節。

例 The rich woman leads a life of luxury: She owns many name-brand bags and

drives a sports car.

這位有錢的女人過著奢華的生活，她有許多名牌包和開跑車。

例 The rules to abide by in our company are as follows: punctuality, loyalty, and hard work.　我們公司需要遵守的規定如下：準時、忠誠和認真工作。

2. 用來引導問題或介紹引言。

例 Jeremy was often asked the question: "What made you hold on to your dream of becoming a basketball player?"

Jeremy 常被問到這個問題：「是什麼讓你堅持成為籃球員的夢想？」

例 John Kennedy delivered his inauguration address in 1961. The speech contained the immortal couplet: "Ask not what your country does for you; ask what you do for your country."　約翰‧甘迺迪在 1961 年發表就職演說。這次演說有不朽的名言：「不要問你的國家能為你做些什麼，而要問你能為你的國家做些什麼。」

3. 連接兩個獨立句子，後面的句子用來解釋或延伸前面句子的意思。

例 Greg finally had his dream come true: He was appointed CEO of the company.　Greg 終於夢想成真：他被任命為公司的總裁。

4. 用於商業書信的稱呼語 (salutation) 後。在私人信函中，通常是用逗號。

例 Dear Ms. Wang: 親愛的王女士：

❼ 破折號 /dash (—)

破折號的前後都不留空格，必須緊接字詞。有以下幾種用法：

1. 用來說明特別的例子或細節。

例 I don't remember when it started annoying me—her hands touching my face that way.　我不記得從何時開始，我對她的手那樣觸摸我的臉感到惱怒。

2. 更進一步解釋，等同於前後加上逗號的用法。

例 Mom had forgiven—and forgotten—long before.
(Mom had forgiven, and forgotten, long before.)

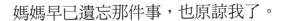

媽媽早已遺忘那件事，也原諒我了。

❽ 引號 /quotation marks (" ")

1. 用在介紹標題、頭銜、名稱、節目、論文、歌名、計畫等。此用法現在也常以斜體字代替。注意，標點必須放在 " 之前。

例 The "Mona Lisa" is one of the most famous paintings in the world.

(The *Mona Lisa* is one of the most famous paintings in the world.)

《蒙娜麗莎》是世界名畫之一。

2. 用在直接引言 (需配合逗號和句號)。

例 "I'll never forget the experience," said Alice.

「我不會忘記這次的經驗。」Alice 說。(引言放在句首。)

例 One night, I finally roared, "Don't do that anymore—your hands are too rough!" 有一晚，我終於大聲怒吼：「別再那樣摸我！妳的手太粗了！」

(引言放在後面。)

例 "It's a wonderful place," Mark said, "and I'm sure to come back."

「這地方真棒，」Mark 說：「我一定會再回來。」(引言被拆成前後。)

3. 用來說明字或片語等的額外含意，引申意義或表示強調。

例 If you are able to put up with the "unique" smell of stinky tofu, you will find it very delicious.

如果你能夠忍受臭豆腐的「獨特」味道，你會發現它很美味。

(表示不是你所想的一般美味的味道。)

> **Tip**
>
> 單引號 (' ') 英文說法為 single quotation marks，用於引句中的引句。
>
> 例 Lisa said, "The proverb says, 'there's no smoke without fire.'"
>   Lisa 說：「俗話說：『無風不起浪。』」

❾ 省略符號 /ellipsis (. . .)

1. 只有 3 個小點，用來表示有所省略。

例 Steve Jobs once said, "Your time is limited, so don't waste it living someone else's life . . . Don't let the noise of others' opinions drown out your own inner voice." 史蒂夫‧賈伯斯曾說：「你們的時間有限，所以不要浪費時間活在別人的人生裡…不要讓旁人七嘴八舌的雜音淹沒了你內在的聲音。」

2. 在對話中，表示中斷或遲疑。

例 Emily： Matt, why don't we buy Mom a new cellphone for Mother's Day?

Matt： Mmm . . . That sounds good.

Emily： Matt，我們何不買一支新手機送媽媽當作母親節禮物？

Matt： 嗯嗯…這是個好主意。

Tip

> 注意，中英文標點符號的寫法有所不同，英文的句點是實心，中文的句號是空心；英文的引號是 " "，中文的引號是「」。

✎ **練習寫寫看 G**

Ⅰ 填入正確的標點符號。

1. More than a hundred people took the examination ____ only five passed ____

2. Sometimes ____ the shooting incident seemed far away ____ However ____ it was always there in the back of my mind ____

3. ____ Why don't you date your cellphone ____ ____ said Vivian.

4. Fred won the championship ____ as a result ____ he was awarded a gold medal as well as the prize money.

5. The angry lady stood up and shouted ____ "Don't ever call me again ____ "

6. To my surprise _____ the living room was tidied up _____ the laundry was done _____ too _____

7. _____ Does an apple a day really keep the doctor away _____ _____ asked the child.

8. Climbing trees used to be something interesting to do _____ at least to the boys like us.

9. Some tips for improving your memory are as follows _____ Set realistic goals _____ cut down on activities that don't require you to think _____ read more _____ and get into the habit of taking notes.

10. Vicky forced a smile and said _____ _____ It's all right _____ Let's order something to eat _____ _____

11. Temperatures change a lot in this area _____ it is like experiencing two seasons in a single day _____ winter in the morning and summer in the afternoon _____

12. What Jeff needs most now _____ in my opinion _____ is our encouragement instead of financial support.

II 填入正確的標點符號。

My husband _____ who believes in avoiding doctors and hospitals at all costs _____ had to have emergency surgery for an inflamed (發炎的) appendix (闌尾) In pain _____ but still protesting the whole idea of an operation _____ he muttered _____ _____ When God gave man an appendix _____ there must have been a reason for putting in there. _____

_____ Oh _____ there was _____ _____ said the surgeon. _____ God gave you that appendix, so I could put my children through college. _____

Unit 2 腦力激盪 (Brainstorming)

寫作文最困難的是不知該從何下筆。當腸枯思竭時，寫作前的暖身活動——腦力激盪 (brainstorming) 就可以幫你發想、構思、組織想法，找出最合適的靈感。只要跟主題相關，想到什麼就先記錄下來，任何想法都可以，因此腦力激盪不需考量邏輯性、一致性或適當性。當沒有任何新想法時，就可結束腦力激盪。之後才從所有想法中縮小主題，篩選出符合該主題的細節。常見的腦力激盪有以下三種方式：自由寫作 (freewriting)、群集 (clustering) 和表列 (listing)。

Tip
> 不論用哪一種腦力激盪的方式都不需考慮拼字、用字或文法，也不用寫出完整的句子。

2-1 自由寫作

有時題目較廣泛，難以聚焦，此時自由寫作 (freewriting) 就很有幫助。只要連續寫 5 至 10 分鐘，想到什麼就寫什麼，即使沒有點子也要一直寫，或重複寫跟前面類似的內容，時間到後再回過頭來，尋找有興趣或可以深入探究的主題，進一步找出相關的細節。

例：以「我的嗜好」為主題，5 分鐘內，寫出所有想到跟此主題有關的點子。

主題：My Hobby

點子：

　　What is my hobbies? I like listening to music, watching magic shows, biking, playing video games, and going to the movies with friends.

　　What else? I have to think. I like to go mountain climbing with my mom. I am a good basketball player.

我的嗜好是什麼？我喜歡聽音樂、看魔術表演、騎腳踏車、打電動以及跟朋友們去看電影。

　　還有呢？我想想。我喜歡跟媽媽去爬山。我籃球打得很好。

將最想寫的點子寫成主題句：My favorite hobby is going mountain climbing with my mom in my spare time.

練習寫寫看 A

> 由 sports (運動)、travel (旅行)、music (音樂) 或 food (食物) 中挑選一主題，在 5 分鐘內，寫出所有想到跟此主題有關的點子。
>
> 主題：＿＿＿＿＿＿
>
> 點子：
>
> 主題句：＿＿＿＿＿＿＿＿＿＿＿＿＿＿＿＿＿＿＿＿＿＿＿＿＿

2-2 群集

群集 (clustering) 是一種將想法圖像化的腦力激盪，由圈圈與圈圈的連結，可看出其中的關聯性。進行群集腦力激盪的步驟如下：

1. 在一張空白紙的中央畫一個圓圈，並於其中寫上主題。

2. 將任何與主題相關的點子寫在主題圓圈周圍的圓圈中。

3. 將這些與新主題相關的點子以線與主題圓圈相連。

4. 根據每個新點子，再想一些相關點子在其周圍圓圈中，並以線連接。

5. 完成後，其中有最多圓圈連接的就是最可能的主題。

（範例）

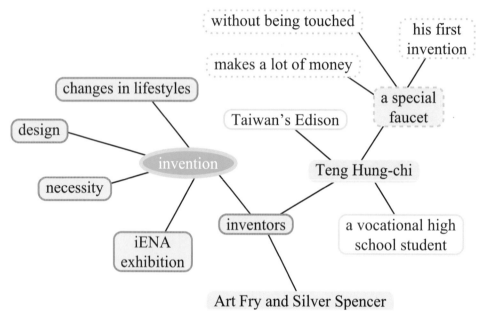

由以上群集腦力激盪的範例發現：

1. 由主題 invention 逐步推敲出以下細節：

- invention (發明) → inventors (發明家) → Teng Hung-chi (鄧鴻吉) → a special faucet (特別的水龍頭) → his first invention (他的第一個發明)、without being touched (無需觸碰)、make a lot of money (賺大錢)

2. 由這些點子寫出一個簡單的主題句。

- Teng Hung-chi invented a special faucet.　鄧鴻吉發明了一種特別的水龍頭。

3. 加上形容詞、副詞、介系詞、連接詞等來加長主題句。

- Teng Hung-chi, a famous Taiwanese inventor, invented a special faucet which could run automatically without being touched when he was 17.　鄧鴻吉，一

位知名的臺灣發明家，在十七歲時，發明了一種無需觸碰即可自動開啟的水龍頭。

練習寫寫看 B

以 holidays 為主題，練習畫出群集腦力激盪的過程圖。

holidays

寫出一個簡單的主題句。

_____

加上形容詞、副詞、介系詞、連接詞等來加長主題句。

_____

2-3 表列

表列 (listing) 的方式可將大主題範圍縮小，順勢找出適當的主題。表列與其他腦力激盪方式相同，都是將未經篩選，直接想到與主題相關的字、詞及點子列出來。跟自由寫作不同之處在於表列所列出來的字、詞常常不是完整句，

只是以較粗略的方式呈現。以「網路的優缺點」為例，可以表列出：

主題： The Advantages and Disadvantages of the Internet

Advantages (優點)	Disadvantages (缺點)
1. faster communication 更快速的溝通	1. theft of personal information 盜用個資
2. information resources 資訊來源	2. spamming 垃圾郵件
3. entertainment 娛樂	3. virus threat 病毒威脅
4. social networking 社群網絡	4. pornography 色情影片
5. online services 線上服務	5. social disconnect 社會脫節
6. e-commerce 電子商務	

Tip

有了點子及方向，即可選擇自己比較瞭解的項目寫出主題句，再進一步發展成段落或文章。

 練習寫寫看 C

以「課堂上是否允許使用智慧型手機？」為題，表列出你的意見

主題： Should Smartphones Be Allowed in Class?

_____

1. _____

2. _____

3. _____

4. _____

5. _____

6. _____

$Unit\ 3$ 句子加長 (Sentence Expansion)

寫作時，是否苦於總是寫出短短的 (choppy) 句子，而句子結構常常只是簡單的「主詞＋動詞＋受詞」？若能讓讀者「看得見」所描述的畫面，就能使文章更吸引讀者，因此有時需寫出長一點的句子。有三種將句子加長的方式較為常見：第一種是利用回答 wh- 問句的方式加長句子；第二種是加入不同詞性的字使句子變長；第三種則是利用不同的句子結構將句子加長。

> **Tip**
> 寫作文時，並非都要寫長句才可以。事實上，句子要有長有短，文章讀起來才更有變化。

3-1 利用回答 wh- 問句將句子加長

利用回答 who、what、where、when、why、how 等問題，加入更多細節到簡單句中。

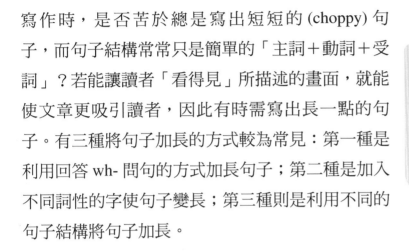

簡單句	I like ice cream.　我喜歡冰淇淋。
Who 是誰	**My sister** and I both like ice cream.　我和妹妹都喜歡冰淇淋。
What kind 哪一種	My sister and I both like **chocolate** ice cream. 我和妹妹都喜歡巧克力冰淇淋。
Where 哪裡	My sister and I both like chocolate ice cream **sold at Honey Dessert**. 我和妹妹都喜歡蜂蜜甜點店賣的巧克力冰淇淋。
How many 幾個	My sister and I both like to have **two scoops of** chocolate ice cream sold at Honey Dessert. 我和妹妹都喜歡來兩球蜂蜜甜點店賣的巧克力冰淇淋。
When 何時	My sister and I both like to have two scoops of chocolate ice cream sold at Honey Dessert **when we feel depressed**. 當我們感到沮喪時，我和妹妹都喜歡來兩球蜂蜜甜點店賣的巧克力冰淇淋。

Why 為什麼	My sister and I both like to have two scoops of chocolate ice cream sold at Honey Dessert when we feel depressed, **because ice cream can cheer us up**. 當我們感到沮喪時，我和妹妹都喜歡來兩球蜂蜜甜點店賣的巧克力冰淇淋，因為冰淇淋能讓我們振奮。

Tip

利用回答 wh- 問句加長句子的方式，可歸納為以下步驟：

1. 加上形容詞來修飾主詞、受詞。　　2. 加上副詞來修飾動詞。　　3. 加上地方副詞。

4. 加上時間副詞。　　　　　　　　5. 加上原因。

利用回答 wh- 疑問句的方式，將簡單句加長。

簡單句	The cat is eating.
What kind	
How	
Where	
When	
Why	

3-2 利用增加不同詞性的字將句子加長

常用來加長句子的字，詞性包括：

1. 形容詞

2. 副詞

3. 介系詞 (如：in、on、at、under、over、above、below)

4. 對等連接詞 (如：for、and、nor、but、or、yet、so)

Tip

形容詞用來修飾名詞；副詞用來修飾動詞；介系詞可引導表時間、地方等的副詞片語；對等連接詞連接對等的字詞、片語或子句；從屬連接詞用來引導表時間、原因、結果等的副詞子句。

5. 從屬連接詞 (如：when、while、before、after、until、unless、as if、as long as、whether)

例 The puppy is playing. 這隻小狗在玩耍。

→ The **cute little** puppy is playing. 這隻可愛的小狗在玩耍。(形容詞)

→ The cute little puppy is playing **happily**. 這隻可愛的小狗快樂地玩耍。
   (副詞)

→ The cute little puppy is playing happily **in the sand**.
   這隻可愛的小狗在沙裡快樂地玩耍。(介系詞所引導的副詞片語。)

→ The cute little puppy is **running, jumping, and** playing happily in the sand.
   這隻可愛的小狗在沙裡快樂地跑、跳和玩耍。
   (用對等連接詞 and 來連接動詞 run、jump。)

→ The cute little puppy is running, jumping, and playing happily in the sand
   while its owner is getting a suntan.
   當主人在做日光浴時，這隻可愛的小狗在沙裡快樂地跑、跳和玩耍。
   (從屬連接詞 while 所引導的副詞子句。)

練習寫寫看 B

用不同詞性的字詞來將下句加長：The man wrote a letter.。

1. 用形容詞來修飾主詞：

   The _____ man wrote a letter.

2. 用副詞來修飾動詞：

   The _____ man _____ wrote a letter.

3. 用介系詞 (to) 來引導副詞片語：

   The _____ man _____ wrote a letter to _____.

4. 用對等連接詞 (and) 來連接對等的字詞、片語或子句：

The _____ man _____ wrote a letter to _____ and

_____.

5. 用從屬連接詞 (because) 來連接從屬子句：

The _____ man _____ wrote a letter to _____ and

_____ because _____.

3-3 利用不同的句子結構將句子加長

一般來說，要將句子加長常用的句子結構有：

1. 對等子句	**2.** 關係子句	**3.** 同位語
4. 副詞子句	**5.** 分詞片語	**6.** 分詞構句

❶ 對等子句

可以用來連接對等子句的單字和片語有：

單字 and、but、or、for、yet、so、nor

例 Some guests came to the party early. (and)

➜ Some guests came to the party early(,) **and** they helped the host to set the table.

一些客人提早抵達派對，他們幫忙主人擺餐具。

片語 both . . . and、either . . . or、neither . . . nor、not only . . . but also、as well as

例 When the typhoon hit Taiwan, it flooded many farms. (not only . . . but also)

➜ When the typhoon hit Taiwan, it **not only** flooded many farms **but also** caused blackouts. 當颱風侵襲臺灣時，它不但淹沒農田，還造成停電。

❷ 關係子句

例 Mr. and Mrs. Green helped us clean the garbage.

→ Mr. and Mrs. Green, **who lived next door**, helped us clean the garbage.

住在隔壁的 Green 夫婦幫忙我們清理垃圾。

例 Lesley hid her toys in the desk drawer.

→ Lesley hid her toys, **which included dolls and some bricks**, in the desk drawer.　Lesley 把她的玩具，包括玩偶和一些積木，藏在書桌抽屜裡。

❸ 同位語

例 Mr. Brent was a retired high school English teacher.

→ Mr. Brent, **my uncle**, was a retired high school English teacher.

我的叔叔，Brent 先生是位退休的高中英文老師。

例 The candy shop will reopen next month.

→ The candy shop, **a paradise for children**, will reopen next month.

這間糖果店，孩子們的天堂，下個月會重新開張。

❹ 副詞子句

副詞子句是指以從屬連接詞開頭的從屬子句，功能為修飾主要子句。副詞子句與主要子句的關係通常由引導副詞子句的從屬連接詞決定，常見的有表示時間、原因、條件、讓步、結果、目的等子句。引導副詞子句的詞語包括：

時間	after、before、when、while、as、as soon as、since、until、till、by the time、once、every time、the first/last/next time 等。
原因	because、now that、since、as 等。
條件	if、unless、only if、whether、as/so long as、in case 等。
讓步	even though、although、though、even if 等。
結果	so that 等。
目的	in order to、in order that、so as to 等。

例 The thief broke into the jewelry shop. (when)

→ **When it was completely dark**, the thief broke into the jewelry shop.

當天色全暗時，小偷潛入這家珠寶店。

例 Oliver will not forgive you. (unless)

→ Oliver will not forgive you **unless you tell him the truth**.

Oliver 不會原諒你，除非你告訴他實話。

例 The girl wore a short skirt. (even though)

→ **Even though it was freezing cold outside**, the girl wore a short skirt.

儘管外面極為寒冷，這女孩卻穿著短裙。

❺ 分詞片語

由關係子句改變而成，關係代名詞為主格，省略的步驟為：

1. 刪去關係代名詞。

2. 動詞為主動時改為現在分詞(V-ing)；動詞為被動時改為過去分詞(p.p.)，例：

例 The speaker **who is delivering a speech** is a famous physicist.

→ The speaker **delivering a speech** is a famous physicist.

正在發表演說的講者是位知名的物理學家。

例 Once in the old house lived a man **who was named Jack**.

→ Once in the old house lived a man **named Jack**.

這間老屋裡曾住著一個名叫 Jack 的男人。

❻ 分詞構句

由從屬子句以及對等子句改變而成，以下分別解說：

從屬子句

省略的步驟為：

1. 可省略或保留從屬連接詞。

2. 從屬子句的主詞若與主要子句相同則可省略，不同則需保留。

3. 動詞為主動時改為現在分詞(V-ing)；動詞為被動時改為過去分詞(p.p.)，例：

例 **When I finished my coffee**, I found I didn't bring money with me.

→ **When finishing my coffee**, I found I didn't bring money with me.

喝完咖啡時，我才發現身上沒帶錢。

(保留從屬連接詞 when，可讓句意更清楚。)

例 **After Amy was encouraged by her teacher**, she had confidence in her ability.

→ **Encouraged by her teacher**, Amy had confidence in her ability.

在老師的鼓勵後，Amy 對自己的能力有信心。

對等子句

對等連接詞 and 用於兩個連續動作，或是第二個動作為第一動作的結果，省略的步驟為：

1. 省略對等連接詞 and，並加上逗號。

2. 對等子句若有主詞，與主要子句相同則省略，不同則需保留。

3. 動詞為主動時改為現在分詞(V-ing)；動詞為被動時改為過去分詞(p.p.)，例：

例 Lisa put on her coat **and rushed out of the door**.

→ Lisa put on her coat, **rushing out of the door**.　Lisa 穿上外套，衝出門。

例 I broke the vase **and was scolded by my mother**.

→ I broke the vase, **scolded by my mother**.　我打破花瓶，被媽媽責罵。

Tip

不想只寫簡單句，可以嘗試寫複合句、複雜句或複合複雜句。

簡單句 (simple sentence)：主詞 + 動詞 (+ 受詞)

例 Kelly stayed home.　Kelly 待在家。

複合句 (compound sentence)：子句 + 對等連接詞 + 子句

例 Kelly stayed home, but her brother went camping with his friends.
Kelly 待在家，但她哥哥跟朋友們去露營。

複雜句 (complex sentence)：主要子句 + 從屬連接詞 + 從屬子句

例 Because the weather was bad, Kelly stayed home.
因為天氣很糟，Kelly 待在家。

複合複雜句 (compound complex sentence)：兩個主要子句 + 從屬子句

例 Because the weather was bad, Kelly stayed home, but her brother went camping with his friends.　因為天氣很糟，Kelly 待在家，但她哥哥跟朋友們去露營。

練習寫寫看 C

I 利用提示的對等連接詞將句子加長。

1. On the hall walls, Jack saw many sports medals. (*and*)

→ _____

2. Do you want to go to the movies? (*or*)

→ _____

3. I'd be glad to play basketball with you. (*but*)

→ _____

II 利用提示的關係子句、同位語或從屬子句將句子加長。

1. The stones looked just like comets. (關係代名詞 that)

→ The stones looked just like comets _____.

2. Peter can speak five different languages. (同位語)

→ Peter, _____, can speak five different languages.

3. I discovered some money inside the envelope. (從屬連接詞 after)

→ I discovered some money inside the envelope _____.

4. The woman is in good health. (分詞片語)

→ The woman _____ is in good health.

5. Andy let out a cry. (分詞構句)

→ Andy let out a cry, _____.

Unit 4 轉折詞 (Transitional Words and Phrases)

轉折詞的主要功能是用來連接句子，為構成句子和句子以及段落和段落之間的橋樑，使文意更加清楚流暢。

〔範例〕

> **In addition to** the superstitions for good luck, some customs that have long been practiced grow out of people's fears. Most people practice these customs to deal with the unknown. In Taiwan, **for instance**, the word for the number "four" sounds like the word for "death." Because of such an association, the number "four" has long been viewed as an unlucky number by most Taiwanese people.
>
> 除了祈求好運的迷信，有些行之已久的習俗乃出自於人們的恐懼。大多數人常遵行這些習俗來處理未知的事物。例如在臺灣，數字「四」聽起來像「死」這個字。因為與「死」有關聯，數字「四」長久以來都被大部分的臺灣人視為一個不吉利的數字。

本段的轉折詞 **in addition to** 讓讀者瞭解迷信除了希望有好運，還有其他的原因 (人們的恐懼)。而 **for instance** 則讓讀者知道接下來為舉例說明：關於臺灣人對數字「四」的迷信。

4-1 常用的轉折詞

以下列出寫作很常用到的轉折詞，依據其意思的不同，共分為 9 項：

❶ 舉例 (Giving examples)

> 例如：for example/instance
>
> 特別：in particular、particularly、especially

例 The poem indicates that friendship requires many different ingredients. **For instance**, trust and similar interests are both very important.

這首詩顯示出友誼需要許多不同的材料。例如,信任與相似的興趣都很重要。

❷ 解釋或說明事實 (Giving explanations or facts)

> 另一方面:(on one hand) . . . on the other hand
> 也就是說:that is (to say)、namely
> 換句話說:in other words、to put it differently
> 事實上:in fact、actually

例 Edison said, "Genius is one percent inspiration, ninety-nine percent perspiration." **That is to say**, success depends on working hard instead of talent. 愛迪生說:「天才是百分之一的靈感,加上百分之九十九的汗水。」也就是說,成功取決於努力工作,而非聰明才智。

❸ 補充說明 (Adding more information)

> 此外:besides、in addition、additionally、moreover、furthermore、what's more
> 更糟的是:what's worse、to make matters worse
> 更好的是:what's better、better still/yet
> 尤其是:above all
> 也:also

例 Jack didn't admit his wrongdoing; **to make matters worse**, he told a lie.
Jack 沒有承認自己的疏失,更糟的是,他說謊。

❹ 表達次序 (Showing order)

首先：first、firstly、first of all、in the first place、to begin with

第二：second、secondly

然後：next、then

同時：at the same time、in the meantime、meanwhile

最後：last、finally

例 You must change your attitude. **To begin with**, you have to be humble.
你必須改變自己的態度。首先，你得謙遜為懷。

❺ 表達結果 (Showing a result)

因此：as a result、therefore、hence、accordingly、in consequence、
　　　consequently、thus

這樣一來：in this way

不用說：needless to say

無疑地：to be sure、without/beyond doubt、doubtlessly

最後：last、finally、in conclusion、in the end

例 The temperature kept dropping. **Consequently**, it was predicted that it would
possibly snow. 氣溫持續下降。因此，預測可能會下雪。

❻ 結論或重複 (Concluding or repeating)

總之：to sum up、in sum、all in all、after all

大體上：on the whole

簡言之：in short、in brief

一般來說：in general、generally speaking

例 **Generally speaking**, those who are active, positive, and optimistic are more
likely to succeed than the shy and timid people.
一般來說，積極、正面和樂觀的人比害羞和膽小的人更可能成功。

Unit
4
轉折詞

❼ 表達證據或資訊 (Showing proof or information)

根據：according to、based on

就像：(just) as、like

不像：unlike

事實上：as a matter of fact、actually、in fact

例 **According to** the weather forecast, there will be heavy rain tomorrow.
根據氣象預報，明天會下大雨。

❽ 表達比較、對比或讓步 (Showing comparison, contrast or concession)

然而：however、nevertheless、nonetheless、yet、whereas、while

相對地：in/by contrast

(與…) 相比較：in/by comparison

儘管：in spite of、despite、in spite of the fact that、despite the fact that

相反地：on the contrary、to the contrary

否則：otherwise、or else

反而：instead

例 **Despite the fact that** Mary is the daughter of the president of the company, she is not spoiled. **Instead**, she is well-mannered and works hard.
儘管 Mary 是這間公司總裁的女兒，但她一點也不驕縱。相反地，她舉止得當且認真工作。

❾ 類比 (Showing analogy)

同樣地：similarly、in the same way、likewise

例 Jeff always complained about his family members; **likewise**, he didn't get along well with his coworkers.
Jeff 總是在抱怨家人；同樣地，他也跟同事們不合。

I 根據文意，選出適當的轉折詞。

1. Unlike most other animals, rabbits touch the ground with their back feet first when they are running. (*Based on/Just as*) this fact, many Westerners think this is unusual and regard a rabbit's foot as a lucky sign.

2. Even though Mom and Dad were unable to go with us, we still had a lot of fun in Penghu. (*Finally/All in all*), it was a pleasant trip.

3. A positive gesture in one country might mean something quite different in another country. (*To make matters worse/Therefore*), it is better for travelers to get to know a country's culture before they visit it.

4. The Post-it note was not a success at first. (*Also/In fact*), it was the result of a failed experiment.

5. There's no such thing as a free lunch; (*that is/better still*), you have to work hard if you want to succeed.

6. Paul never burns the midnight oil. (*In other words/In particular*), he never stays up late.

7. Take an umbrella with you; (*namely/otherwise*), you'll be caught in the rain.

8. David made the same mistake again. (*First/Accordingly*), he was punished by his mother.

9. (*In general/What's worse*), people in Taiwan are friendly and hospitable.

10. In the past, women would do all the housework, (*similarly/while*) men were not encouraged to get involved.

11. (*Despite/Unlike*) her father's encouragement, May is still too shy to talk in public.

12. Our teacher didn't blame us for being unable to answer the questions. (*Instead/Likewise*), he gave us some hints in an interesting way.

Ⅱ 根據文意，從選項 (A) 至 (F) 中選出適當的轉折詞

(A) However (B) That is (C) As a result

(D) Also (E) For example (F) On the other hand

It is said that a quick look at our closet can help us know more about ourselves because the color we often wear indicates what kind of person we are. 1.____, one afternoon I decided to open up my closet and look inside. I found that I was drawn to my gray clothes—I believed that I looked great in gray. I have thought that I am willing to share my ideas with others most of the time. 2.____, I have heard that people who like to wear gray clothes seldom have opinions about things around them. 3.____, I have heard that people who wear gray tend to hide their emotions from other people. 4.____, people who are fond of red clothes are full of energy and good at expressing themselves. They are likely to enjoy getting up early in the morning to start an active day. It seems that they never "feel blue." Are these ideas true? I'm not sure. At least, it does not fit my case. I still think the colors we like to wear are very important. 5.____, I believe we will look great and feel good when we wear the colors we like.

4-2 搭配轉折詞的標點符號

1. 轉折詞置於句首時，必須大寫，並在其後加上逗號，再連接另一個句子。

例 Chris is good at painting. **Besides,** he plays the violin very well.

Chris 擅長畫畫。此外，他小提琴也拉得很好。

例 Mr. Wang is a nice neighbor. He picks up trash in the community. **What's better,** he will share the fruit he plants with the neighbors. 王先生是個好鄰

居。他撿拾社區的垃圾。更好的是,他還會分享自己種的水果給鄰居們。

2. 當轉折詞置於句中連接前後的句子時,前面的句子以分號結束,接著以小寫的轉折詞和逗號連接後面的句子。

例 Tim is a five-year-old boy**; however,** he helps do a lot of housework.
Tim 是個 5 歲男孩。然而,他幫忙做許多家事。

例 Success belongs to those who work hard**; in other words,** fooling around will get you nowhere.

成功是屬於努力的人。換句話說,遊手好閒讓你一事無成。

3. 轉折詞當作插入語置於句子中間時,轉折詞的前後需以逗號隔開。

例 We think that people nod their heads to mean "Yes." However, this is not the same all over the world. In India**, for example,** people use the head bobble to express their approval.

我們認為人們會點頭來表示「贊同」。然而,這不是放之四海而皆準。譬如,在印度,人們會搖頭來表示同意。

例 Jamie's brother is a spoiled child. Jamie**, on the contrary,** is a considerate and polite girl.　Jamie 的弟弟是個被寵壞的小孩。相反地,Jamie 是個體貼、有禮貌的女孩。

Tip
轉折詞運用得當可以增進句子的文意表達,使其增色不少,讓讀者更容易了解,可以多多運用。

Unit
4
轉折詞

I 根據轉折詞的使用規則，選出符合句意且正確的選項。

_____ 1. Greg plans to marry his girlfriend _____ his parents object to their marriage.

(A) instead,　　(B) ; instead,　　(C) ; however,　　(D) however,

_____ 2. The floods damaged the rails. _____ all the trains had to be suspended.

(A) Therefore　　(B) Therefore,　　(C) Instead　　(D) Instead,

_____ 3. Professor Lee is an expert in electronics _____ she has much knowledge of American culture.

(A) ; moreover,　　(B) ; moreover　　(C) ; otherwise　　(D) . Otherwise,

_____ 4. Victoria is mean and self-centered. _____ her twin sister is kind and generous.

(A) Generally speaking,　　　　(B) Needless to say,

(C) On the contrary,　　　　　(D) At the same time,

II 根據提示的轉折詞，寫出文意完整的段落。

1. The typhoon brought heavy rain to this island, and many places were flooded. *As a result,* _____.

2. Henry was late for school and didn't hand in the assignment yesterday. *To make matters worse,* _____. *Therefore,* _____.

3. I helped an old woman cross the road. She thanked me and said that I was a good boy. It made me feel happy. *Needless to say,* _____.

4. With my cellphone, I can keep in contact with my family members and friends at all times. *Besides,* _____. *Consequently,* _____.

5. How colors affect appetite is something that most people probably do not notice. *According to studies,* _____.

6. My neighbor, John, works as a volunteer on weekends. He says that he gets happiness out of helping others.

In addition, _____

_____.

Better still, _____

_____

_____.

Unit 5 段落寫作 (Paragraph Writing)

5-1 段落格式

前面 4 個單元討論了句子的結構、標點符號等,從這個單元進入段落的寫作。本單元開始介紹段落的基本格式。從句子組成段落,段落組成文章,而正確的段落格式是文章寫作的重要要素之一。以下是基本的段落格式:

1. 每一段的開始通常縮排五個字母。

Tip

現在有些正式的出版品 (如商業信件或報章雜誌) 並無縮排,而是以跟上、下段空行代替,稱作齊頭式 (block style),但縮排還是比較普遍的段落格式。

2. 每一個句子以大寫字母開始,以正確的標點符號結束,如句點、問號或驚嘆號。

3. 每一個句子與前後句子的順序必須合乎邏輯,使文意連貫直到段落結束。

〔範例〕

將下列句子組成完整的一個段落,包括大小寫、標點符號等。

本段的主題在介紹一位女服務生。從文法邏輯來看,第一次出現的普通名詞是以「不定冠詞 a(n) + 名詞」,再次提到才用「定冠詞 the + 名詞」;從文意上來看,先提到一位女服務生,然後加以描述她,接著再說明婦人對該女服務生的看法。

- a waitress opened the door and gave the elderly lady a clean towel for her wet hair
- the lady noticed that the waitress was heavily pregnant
- she wondered how a person like this waitress could be so thoughtful to a perfect stranger

• the waitress had a sweet smile, one that even being on her feet for an entire day couldn't erase

A waitress opened the door and gave the elderly lady a clean towel for her wet hair. The waitress had a sweet smile, one that even being on her feet for an entire day couldn't erase. The lady noticed that the waitress was heavily pregnant. She wondered how a person like this waitress could be so thoughtful to a perfect stranger.

一位女服務生開門並且拿了一條乾淨的毛巾給這位老太太,讓她擦乾淋溼的頭髮。這位女服務生面帶甜美的微笑,那種儘管站了一整天也不會消失的微笑。老婦人注意到這位女服務生即將臨盆。她納悶怎麼會有人像這位女服務生一樣,可以對一個完全陌生的人如此體貼。

Tip

段落標題的注意事項:
1. 以置中的方式將段落標題置於首行。
2. 出現在標題的第一個字都得大寫。在標題裡面,冠詞 (a、an、the)、連接詞以及少於五個字母的介系詞則需小寫。但五個字母以上的介系詞 (如:during、among、about、under、between、 through) 的第一個字要大寫。最後一個字不管幾個字母,第一個字都要大寫。
3. 標題後不加句點。
4. 標題與正文間需要空一行。

請將下面的句子重新排列，組成文意通順的段落，並注意大小寫以及標點符號的正確性。

1. • once upon a time a stingy man hid all of his money in a hole and put a heavy stone to the top

   • he cried so loudly that his neighbors came out to see what was going on

   • one day, he lifted the stone but found no money there

   • one of the neighbors told him that he didn't need to be unhappy at all

   • since he never thought of what to do with the money

   • there is a French proverb that says, "A stingy man is always poor"

_____

_____

_____

_____

_____

_____

_____

_____

2. • in Chinese, for example, dogs represent loyalty, and tigers are a symbol of authority

   • likewise, animal imagery can be found in many English expressions

   • the imagery does give color to the language

   • in many languages, certain animals have specific characteristics

   • "as busy as a bee" and "as quiet as a mouse" vividly describe a busy person and a quiet person

3. • thus, it is common to find pineapples placed in houses during Chinese New Year

  • baozi and zongzi are another example

  • as a result, many Chinese people give those who are going to take an exam baozi and zongzi as gifts

  • the pronunciation of the word for "pineapple" in Taiwanese means "prosperity or good luck will come"

  • the pronunciation of the two words "bao zong" sounds like "a sure victory"

  • naturally, it has become a symbol of wealth in Chinese culture

  • pineapple, baozi, and zongzi are considered good luck in Chinese culture

4. • to make more money, Della had her long hair cut off and sold

   • for Christmas, Della decided to buy Jim a chain for his cherished pocket watch given to him by his father

   • Jim and Della were a young couple who loved each other so much, but they were very poor

   • meanwhile, Jim decided to sell his watch to buy Della a beautiful set of combs for her long hair

   • although disappointed to find the gift they chose became useless, they were all pleased

---

5-2 主題句

何謂主題句 (topic sentence)？一個段落通常是主題句加上一個或數個跟主題句相關的句子組合而成。主題句就是一段的主要論點，點出這一段所要表達的主要內容。主題句不僅點出一段要敘述的主題，也掌控其他句子要表達的訊息。好的主題句能夠說明整體的方向，預告或概述一段的內容，引導發展的方向，並避免跟主題無關的內容。主題句必須廣泛且簡單扼要地概述所要表達的觀點，不做細節的描述。

主題句常見的問題是：

1. 內容過於廣泛，缺乏明確的論述方向。

例 Many children like to play.　許多小孩喜歡玩。

（內容過於廣泛，並且缺乏明確的論述方向。）

2. 內容為事實，無法發展成論點。

例 I walk to work every day.　我每天走路上班。

（內容為事實，難以發展成論點。）

3. 缺乏作者觀點。

例 This chapter is about the invention of cellphones.

這個章節是關於手機的發明。（主題明顯，但缺乏作者觀點。）

主題句通常會在段落之初，多為段落的第一句。雖然也能置於最後一句，但一般而言，還是建議以第一句的位置為佳。

《範例》

In Japan, a person's blood type is popularly believed to determine his or her own personality traits. People with blood type A are generally considered responsible and cautious, but over-anxious. Those who with blood type B are cheerful, but irresponsible and forgetful. People having blood type AB are suggested to be rational, but critical and indecisive. On the other hand, people with blood type O are curious and confident, but stubborn. Even though there is no scientific evidence to support this belief, it is widely seen in books, magazines, and television programs.

在日本，一個人的血型普遍被認為能決定其人格特質。A 型人大多被認為是負責且謹慎的，但會過度焦慮。B 型人是開朗的，但較不負責任且健忘。AB 型人很理性，但挑剔且優柔寡斷。另一方面，O 型人好奇心強且有自信，但是固執己見。即使沒有科學證據支持這個論點，還是常見於書本、雜誌和電視節目上。

可以明顯看出這個段落的主題句是："In Japan, a person's blood type is popularly believed to determine his or her own personality traits."，知道本段的中心思想是血型決定人的人格特質。主題句是個概述，進而可以瞭解本段接著會說明細節，陳述各種血型有著不同的個性。

Tip
偶爾主題句也會出現在段落的最後一句。在寫法上會先鋪排支持句的相關例子，最後由主題句概括整段資訊，同時製造出戲劇化的效果。

I 選出最適合當主題句的句子。

_____ 1. (A) Colors play a more important role in your life than you can ever imagine.

(B) Among my friends, those who like red color seem to be more active.

(C) My sister doesn't like purple because she thinks it disgusting.

(D) Red light is also a symbol of danger and warning.

_____ 2. (A) You have to add some seasonings to make the soup a tasty dish.

(B) Making friends can be a lot like making soup.

(C) First, you need a special recipe to tell you the things that you need.

(D) Next, you have to prepare everything properly and then cook it with care.

_____ 3. (A) If you believe that opera can be fun to watch, you will surely enjoy it.

(B) You can start with short, well-known operas and avoid long, difficult ones.

(C) It is important for you to learn the story of the opera before you watch it.

(D) Here are some useful tips for you to learn how to enjoy operas.

Ⅱ 閱讀各段內容後，寫出適當的主題句。

1. _____

Most Americans show affection by kissing and hugging. The Inuit rub noses. Instead of giving cards or roses, Koreans give chocolate-covered cookie sticks to their loved ones.

2. _____

They feel good about themselves while wearing, using, or eating brand-name items. For instance, some think they look slimmer and more attractive in jeans from a company that has hired famous models as its brand ambassadors. Others trust only Nike or Adidas shoes, for they believe their feet will not be protected in shoes without those brand names. Still others consider that only drinks sold by Starbucks provide them with the refreshment they need.

3. _____

Have you ever thought about why school buses and taxis are painted yellow, and stop signs red? This is because yellow is bright enough to attract people's attention, even in heavy traffic. As for red, it is usually used to indicate warning. Therefore, most traffic signs use this color.

Unit

5

段落寫作

4. _____

I broke Mr. Wang's window last Sunday, but I didn't tell him about this. Instead of saying sorry to him, I ran away. After that day, I was afraid to look Mr. Wang in the eye. Yesterday, I decided to tell him what had happened. To my surprise, Mr. Wang wasn't angry. He said he was proud that I had told the truth. As a result, I made up my mind that I would be honest with other people.

5. _____

Fresh onions are available in yellow, red, and white throughout their season, March through August. They can be identified by their thin, light-colored skin. Because they have a higher water content, they are typically sweeter and milder tasting than storage onions. This higher water content also makes it easier for them to bruise. With its delicate taste, the fresh onion is an ideal choice for salads and other lightly-cooked dishes. Storage onions, on the other hand, are available August through April. Unlike fresh onions, they have multiple layers of thick, dark, papery skin. They also have an intense flavor and a higher percentage of solids. For these reasons, storage onions are the best choice for spicy dishes that require longer cooking times or more flavor.

5-3 支持句

一個段落有了主題句，接著必須提供資訊來支持主題句，這些句子稱為支持句 (supporting sentences)。支持句能為主題句提供解釋、細節、訊息、舉例或佐證，使讀者能更加瞭解段落的主題。跟主題句密切相關的支持句越多，主題就越清楚，也會更具說服力。主題句通常是廣泛的陳述，而支持句是針對主題句提出明確、深入且肯定的論述。

以下為常見的支持句內容：

1. 舉例、個人經驗、解釋和提供細節。

2. 根據新聞報導、歷史事實、研究報告、科學證據和統計資料。

3. 引用文學作品、諺語和名言。

4. 引用故事或寓言。

〔範例 1〕

　　Believe it or not, baby oil, medicated oil, or even oil from potato chips can help remove stubborn stains effectively. Just follow these steps. First, prepare some baby oil. Then, put a few drops of the oil on the stain. Two minutes later, wipe it up with some tissues. Amazingly, the stained area will look clean again. The secret behind the magic is that the organic substances from these kinds of oil can help break down the stains, and thus, make them easier to remove.

　　信不信由你，嬰兒油、藥油或甚至是洋芋片上的油都能有效清除頑固污漬。只要跟著這些步驟。首先，準備一些嬰兒油。然後，滴幾滴油在污漬上。兩分鐘過後，用衛生紙擦拭該處。出乎意料地，髒汙的地方又再度變乾淨了。這個魔法的祕訣在於這幾種油的有機物質能夠分解汙漬，也因此能夠更輕鬆清除掉。

主題句： Believe it or not, baby oil, medicated oil, or even oil from potato chips can help remove stubborn stains effectively.

支持細節 1： First, prepare some baby oil. Then, put a few drops of the oil on the stain. Two minutes later, wipe it up with some tissues. (說明步驟。)

支持細節 2： The secret behind the magic is that the organic substances from these kinds of oil can help break down the stains, and thus, make them easier to remove. (解釋原因。)

〔範例 2〕

There is no doubt that travel opens people's eyes, but how can this possibly be true if the explosive growth of tourism eventually leaves nothing but ruins for visitors to see? Governments and tourists must take action now to help preserve the cultural and natural treasures because these precious things cannot be restored once they have been spoiled. To prevent further destruction, it is important that governments lay down clear guiding principles to encourage more public participation in environmental conservation. Tourists, too, must act with a stronger sense of responsibility and morality than they do now. After all, visiting these unique and amazing places around the world is a privilege, rather than something that is taken for granted.

毫無疑問地，旅遊可以增廣見聞，但如果急遽擴張的旅遊業最終只留下斷壁殘垣給旅客欣賞，這還是事實嗎？政府和觀光客現在必須採取行動來保護文化和自然的珍寶，因為這些珍貴的東西一旦受損就無法復原了。為了避免更嚴重的破壞，重要的是政府應該設立明確的指導原則來鼓勵大眾參與環境保育。觀光客，同樣地，必須表現得比現在更有強烈的責任感和公德心。畢竟，參訪世界上這些獨特且令人驚豔的地方是一種殊榮，而非理所當然的事。

主題句：Governments and tourists must take action now to help preserve the cultural and natural treasures because these precious things cannot be restored once they have been spoiled.

支持細節 1：To prevent further destruction, it is important that governments lay down clear guiding principles to encourage more public participation in environmental conservation.

（針對政府的部分，提供補救方法。）

支持細節 2： Tourists, too, must act with a stronger sense of responsibility and morality than they do now.

(針對觀光客的部分，提供補救方法。)

根據主題，選出**不適合**做為支持句的句子。

_____ 1. Citrus peel can be used to remove stubborn stains.

(A) Squeeze some juice from the peel on the stains and rub the stains with the peel.

(B) Citrus fruits, such as oranges and lemons, are good for your health.

(C) The acid contents from citrus peel can help break down the stains.

(D) Wait for a few minutes, and the stains will gradually come off.

_____ 2. It is interesting to go traveling in a foreign country.

(A) We can visit popular tourist attractions.

(B) We can learn different customs.

(C) We should book the plane tickets before we set off.

(D) We can meet people from different cultures.

_____ 3. There are several Halloween traditions.

    (A) Halloween and Christmas are national holidays in the U.S.

    (B) Children would go trick-or-treating.

    (C) People use pumpkins to make jack-o'-lanterns.

    (D) Children dress up in special costumes.

_____ 4. Necessity is the mother of invention.

    (A) Many times, people come up with ideas to meet their own needs.

    (B) The solutions to the problems become great inventions that change people's lives.

    (C) Teng Hung-chi invented a faucet controlled by a built-in sensing device because he did not want to touch the faucet with his dirty hands.

    (D) There have been many great inventors throughout history, such as Isaac Newton, Thomas Edison, and Steve Jobs.

_____ 5. It is not advised to heat a baby's bottle in a microwave.

    (A) The bottle may seem cool to the touch, but the liquid inside may become too hot to drink.

    (B) Heating the bottle of milk in a microwave can cause changes in the milk.

    (C) Breast milk is better for babies because it is said to encourage healthy brain development.

    (D) The nutritional value of milk may be destroyed.

I 寫出各段的主題句和支持細節。

1. Things often have more uses than you could ever imagine. Some common items that we use every day can seem to perform magic when you know how to use them. Take sugar cubes, for example. You can add a sugar cube to coffee or tea to make the drink sweet. However, most people don't know that there's another thing that sugar cubes can do—keep cookies crisp!

主題句：_____

支持細節 1：_____

支持細節 2：_____

支持細節 3：_____

2. Many patients have reported a decrease in pain after a good laugh. This reduction in pain may result from chemicals produced in the blood. Also, patients might feel less pain because their muscles are more relaxed, or because they are simply distracted from thinking about their pain. It doesn't matter what the truth may be, since there are plenty of people who would agree with the comedian Groucho Marx, who once said, "A clown is like aspirin, only he works twice as fast."

主題句：_____

支持細節 1：_____

支持細節 2：_____

支持細節 3：_____

Unit

5

段落寫作

II 根據各題的主題句,寫出 3 個支持細節。

1. For people who live in cities, a fast-food restaurant is a good place to have meals in.

支持細節 1:＿＿＿＿＿＿＿＿＿＿＿＿＿＿＿＿＿＿＿＿＿

支持細節 2:＿＿＿＿＿＿＿＿＿＿＿＿＿＿＿＿＿＿＿＿＿

支持細節 3:＿＿＿＿＿＿＿＿＿＿＿＿＿＿＿＿＿＿＿＿＿

2. Taiwan's birth rate has been decreasing in recent years. In fact, Taiwan has one of the lowest birth rate in the world.

支持細節 1:＿＿＿＿＿＿＿＿＿＿＿＿＿＿＿＿＿＿＿＿＿

支持細節 2:＿＿＿＿＿＿＿＿＿＿＿＿＿＿＿＿＿＿＿＿＿

支持細節 3:＿＿＿＿＿＿＿＿＿＿＿＿＿＿＿＿＿＿＿＿＿

3. There are advantages for college students to work part-time.

支持細節 1:＿＿＿＿＿＿＿＿＿＿＿＿＿＿＿＿＿＿＿＿＿

支持細節 2:＿＿＿＿＿＿＿＿＿＿＿＿＿＿＿＿＿＿＿＿＿

支持細節 3:＿＿＿＿＿＿＿＿＿＿＿＿＿＿＿＿＿＿＿＿＿

4. There are disadvantages for college students to work part-time.

支持細節 1:＿＿＿＿＿＿＿＿＿＿＿＿＿＿＿＿＿＿＿＿＿

支持細節 2:＿＿＿＿＿＿＿＿＿＿＿＿＿＿＿＿＿＿＿＿＿

支持細節 3:＿＿＿＿＿＿＿＿＿＿＿＿＿＿＿＿＿＿＿＿＿

結論句通常置於段落的最後一句,跟主題句相互呼應,讓讀者對整段文章有完整的概念。有幾種方法來寫結論句,通常作者也會同時混用數種。但不論用何種方法,都不能偏離主題。好的結論句能夠引導讀者對本段內容有更清楚的瞭解和更深刻的印象,並能總結前面所述。以下列出幾種常用的結論寫法:

1. 簡單扼要地重述本段主旨。

2. 提出個人的意見、想法或評論。

3. 提供結果、答案或解決方法。

範例 1

We sometimes lie to cover up our mistakes. While it is true that we make errors from time to time, some of us don't have the courage to admit that we've made them. For example, some students might deceive their teacher about their unfinished homework. They might say that they left it at home when in fact, they didn't even do it. These students don't want to seem irresponsible, so they make up an excuse—that is, a lie—to save face.

有時候我們說謊是為了掩蓋我們的錯誤。雖然事實上我們偶爾會犯錯,有些人卻沒有承認過錯的勇氣。舉例來說,有些學生可能功課沒有寫完,欺騙老師說他們將功課留在家裡了。事實上,他們根本沒有寫功課。這些學生不想表現出不負責任的樣子,所以他們編造藉口,也就是說謊,來保留顏面。

主題句: We sometimes lie to cover up our mistakes.

支持句: While it is true that we make errors from time to time, some of us don't have the courage to admit that we've made them. For example, some students might deceive their teacher about their unfinished homework.

Unit **5** 段落寫作

They might say that they left it at home when in fact, they didn't even do it. (說明原因。)

結論句： These students don't want to seem irresponsible, so they make up an excuse—that is, a lie—to save face. (重述本段主旨。)

範例 2

Sending teenagers to study abroad might not be a good idea. When teenagers are sent abroad, they may have to live alone. Without their parents taking care of them, they are very likely to feel lonely and may hang out with some friends. Besides, teenagers are always curious. They tend to try something new and strange without a second thought. They may be attracted to drugs and get involved in drug use. Therefore, in my opinion, parents should think very carefully about sending their children abroad.

送青少年出國念書可能不是個好主意。當青少年被送出國，他們可能得獨自生活。少了父母親的照顧，他們很可能感到孤單，並且跟朋友四處鬼混。此外，青少年總是好奇。他們不假思索地嘗試新奇的事物。他們可能會受毒品吸引和吸毒。因此，在我看來，父母親對送孩子出國一事應該要好好考慮。

主題句： Sending teenagers to study abroad might not be a good idea.

支持句： 1. Without their parents taking care of them, they are very likely to feel lonely and hang out with some friends.

2. Teenagers are always curious. They tend to try something new and strange.

3. They may be attracted to drugs and get involved in drug use.

結論句： Therefore, in my opinion, parents should think very carefully about sending their children abroad. (提出個人意見。)

I 以下各題的選項 (A)、(B)、(C) 和 (D) 可組成一個段落，請從這 4 個選項中選出該段最適合做為結論句的句子。

_____ 1. (A) The idea of a perfect gift varies from culture to culture

(B) For example, it is not proper to give fans in Chinese culture.

(C) The Chinese word for "fan" has a similar pronunciation as that of "separation."

(D) You'd better ask the locals for advice before giving gifts to a foreigner.

_____ 2. (A) Unlike most people who work for a living, there are some people who really enjoy their work.

(B) In a word, some people are devoted to their jobs.

(C) They are willing to spend extra hours on the job.

(D) They even work at home.

_____ 3. (A) Both bookworms and human bookworms enjoy having books around.

(B) Bookworm is the name given to the insects feeding on the binding and paste of books.

(C) Human bookworms, however, feed on the words and ideas contained in the book.

(D) The reason they share the same nickname is most likely that they spend most of their time with books.

Unit **5** 段落寫作

II 選出最適當的結論句。

_____ 1. People sometimes lie to get out of situations that they don't want to be involved in or can't manage. For instance, if one would rather sleep in on the weekend than go camping with his or her family, the person might say "I have stayed up late recently to finish a company project, so I need to get some rest." This type of lie is also told by students quite often. For instance, a boy who has been caught cheating on a test might not reveal what has happened at school to his family. This student may choose not to tell the truth because he isn't confident enough to deal with the anger that he might face.

_____

(A) In short, people who have the habit of sleeping in on weekends often tell a lie.

(B) When we don't want to face the consequences, lies are convenient ways to avoid such difficulties.

(C) Therefore, lies can be useful in maintaining good relationships between teachers and parents.

(D) When people are not confident about themselves, they have no choice but to tell a lie.

_____ 2. We sometimes tell "protective lies" so as to keep ourselves out of dangerous situations. Parents may teach their children to use this type of lie in certain circumstances. Some parents, for example, ask their children to say that their mom and dad are too busy to come to the phone if a stranger calls while they are out. _____

(A) In this way, children may learn the right time to tell lies.

(B) In addition, they must not tell the stranger where their parents are.

(C) Children should be taught not to pick up the phone when they stay home alone.

(D) As a result, protective lies may prevent harm from happening.

_____ 3. Personal space can be a very sensitive issue. Have you been disturbed by someone standing too close in line, talking too loud or making eye contact for too long? Or, they may have offended you with the loud music from their earphones, or by taking up more than one seat on a crowded subway cabin. _____

(A) You feel unhappy because your personal space has been violated.

(B) It is obvious from their body language that they are nervous.

(C) You shouldn't argue with impolite people.

(D) Some people easily get angry, while others are not.

_____ 4. John Harrison has an enviable job in most people's opinion. He's the official taster for Dreyer's Grand Ice Cream, one of the best-selling ice-cream brands in the United States. On an average day, Harrison has to sample sixty ice creams at the Dreyer's headquarters. It is important for Harrison to keep a sharp palate. That is to say, he must avoid eating onions, garlic or pepper. Besides, he can't have any caffeine, since this blocks the taste buds. Thus, he usually has a cup of caffeine-free herbal tea for breakfast so that his job will not be affected. _____

Unit

5

段落寫作

(A) Undoubtedly, ice cream is one of the favorite desserts for people of all ages.

(B) However, he has to try hard to control his weight and keep fit.

(C) But to Harrison, this is just a small price to pay for what he calls "the world's best job."

(D) As a result, Dreyer's Grand Ice Cream has become popular all over the world.

Ⅲ 根據文意，寫出結論句。

1. When we were kids, we were taught the virtue of honesty through fairy tales and stories. The story of *Pinocchio* (木偶奇遇記) showed us the importance of telling the truth. The boy who cried wolf finally lost all his sheep as well as the trust of his fellow villagers. _____

_____

2. Some parents believe that watching TV is not good for their children. However, it can be an educational tool. One way to use TV for learning is to watch programs produced specifically for education. Public broadcasting channels have many educational shows for children, and cable TV is full of programs about nature, travel, and history, which contain many good lessons for children. Additionally, TV shows with subtitles or "closed captioning (隱藏字幕)" for the deaf can help children enlarge their vocabulary and improve their reading ability. Parents can make watching TV with their children into an active activity by asking their children to express their opinions about the show. After the show has finished, parents can also ask children to summarize what has happened. _____

3. When it comes to communication, many people agree that men and women seem to come from different worlds. For most women, it is important to talk and share feelings with friends. By comparison, men prefer to share facts and specific information. Moreover, when men are under stress, they tend to remain silent because it is not easy for them to show their emotions. _____

_____

4. When I was in the first grade in high school, I went to Japan as an exchange student (交換學生) with some of my classmates. We visited schools there and talked to local students. However, my Japanese was not that good at that time, so I had to talk both in Japanese and English and used a lot of body language. It was really fun. _____

5. Sunburn is a form of burn that affects living tissue, such as skin. It is caused by long exposure to ultraviolet radiation (紫外線輻射) coming from the sun. Common symptoms include red skin, pain, tiredness, headache, and fever. Too much UV radiation can be life-threatening in some extreme cases.

_____

5-5 文章寫作

本單元前面討論了段落寫作，一個段落中包含了主題句、支持句以及結論句。文章寫作是段落寫作的放大版，把主題句放大為主題段 (introduction)，支持句成為一段或數段的支持段 (supporting paragraph)，最後一段為結論段 (conclusion/concluding paragraph)。

❶ 文章寫作的結構

英文文章寫作的結構包括三個部分：第一段主題段是文章的開始，介紹文章要談論的主題 (main idea)；內文 (body) 部分是支持段，可以是一段或多段；

段落寫作

最後一段結論段是文章的結尾。英文文章一般會分成三段——主題段、支持段以及結論段。

❷ 文章格式

題目置中，每段的開始一般會縮排五個字母，每段之間可以間隔一行或不間隔。

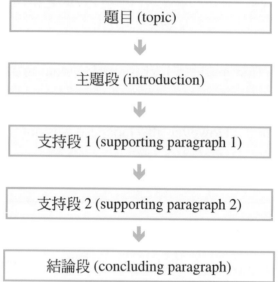

❸ 寫作技巧

1. 每一段都要有主題句，全段說明跟主題句相關的論述。

2. 第一段是整體概括的論述，點出文章的主旨，使讀者預知本文要談論的內容。

3. 支持段提出的細節可以是多元的，如：個人經驗、意見、想法、報導、研究等，可以每段談論一個支持細節，也可以一段包含所有的支持細節。

4. 結論段可以重點概述本文重點、提供結果、解決方法或引導未來發展等。

本文分成五段：

The Wonderful World of Hayao Miyazaki

Many people may have either heard of Hayao Miyazaki, a well-known Japanese animator, or seen his internationally praised films. His films, such as *My Neighbor Totoro, Princess Mononoke*, and *Howl's Moving Castle*, have attracted the interest of people of all ages around the world. When moviegoers steep themselves in Miyazaki's films, they easily note three marked characteristics.

First, the main characters are often tough females who always face difficulties bravely and try to overcome them. Take Satsuki, the twelve-year-old main character in *My Neighbor Totoro*, for example. She has to take care of her younger sister and do piles of housework because her father is busy working while her mother is being treated in a hospital. . . .

Second, flying is a major theme in many of Miyazaki's works. Miyazaki's father worked in aviation, and this led to Miyazaki's interest in flying. . . .

Third, Miyazaki's films consist of characters that are very different from the characters in typical Hollywood animations. The characters he created reflect reality. They are neither totally good nor absolutely wicked, which is true to life. . . .

Unit
5
段落寫作

第五段
(結論段)：
談論宮崎駿的成就
和影響力。

With these special characteristics, Miyazaki's films have not only hit it big in Japan, but also impressed audiences and critics alike from the four corners of the earth . . . Without a doubt, with the wonderful worlds he creates in his movies, this imaginative animator as well as his brilliant films will always fill people with awe.

宮崎駿的美妙世界

許多人可能曾聽聞有名的日本動畫家宮崎駿，或看過他享譽國際的電影作品。他的電影如《龍貓》、《魔法公主》與《霍爾的移動城堡》，吸引了全球各年齡層民眾的興趣。當電影迷沉浸在宮崎駿的影片時，他們容易注意到三個鮮明的特色。

首先，主角通常是堅毅的女性，她們總是勇敢面對、並試著克服困難。以《龍貓》中的十二歲主角—小月為例，因為爸爸忙於工作，而媽媽正在醫院接受治療，她必須照顧妹妹並做成堆的家事。…

第二，飛行是宮崎駿很多作品中的重要主題。宮崎駿的父親在航空業工作，這促使他對飛行產生興趣。…

第三，宮崎駿電影中的角色與好萊塢典型動畫片中的角色非常不同。他創造的角色反映出現實，既非絕對的善良，也非全然的邪惡，這點相當寫實。…

因為這些特色，宮崎駿的電影不只在日本得到成功，也讓全球各地的觀眾與影評都留下深刻印象。…無疑地，憑著在他的電影中所創造的美妙世界，這位想像力豐富的動畫家與其出色的作品總是讓人們驚嘆。

根據英文文章的寫作結構，將下列句子組合成一篇主題段、支持段和結論段的文章。

1.

題目：The Influence of Weather on People's Moods

(1) However, there is a surprising link between such beliefs and the actual effect of weather on people's work performance.

(2) Thus, many people believe that bad weather can reduce productivity and efficiency.

(3) The findings conclude that workers are actually most productive when the weather is lousy—and only if nothing reminds them of good weather.

(4) Research has proven that weather plays a part in people's moods.

(5) Warmer temperatures and exposure to sunshine can help increase positive thinking, while cold, rainy days bring anxiety.

(6) Through data from laboratory experiments as well as observations of a Japanese bank in real life, researchers find that weather conditions indeed influence a worker's focus.

(7) Workers can be greatly distracted by photos showing outdoor activities, such as sailing on a sunny day or walking in the woods, and thus lower their productivity.

(8) To many people's surprise, when the weather is bad, individuals tend to focus more on their work rather than thinking about activities they could engage in outside of work.

Unit

5

段落寫作

_____

_____

_____
_____
_____
_____
_____
_____
_____
_____
_____
_____
_____
_____

2.

題目：As a High School Senior

(1) It was stressful for me because this was the first week that I became a high school senior.

(2) In this week, I took tests every day and spent most of my time studying.

(3) To sum up, life in the third year of senior high school is completely different from the first two years.

(4) I knew that health meant everything.

(5) I was advised to prepare for the college entrance examination as soon as possible. Thus, I had to plan my study schedule.

(6) Most of all, I exercised to stay healthy.

(7) Clearly, I should make good use of my time to face a challenging future ahead of me.

(8) First, I made a study plan.

(9) Second, I had to review previous lessons and preview new ones.

(10) Besides, I changed my study habits so that I could do things more efficiently.

(11) I did the review in order to move information into my long-term memory. I also did the preview, and thus I could gain a better understanding of new lessons.

NOTE

PART II

實用寫作文體

(Writing Genres)

Unit 6 敘述文 (Narrative Writing)

敘述文 (narrative writing) 是描述人物經歷或事件發生過程的文體，也就是俗稱的說故事 (story telling)。其實日常生活中，很多說話的內容就具有敘述性質，譬如敘述一位值得尊敬的人、一件難忘的事、朋友間分享的親身經歷、生活札記、電影情節、小說、童話故事、名人傳記、新聞報導等。說故事，尤其是真人真事的故事，是一種很具說服力的寫作文體。作家常用敘述文來分享重要的人生經驗或用來說明自己的觀點。因此，敘述文可說是一種應用最頻繁的文體。

在題材方面，一個人的經驗、事蹟，一件事的發生，尤其是具有啟發性、警惕性、感動性等往往是很好的寫作題材，因為它有人類經驗的共同性，他人也許會因有類似的經驗而產生共鳴，所以生動的敘述文有其獨特性和渲染力。

6-1 敘述文的寫作技巧

❶ 設定情節 (plot)

第一步先設定好主角和故事，如何開始 (beginning) → 問題、事情或衝突 (conflict/rising action) → 過程 / 問題 / 衝突等如何發生 (climax) →解決方法 (falling action) → 結果 (result)。

❷ 設定觀點 (point of view)

最常見的敘事身份與角度為第一人稱和第三人稱。第一人稱是以「我」的口吻或角度來敘述。一般敘述文中，「我」即敘事者 (narrator)，透過「我」的眼睛和感受，給讀者第一手資訊，讓讀者更真實自然體會「我」的經歷。而第三人稱是以旁觀者的角度來敘述文章中的人物、事件、場景等，可以不受空間及時間的限制，以較自由廣闊的角度來做客觀的描述。不論是第一人稱還是第三人稱的敘述都有其優缺點，但重要的是，初學者在寫作練習中，應該選擇一種觀點來描述，人稱千萬不可換來換去，否則容易沒有一致性，讓讀者感覺混亂、無所適從。比較下列範例 1 和 2：

（範例 1）

本段文章以第一人稱敘述和 Jim 爭吵的原因、過程和結果。

Jim and **I** got into another fight over the mess he made in the living room again. **I** was trembling with rage after he told **me** to "stop nagging." With his eyes closed, he said that he had been stressed out and needed some silence. **I** stood still next to the sofa and waited for an apology from him. However, **I** almost hit the roof because he just sat there and kept changing channels.

我和 Jim 又因為他把客廳弄得一團亂而吵架了。在他跟我說：「不要再嘮叨了。」後，我氣得直發抖。他閉上眼睛，說他最近壓力很大，需要安靜。我靜靜地站在沙發旁，等著他向我道歉。然而，我快氣炸了，因為他只是坐在那裡，不停地切換電視頻道。

（範例 2）

本段文章以第三人稱述說一個助人的故事，以第三人稱敘述雖然沒有直接涉及情節發展，卻能以客觀的角度來描述 Joe 的善行。

It was starting to get dark. Although snow flurries drifted in the dim light of day, **Joe** could still notice an elderly lady stranded by the roadside. Apparently, she needed some help. So, **he** pulled up in front of her Mercedes-Benz and got out. When **he** approached her, she was worried. Realizing that she was frightened, **he** said quickly, "**I'm** here to help, ma'am. By the way, **my** name is Joe."

All she had was a flat tire, but for an old lady, that was bad enough. She thanked **him** for coming to her aid. **Joe** just smiled as **he** put the flat tire into the

trunk. She asked **him** how much she owed **him**. **Joe**, however, never thought twice about helping others. **He** certainly never thought about any kind of payment or reward. To **him** this wasn't a job, but rather a way to help someone in need, just like those who had given **him** a hand in the past. **He** told the lady that if she really wanted to repay **him** she could help someone else that was in need.

He waited until she started her car and drove off. It had been a cold and depressing day, but **he** felt content as **he** headed for home.

天色漸漸暗了。雖然飄著陣陣細雪，Joe 還是注意到有一位老婦人受困在路旁。顯然地，她需要幫助。所以他把車子停在她的賓士車前面，然後下車。當他靠近她時，她很擔心。看出她的恐懼，他立刻說：「女士，我是來幫妳的。對了，我的名字是 Joe。」

她的問題只不過是輪胎爆胎罷了，但對一位老婦人而言，這就夠糟了。她感謝他能來幫助她。Joe 只是微笑著把洩氣的輪胎放進後車廂。她問他該付多少錢。然而，對於助人，Joe 從來不曾猶豫。他從未想過任何報酬或回報，對他來說，這不是工作，而是幫助需要的人，就像那些曾經對他伸出援手的人一樣。他告訴那位老婦人，如果她真的想要報答他，她可以幫助其他需要幫助的人。

他等著老婦人發動車子並把車子開走。這原本是個既寒冷又令人沮喪的一天，但 Joe 在回家的路上卻感到心滿意足。

❸ 時間順序 (time order)

順敘法：順敘法 (chronological order) 於敘述時通常照時間的先後順序來說明事情的發展經過，先發生的事先說明，接著依次寫後續發生的事，也是敘述文最常用的敘事順序。

《範文》

本篇文章依時間先後順序說明事情發生的原因、內心的不安、補救的辦法，最後得到原諒和鼓勵。

On a quiet Saturday afternoon, my friend and I were bored, so we played the game of throwing stones. I found a stone and threw it. Unfortunately, it was so smooth that it slipped out of my hand and hit my neighbor's window. We were frightened and escaped at the sound of the broken window.

For the next few days, I was so worried about myself that I did not think of the old lady and her broken window. **Later on**, I started to feel guilty. Every day, the old lady greeted me with a warm smile as I passed her the newspaper, but I didn't feel comfortable in her presence anymore.

Finally, I made up my mind to save the money which I made from delivering newspapers. **In three weeks**, I collected seven dollars and put the money in an envelope with an apology letter. I slipped the envelope under her door. After I did so, I felt relieved and couldn't wait to look her straight in the eye once again.

The next day, I could happily hand her the newspaper and return the warm smile that I received from her. She thanked me for the newspaper and gave me a bag of cookies. I walked away and opened the bag. I discovered an envelope inside. I opened it up. I was very surprised. There were the seven dollars and a short note that said, "I'm proud of you!"

　　一個安靜的星期六午後，我和朋友覺得無聊，所以我們玩起丟石頭的遊戲。我找到一顆石頭，然後一扔。不幸的是，石頭太滑而從我手中滑出，打破我鄰居家的窗戶。一聽到窗戶玻璃的破碎聲，我們害怕得逃跑了。

　　接下來幾天，我太擔心自己以致於我根本沒有想到老婦人以及她破掉的窗戶。後來，我開始感到愧疚。每天，當我送報紙給老婦人時，她都

以溫暖的微笑跟我打招呼，但我在她面前卻不再自在了。

最後，我下定決心要把送報賺得的錢存起來。在 3 週後，我準備好 7 塊錢，把錢放在信封裡，並附上一封道歉信。我悄悄地把信封從門下塞入。完成此事後，我感到如釋重負，迫不及待能再次坦然地直視她的雙眼。

翌日，我開心地將報紙遞給老婦人，並回應她那溫暖的笑容。她謝謝我的報紙，並給我一袋餅乾。我離開後、打開袋子，發現袋子裡有一個信封，當我打開信封時，我非常地驚訝，信封裡有那 7 塊錢和一張簡短的便條，上面寫著：「我以你為榮！」

倒敘法：除了順敘法外，敘述文也可用倒敘法 (flashback) 的技巧，亦即從現在時間上的一點回溯到過去，然後再回到現在。倒敘法會在文章開頭先描寫事情的結果，接著才敘述事情的開始及經過，因此文章會根據發生時間出現現在式和過去式混用的情況。倒敘法把結果放在故事開頭，能營造出懸疑的氣氛，引起讀者一探究竟的興趣。

◖範文◗

本篇文章是用倒敘法，由現在偶然間發現一張全家出遊照片，回溯到拍攝照片的那一天，並敘述當天的情形，結尾再回到照片，表示睹物思人。

While we were doing the cleaning, my daughter accidentally found a picture and asked me who the girl in the picture was. Taking a glimpse at it, I recognized that the picture was taken when I attended a singing contest for the first time. **At once, I was brought back to thirty years ago** ...

當我們打掃時，我女兒無意間發現一張照片，問我照片中的女孩是誰。我看了一眼，認得那是自己第一次參加歌唱比賽的照片。我一下子回到 30 年前…

無論順敘或倒敘，最好能用表示時間或先後次序的轉折詞或時間副詞，把時間順序交代清楚，以免讓讀者感到困惑。常用的轉折詞或時間副詞列表於下：

back to (回溯到…)	afterwards (後來)	in the long run/at last/in the
first/to begin with (首先)	before (在…之前)	end/finally (最後)
at first (一開始)	after (在…之後)	until (直到)
second (第二)	at that moment (那時)	from now on (從現在起)
then (接著，然後)	meanwhile (同時)	before long (不久)
next (接著)	at the same time (同時)	a few days later (幾天之後)
the next day (第二天)	as soon as (一…就)	while/when/as (當)
later (後來)	nowadays (現今)	after a while (過了一會兒)

練習寫寫看 A

第一人稱的觀點敘述法填 FN (a first-person narrative)，第三人稱的觀點敘述法則填 TN (a third-person narrative)。接著改變人稱 (第一人稱改為第三人稱，第三人稱改為第一人稱) 來重寫各題。第一題為示範。

__TN__ 1. Harrison's family has been in the ice-cream business for four generations, and Harrison himself has spent almost his whole life in it as well. <u>My family has been in the ice-cream business for four generations, and I myself have spent almost my whole life in it as well.</u>

_____ 2. Jack Wang is standing at the gate of his new school. He is so nervous that his heart is pounding because today is his first day at an American high school.

_____

_____

_____ 3. At that time, I was a primary school student. One day, when I was cleaning the classroom, I picked up a five-dollar bill. Without thinking, I put it in my pocket. Later, Helen, one of my best friends, told me she had lost her money with tears in her eyes. I comforted her and felt regret. I decided to wait until there was no one in the classroom. Then, I put the money in Helen's drawer.

_____

_____

_____

_____

_____

_____

_____

_____

6-2 敘述文的寫作原則

❶ 主旨要清楚

主旨是一篇文章的重點,寫敘述文就是藉由說故事的方式,把主旨傳遞給讀者。敘述文的主旨可以是作者對某一經歷的見解或態度,或是某一經歷對作者的意義或影響。舉一篇以地震為題的敘述文為例,它的主旨可以是純粹敘述一起可怕的天災,也可能是作者從可怕的逃生經驗中體會到生命的脆弱、表達失去親人的悲傷等。

❷ 必須掌握的六個要素

在敘述人物經歷或事情經過的時候,有六個要素,也就是人物 (who)、地點 (where)、時間 (when)、事件 (what)、經過 (how) 和起因 (why),這些要素必須交代清楚。以一篇敘述從地震經驗中體會到家人重要性的文章為例,作者可以在敘述文中說明何時發生地震 (when)、當時作者人在哪裡 (where)、誰

跟作者在一起 (who)、地震時發生了什麼事 (what)、經過如何 (how)、作者為什麼會因地震而領悟家人的重要性 (why) 等。

❸ 選擇相關事件來呈現事情發生經過

敘述文不是記流水帳，並不需要把大大小小經過的事情從頭到尾寫下來。作者須仔細選擇與主旨相關的事件來敘述。

❹ 描寫人、事、物的細節

敘述文中常有重要的人物或場景，清楚的描寫可讓讀者有身歷其境的感覺。例如敘述地震時，可以描寫作者所在之處天搖地動的情形，這樣可以讓讀者體會作者的恐懼和思念家人的心情。

❺ 適時的應用對話

人物之間的對話可以讓讀者彷彿能夠聽到故事中的人物說話一樣，進而拉近讀者與人物之間的距離，使人物更加真實生動。

比較以下範例 1 和 2，母女間的衝突在範例 1 以對話直接呈現，範例 2 以平述句間接敘述。相較之下，範例 1 讓讀者更有臨場感、衝突畫面的感受更加強烈，而範例 2 的衝突畫面就顯得平淡許多。

C範例 1 ᗡ

My mother was waiting for me in the living room when I arrived home at midnight. "Where have you been all night?" she almost yelled. "I was at a friend's place," I said. "Don't you know I am worried about you?" she complained. "I am not a child anymore," I said impatiently.

當我半夜回到家時，我媽媽在客廳裡等我。她吼說：「妳整晚去哪了？」我說：「我在朋友家。」「妳不知道我在擔心妳嗎？」她抱怨著。我不耐煩地說：「我又不是小孩了。」

範例 2

> My mother was waiting for me in the living room when I arrived home at midnight. She asked me angrily where I had been all night. I said that I was at a friend's place. She complained that she was worried about me. I said to her impatiently that I was not a child anymore.
>
> 當我半夜回到家時,我媽媽在客廳裡等我。她生氣地問我整晚去哪了。我說自己在朋友家。她抱怨說她很擔心我。我不耐煩地回她,自己又不是小孩了。

❻ 句子結構多變化

除了簡單句外,可以善用對等連接詞形成複合句 (compound sentence),或善用從屬連接詞形成複雜句 (complex sentence)。但句子並非越長越好,應視需要長短句交替使用,這樣文章才不會單調無變化。

❼ 使用生動的動詞

動詞的精確與否能給讀者不同的感受,精確的動詞能讓故事更有活力,讓讀者更清楚故事內容、角色的性格及感受,例:

例 On hearing the joke, all the girls **giggled**.

　　一聽到這個笑話,所有的女孩們咯咯地笑。(表現出女孩們的嬌羞。)

例 The little girl **murmured** in my ear.

　　這個小女生在我耳邊低聲說話。(表達更生動。)

❽ 善用有關感覺的表達

敘述文中有許多關於情感的敘述,可以引起讀者共鳴,讓讀者感同身受。常用的形容詞有:

1. 敘述人的感覺

1. 驚訝的 / 害怕的：surprised/shocked/astonished/frightened/scared
2. 抱歉的 / 後悔的：bad/sorry/sad/guilty (罪惡感)/regret
3. 興奮的 / 高興的：pleased/excited/satisfied
4. 厭煩的 / 煩惱的：annoyed/tired/disgusted/irritated/worried
5. 困擾的：puzzled/confused/troubled/embarrassed (尷尬)
6. 感動的：moved/touched

2. 描述某事物令人感覺的形容詞

1. 令人驚訝的 / 害怕的：surprising/shocking/astonishing/frightening/scary
2. 令人興奮的 / 高興的：pleasing/exciting/satisfying
3. 令人厭煩的 / 煩惱的：annoying/tiring/disgusting/troublesome
4. 令人困擾的：puzzling/confusing
5. 令人感動的：moving/touching

 練習寫寫看 B

1. 從 A 至 I 根據邏輯順序，組成一篇敘述童年的文章。

A. In the daytime, my cousins and I usually did nothing but play. We liked to play hide-and-seek the most.

B. When it was time for bed, I looked forward to some bedtime stories.

C. We might also play basketball or baseball.

D. My parents would come to my room and take turns telling bedtime stories.

E. My childhood was the sweetest time of my life.

F. I lived in an extended family with my grandparents, parents, uncle, aunt, and cousins.

G. Once in a while, I would go to grocery stores with my grandparents.

H. In the evenings, while children were watching TV, the adults were chatting.

I. I wish I could go back to the sweet, carefree childhood.

句子順序為：＿＿ → ＿＿ → ＿＿ → ＿＿ → ＿＿ → ＿＿ → ＿＿ →

＿＿ → ＿＿

2. 從 A 至 I 根據邏輯順序，組成一篇敘述邵族傳奇故事的文章。

A. Finally, the spirit got a chance to explain. It complained that the Thao have been blinded by their greed, and they were emptying the lake of its fish.

B. Numa then told the tribe's elders what had happened in the lake.

C. One day, a group of Thao fishermen found that their fishing nets had been seriously damaged, but no one knew the reason for this.

D. To avoid catching baby fish, the Thao no longer used small-mesh nets from then on.

E. After he jumped into the water, he headed directly for its deepest area and came upon the answer there—a long-haired spirit was destroying the Thao's fishing nets.

F. He made peace with the long-haired spirit before he returned to his tribe.

G. Numa, a strong Thao hero, volunteered to go into the lake to find out the cause of it.

H. When Numa heard what the spirit said, he was shocked and embarrassed. It dawned on him that the lake had supported his tribe for generations.

I. Numa swam quickly toward it and tried to stop it from tearing more of the nets. The two then had a fierce fight underwater for three days.

句子順序為：＿＿ → ＿＿ → ＿＿ → ＿＿ → ＿＿ → ＿＿ → ＿＿ →

＿＿ → ＿＿

6-3 敘述文的寫作練習

1. 腦力激盪：先構想一個故事，並盡量寫出所有想到的支持細節或相關細節，之後去除跟主題沒有相關的細節，再把留下來的細節依邏輯來分類或分段。

敘述人物主角 (who)：家庭、成就、個性／態度、想法、影響、才華／能力、經歷／教育。

敘述事件 (what)：時間、地點、相關人物、發生經過、原因、事件、影響、結果。

2. 寫大綱：根據分類的細節擬定大綱和分段，決定每段的主題句、支持句和結論。

3. 組織文章：根據敘述文的寫作技巧來組織文章。

範文 1

題目：Watching a Horror Movie

1. 腦力激盪

1. dead people came alive and turned into zombies　死人們活過來、變成殭屍

2. zombies look no different from living people　殭屍看起來跟活人一樣

3. frightened by the bloody scenes　被血腥的畫面嚇到

4. turned the volume up　將音量調大

5. turned off the TV　關掉電視

6. headed back to my room　回去我的房間

7. scared to death and nearly passed out　嚇到快昏厥過去

8. the darkness of the room made it creepier　屋裡的黑暗讓這部片更令人毛骨悚然

9. heard footsteps behind me and a voice whispering my name

　　聽到身後有腳步聲，而且有聲音低聲呼喚我的名字

10. my heart pounded wildly　我的心臟狂跳

11. the ghost-like figure was my mom　　鬼魅般的人物是我媽媽

12. I turned off the light, lay down on the sofa, and watched the film by myself

　　我關掉電燈、躺在沙發上、獨自看電影

13. at first, I didn't think it would be too scary　　起初，我不認為片子會太恐怖

Group A:

13. at first, I didn't think it would be too scary

12. I turned off the light, lay down on the sofa, and watched the film by myself

1. dead people came alive and turned into zombies

3. frightened by the bloody scenes

8. the darkness of the room made it creepier

Group B:

5. turned off the TV

6. headed back to my room

Group C:

7. scared to death and nearly passed out

9. heard footsteps behind me and a voice whispering my name

10. my heart pounded wildly the ghost-like figure was my mom

11. the ghost-like figure was my mom

2. 寫出大綱

主題句： Last Friday night, I watched a horror movie alone at home.

支持細節： Group A: I was scared to watch the horror movie

Group B: I decided to stop watching

Group C: I was frightened by a ghost-like figure and then discovered

who it really was

3. 組織文章

主題句 (1)

支持句 (2-12)

結論句 (13)

¹Last Friday night, I watched a horror movie alone at home. ²At first, I did not think it would be too scary, so I turned off the light, lay down on the sofa, and watched the film by myself. ³However, right after the movie started, I found out that I was wrong—it was really scary. ⁴I was really terrified when the dead people came alive and turned into zombies. ⁵As blood splattered everywhere on the TV screen, the darkness of the room made it even creepier. ⁶Finally, I decided to turn off the TV. ⁷Just as I was about to head back to my room, I heard footsteps behind me and a voice whispering my name. ⁸I tried to tell myself that it was only my imagination, but the voice kept coming back. ⁹My heart pounded wildly, and I was very afraid. ¹⁰It was not my imagination! ¹¹There really was someone behind the sofa! ¹²At the moment I was just about to pass out, that "someone" turned the light on. ¹³To my great relief, it was my mom, saying that she had heard some noise in the living room.

上週五晚上，我獨自在家看恐怖片。起初，我不認

為片子會太恐怖，所以我關掉電燈、躺在沙發上、獨自看電影。然而，電影才剛開演，我就發現自己錯了——這部片相當嚇人。當死人們變成殭屍活過來時，我真的嚇到了。電視螢幕裡鮮血四濺，屋裡的黑暗讓這部片更令人毛骨悚然。最後，我決定關掉電視。正當我要回房間時，我聽到身後有腳步聲，而且有聲音低聲呼喚我的名字。我試著告訴自己那只是幻想，但是聲音一直傳來。我的心臟狂跳，感到十分害怕。這不是我的幻想！沙發後面真的有人！就在我幾乎快昏厥的時候，那個人打開燈。令我鬆了一口氣，那是我媽媽，她說她聽到客廳裡有聲音。

（範文 2）

以下範文的文章是以第三人稱敘述 Toni Morrison 的生平。文章依時間順序敘述作家 Toni Morrison 從小到老，從家庭、結婚到工作，對寫作的投入，最後得到諾貝爾獎的殊榮，敘述條理清楚。可以做為敘述人物的參考。

題目： Toni Morrison: The First African American Woman to Win the Nobel Prize

主題段 (1-3)

¹American writer Toni Morrison was born in 1931 in Ohio. ²She was brought up in an African American family filled with songs and happiness. ³Her happy family life led to her excellent performance in school.

支持段
(故事鋪陳 1) (4-10)

⁴After graduating from college, Morrison worked as a teacher and got married in 1958. ⁵Several years later, her marriage began to fail. ⁶For a temporary escape, she joined a small writers' group. ⁷In the group, each member was required to bring a story for discussion. ⁸She wrote a story

based on the life of a girl she knew in childhood. [9]The girl had prayed to God for blue eyes. [10]The story was well received by the group, but then she put it away.

[11]In 1964, she got divorced and devoted herself to writing. [12]One day, she dusted off the story and decided to make it into a novel. [13]She drew on her memories from childhood and expanded upon them using her imagination so that the characters developed a life of their own. [14]*The Bluest Eye* was eventually published in 1970. [15]From 1970 to 1992, Morrison published five more novels.

[16]In her novels, Morrison brings in different elements of the African American past, their struggles, problems and cultural memory. [17]In *Song of Solomon*, for example, Morrison tells the story of an African American man and his search for identity in his culture. [18]The novels and other works won her several prizes. [19]In 1993, Morrison received the Nobel Prize in Literature. [20]She is the eighth woman and the first African American woman to win the honor.

美國作家Toni Morrison在1931年出生於俄亥俄州。她在一個充滿歌曲與快樂的非裔美國家庭中成長。快樂的家庭生活使 Morrison 在校表現優異。

大學畢業後，Morrison 從事教職並於 1958 年結婚。幾年後，她的婚姻卻出現狀況。為了暫時逃避，她參加一個小型的寫作團體。團體中，每個團員都被要求準備一個故事來參與討論。她寫了一篇取材自一個她兒時認識的小女孩的故事，那個小女孩為了擁有一雙湛藍的雙

眼而向上帝祈禱。這個故事受到寫作團體的好評，然而 Morrison 將其擱置一旁。

在 1964 年，Morrison 離婚並致力於寫作。某天，她重拾為寫作團體所寫的故事，並決定把它寫成一部小說。她以兒時回憶為藍本，並運用她的想像力將故事情節加以發展，使得其中的人物栩栩如生。《至藍之眼》最後於 1970 年出版。在 1970 到 1992 年，Morrison 還出版其他 5 本小說。

在她的小說中，Morrison 帶入非裔美國人過去歷史的不同元素，其困境、問題與文化記憶。例如在《所羅門之歌》，Morrison 道出一名非裔美國男子在自身文化中找尋自我認同的故事。Morrison 的小說和其他作品為她贏得諸多獎項。在 1993 年，Morrison 獲頒諾貝爾文學獎。她是第 8 名女性，也是第一位非裔美國女性得到這份殊榮。

NOTE

練習寫寫看 C

根據題目寫出一篇敘述文，其寫作步驟為：腦力激盪 → 寫出大綱 → 寫出文章 (至少 120 個單詞)。

題目：A Bad Day in My Life

1. 腦力激盪

➜

2. 寫出大綱

主題句：_____

支持細節：_____

_____

_____

3. 寫出文章

_____
_____
_____
_____
_____
_____

(blank lined writing space)

Tip

練習寫敘述文時,人、事、物皆可入題,如:A Person Who Influences Me Most (影響我最深的人)、An Unforgettable Experience/Lesson (一個難忘的經驗 / 教訓)、A Wonderful/Busy/Lucky Day (很棒 / 很忙 / 幸運的一天)、A Gift/Present I Treasure Most (我最珍惜的禮物)、An Impressive Movie/Book (印象深刻的電影 / 書籍)、My First Date (我的第一次約會)、My First Watch (我的第一支手錶) 等。

重要的是,多多練習才能熟能生巧。多讀多寫是寫作進步的不二法門。

Unit 7　描寫文 (Descriptive Writing)

描寫文通常描述人、地方或物品,為讀者創造「字的圖畫」,
讓他們能夠清楚地「看」。

如何寫出一篇好的描寫文,寫作的重點於下:

❶ 提供足以吸引讀者感官 (視覺、聽覺、嗅覺、味覺、觸覺) 的描述

例 The golden sun shed tender light across the grass as it peeked out from behind the clouds.

當金色的太陽從雲後露臉時,柔和的光線灑落在草地上。(視覺)

例 The squeaky bicycle wheels are extremely annoying.

嘎吱作響的腳踏車輪令人十分討厭。(聽覺)

例 I can smell the aroma of freshly brewed coffee.

我能聞到剛煮好的咖啡香味。(嗅覺)

例 The sour cream soup tastes like spoiled milk.

這酸奶油湯喝起來像壞掉的牛奶。(味覺)

例 The texture of the wall is like coarse paper.

這牆壁的材質像粗糙的紙。(觸覺)

> **Tip**
> 在寫描寫文之前,可先問自己:What did I see/hear/smell/feel/taste?
> 我看 / 聽 / 聞 / 感覺 / 嚐到什麼?

❷ 可利用修辭法 (明喻、暗喻、誇飾、擬人法等)

明喻 (simile):利用 like 或 as 等字詞明確地比喻某物,例:

例 The bed is **as** hard as a rock.　這張床像石頭一樣硬。

例 The blonde girl looks **like** a Barbie doll.　這個金髮女孩看起來像芭比娃娃。

暗喻 (metaphor):不用 like 或 as 等字詞來比喻某物,句子所延伸的意義本

身不見得能從字面上看出來，而是用「是」、「為」、「也」、「等於」、「成了」等來表示隱藏的比喻手法。

例 Knowledge **is** power. 【諺】知識就是力量。

誇飾 (hyperbole)：將原有的情形加以誇大描述，藉此加深讀者印象，同時製造輕鬆幽默的氛圍，例：

例 Lucas spoke so loudly that I could hear his voice from miles away.
Lucas 講話如此大聲，以致於我在幾英里外就聽得到他的聲音。

擬人法 (personification)：把動植物或無生命之物用人來做比喻，例：

例 The flowers were begging for water. 這些花朵渴求水分。

❸ 使用更精確的形容詞、副詞、名詞及動詞

例 Sitting on the chair, I drank coffee. 坐在椅子上，我喝咖啡。

→ Leaning on my favorite crushed velvet sofa, I leisurely sipped a cup of latte.
斜靠在我最愛的壓花絲絨沙發上，我悠閒地啜飲一杯拿鐵。

加上更精確的形容詞、副詞、名詞及動詞來描寫後，句子更加生動有趣。

例 The boy went to the playground when he heard the bell ring.
聽到鐘響，這男孩去操場。

→ The active boy rushed to the outdoor playground immediately when he heard the recess bell ring.
聽到下課鐘響，這個好動的男孩立刻衝到戶外操場。

(用形容詞 (active、outdoor) 分別來修飾 boy 和 playground，更精確的動詞 (rushed) 來代替 went，並用副詞來修飾動詞。)

❹ 依實際需要，有組織的呈現描寫的細節，可按空間順序、時間順序、地方順序或重要性來加以排列

例 The department store is located in the busiest area of the city. It is near the train station and the bus terminal.
這家百貨公司位於城裡最繁華的地段。它在火車站和客運站附近。

7-1 描寫人物

以下為描寫文中描述人物時需注意的原則以及寫作的步驟：

❶ 利用形容詞來表示人物的外表特徵和內在特質

利用形容詞，以自由聯想、列表或問答等各種方式得到更多可用的細節，針對描寫對象將所有可以想到的資訊列出來。以下為人物的外表特徵和內在特質的形容詞列表：

外表	attractive (迷人的)、brown-eyed (棕色眼珠的)、fit (健康的)、good-looking (好看的)、handsome (帥的)、ordinary (一般的)、pale (蒼白的)、plain (平凡的)、pretty (漂亮的)、overweight (過重的)、slim (苗條的)、ugly (醜陋的)、well-built (結實的)
性格	正面性格： clever (聰明的)、confident (有自信的)、easy-going (隨和的)、energetic (精力充沛的)、generous (慷慨的)、honest (誠實的)、humorous (幽默的)、patient (有耐心的)、rational (理性的)、thoughtful (體貼的)、trustworthy (值得信賴的) 負面性格： big-headed (自負的)、boring (無趣的)、careless (粗心的)、cowardly (膽小的)、cruel (殘忍的)、irresponsible (不負責任的)、jealous (嫉妒的)、lazy (懶惰的)、mean (卑鄙的)、selfish (自私的)、stubborn (固執的)

❷ 描寫順序的安排

1. 可以從頭到腳或由腳到頭，也可以從最重要的外表特徵開始描寫。

例 My mother is very beautiful. She has short hair, a small waist, and long legs.
我媽媽很漂亮。她有一頭短髮、細腰和長腿。(從頭到腳描寫。)

例 My mother looks younger than people of the same age. Tall and thin, she is very beautiful with the brightest eyes I have ever seen.
我媽媽看起來比同年齡的人來得年輕。又高又瘦，她很漂亮，有我見過最明亮的眼睛。(從最重要的外表特徵描寫。)

2. 除了描寫外表特徵，也可以描述人物的內在特質。

例 My mother has a pleasant personality. With a smile on her face, she makes people around her feel at ease.

我媽媽有親和力。臉上掛著笑容，她讓周遭的人感到輕鬆自在。

3. 可以加入作者與描寫對象的關係，或彼此相處時所擁有的特殊經歷和回憶。

例 My mother took good care of my brother and me when we were little. In order not to make her sad or worried, we would do anything to bring a smile to her face. 我媽媽在我和弟弟小時候悉心照顧我們。為了不讓她難過、煩惱，我們願意做任何事來讓她開心。

❸ 利用五種感官 (five senses) 來描寫

描寫人物時，必須得生動逼真。訴諸讀者的五種感官：視覺 (sight)、聽覺 (hearing)、嗅覺 (smell)、味覺 (taste) 以及觸覺 (touch)，是最好用、也是最常用的方法。

例 The handsome young man wears a pair of dark blue jeans.
這帥氣的年輕人穿著一條深藍色牛仔褲。(視覺)

例 Helen couldn't sleep because of her husband's deafening snores.
因為她先生震耳欲聾的鼾聲，Helen 無法入睡。(聽覺)

例 The cheap perfume of the woman made me unable to breathe.
這女人的廉價香水讓我無法呼吸。(嗅覺)

例 Linda's glossy lips taste like strawberries.
Linda 的水亮雙唇嚐起來像草莓一樣。(味覺)

例 On touching Mom's rough hands, I could feel her deep love for me.
一碰到媽媽粗糙的雙手，我就感受到她對我濃濃的愛。(觸覺)

❹ 利用比喻法，使描述能更加生動

例 Tommy is as stubborn as a mule.　Tommy 像騾子一樣固執。(明喻)

例 Hank is a wolf in sheep's clothing.　Hank 是披著羊皮的狼。(暗喻)

例 I am so hungry that I could eat a horse.　我餓到可以吃下一匹馬了。(誇飾)

Tip
除了明喻、暗喻、誇飾及擬人法之外，描寫文也可用：
1. 擬聲 (onomatopoeia)
例 The rough wind rattled the windows.　狂風讓窗戶嘎嘎作響。
2. 象徵 (symbol)
例 Sam offered an olive branch to his enemy in the company and agreed to write a letter of apology.　Sam 向他公司的對頭伸出橄欖枝，並同意寫一封道歉信。

描寫人物的寫作步驟：

1. 腦力激盪所有跟描述人物有關的細節，歸類想寫的細節，刪除無關的細節，然後開始書寫。

2. 於主題句中告訴讀者主角是誰，並寫下對此人的綜合印象。

3. 於支持句中描寫此人的外表、性格、與描寫對象的關係或特殊經歷等，善用感官和比喻法，並使用精確的文字。

4. 於結論句中告訴讀者此人對你造成的影響。

〔範文〕

題目：My Mother 我的母親

1. 腦力激盪：先將所有想得到與媽媽有關的細節都先記錄下來，然後將細節分類，再刪除不相關的細節。

1. tall and thin 高瘦的

2. short hair 短髮

3. looks young 看起來年輕

4. takes exercise twice a week
   ~~一週運動兩次~~

5. pretty 漂亮的

6. in her mid-forties
   45 歲左右

7. thoughtful and sympathetic
   體貼且富同情心

8. works hard 工作努力

9. takes good care of the family
   照顧好家庭

10. does voluntary work 做志工

11. my role model 我的榜樣

1. ① tall and thin

2. ① short hair

3. ① looks young

5. ① pretty

6. ① in her mid-forties

7. ② thoughtful and
   sympathetic

8. ② works hard

9. ③ takes good care of the
   family

10. ③ does voluntary work

11. ③ my role model

2. 寫出大綱

主題句：My mother is a very special woman in many ways.
　　　　我媽媽在許多方面都很特別。

支持細節：① her looks　她的長相
　　　　　② her personality　她的個性
　　　　　③ her behavior　她的行為

3. 寫出段落

主題句 (1)

支持句 (2-8)

結論句 (9)

¹My mother is a very special woman in many ways. ²She has short hair. ³Tall and thin, she often wears jeans when she goes out. ⁴Because she looks so young and pretty, she is often mistaken for my elder sister, even though she is now in her mid-forties. ⁵Having grown up in a poor family makes my mother cherish what she has now. So, she works hard to make sure we have a better home environment than she had. ⁶As a busy working mother, she not only does her job very well, but also helps to take good care of her family all the time. ⁷What's more, she is very thoughtful and sympathetic, and she does voluntary work to help people in need. ⁸She believes that it is more blessed to give than to receive. ⁹Without doubt, my mother is a role model to me, and it's great to have a perfect mother like her.

Unit

7

描寫文

我媽媽在許多方面都很特別。她有著一頭短髮。又高又瘦，她常穿牛仔褲出門。因為她看起來如此年輕漂亮，常被誤認為是我姊姊，即使她現在已經 45 歲左右了。成長在貧困的家庭讓媽媽很珍惜現在她所擁有的一切。因此，她努力工作，確保我們有比她以前更好的家庭環境。身為一名忙碌的職業婦女，她不只做好工作，還總是照顧好家庭。此外，她非常體貼且富有同情心，更擔任志工幫助需要的人。她認為施比受有福。無疑地，我媽媽是我的模範，我能有像她這樣完美的媽媽，真是太棒了。

以「我最好的朋友」為題,寫一段描寫文。依照上面的例子,先腦力激盪出關於其長相、性格或行為等細節,然後寫出大綱,善用五種感官和比喻法,並使用精確的文字,寫出包含主題句、支持句及結論句的完整段落。

題目: My Best Friend

1. 腦力激盪

→

2. 寫出大綱

主題句:＿＿＿＿＿＿＿＿＿＿＿＿＿＿＿＿＿＿＿＿＿＿＿＿＿

支持細節:＿＿＿＿＿＿＿＿＿＿＿＿＿＿＿＿＿＿＿＿＿＿＿＿

3. 寫出段落

＿＿＿＿＿＿＿＿＿＿＿＿＿＿＿＿＿＿＿＿＿＿＿＿＿＿＿＿＿＿＿＿＿＿＿

＿＿＿＿＿＿＿＿＿＿＿＿＿＿＿＿＿＿＿＿＿＿＿＿＿＿＿＿＿＿＿＿＿＿＿

＿＿＿＿＿＿＿＿＿＿＿＿＿＿＿＿＿＿＿＿＿＿＿＿＿＿＿＿＿＿＿＿＿＿＿

＿＿＿＿＿＿＿＿＿＿＿＿＿＿＿＿＿＿＿＿＿＿＿＿＿＿＿＿＿＿＿＿＿＿＿

＿＿＿＿＿＿＿＿＿＿＿＿＿＿＿＿＿＿＿＿＿＿＿＿＿＿＿＿＿＿＿＿＿＿＿

＿＿＿＿＿＿＿＿＿＿＿＿＿＿＿＿＿＿＿＿＿＿＿＿＿＿＿＿＿＿＿＿＿＿＿

＿＿＿＿＿＿＿＿＿＿＿＿＿＿＿＿＿＿＿＿＿＿＿＿＿＿＿＿＿＿＿＿＿＿＿

以「我最喜歡的老師」為題，寫一段描寫文。先腦力激盪出關於老師的長相、性格、教學風格或難忘的經歷等細節，然後寫出大綱，善用五種感官和比喻法，並使用精確的文字，寫出包含主題句、支持句及結論句的完整段落。

題目： My Favorite Teacher

1. 腦力激盪

→

2. 寫出大綱

主題句：＿＿＿＿＿＿＿＿＿＿＿＿＿＿＿＿＿＿＿＿＿＿＿＿＿＿＿

支持細節：＿＿＿＿＿＿＿＿＿＿＿＿＿＿＿＿＿＿＿＿＿＿＿＿＿

3. 寫出段落

＿＿＿＿＿＿＿＿＿＿＿＿＿＿＿＿＿＿＿＿＿＿＿＿＿＿＿＿＿＿＿＿

＿＿＿＿＿＿＿＿＿＿＿＿＿＿＿＿＿＿＿＿＿＿＿＿＿＿＿＿＿＿＿＿

＿＿＿＿＿＿＿＿＿＿＿＿＿＿＿＿＿＿＿＿＿＿＿＿＿＿＿＿＿＿＿＿

＿＿＿＿＿＿＿＿＿＿＿＿＿＿＿＿＿＿＿＿＿＿＿＿＿＿＿＿＿＿＿＿

＿＿＿＿＿＿＿＿＿＿＿＿＿＿＿＿＿＿＿＿＿＿＿＿＿＿＿＿＿＿＿＿

＿＿＿＿＿＿＿＿＿＿＿＿＿＿＿＿＿＿＿＿＿＿＿＿＿＿＿＿＿＿＿＿

Unit 7 描寫文

_____

_____

_____

7-2 描寫地方

描述地方的描寫文要讓讀者彷彿身歷其境,因此必須提供足以吸引讀者感官 (視覺、聽覺、嗅覺、味覺、觸覺) 的描述,使文章生動活潑。寫作時可依照空間配置,或是從一般印象到特別細節的順序來加以描述。以下提供 4 點描寫文中描述地方的寫作原則:

❶ 提供描寫主題的背景資料

描寫文通常會先簡單地勾勒出描寫對象的背景,如作者何時到過該地。此外,最好能同時讓讀者對將要描寫的地方產生興趣,如利用一些帶有情感的語句做為開頭來吸引讀者,例:

例 I will never forget . . .　我永遠不會忘記…

例 I still remember very clearly . . .　我仍然清楚記得…

這樣的句型能表達出對某地難以忘懷的心情,使讀者因此產生好奇心。

❷ 描繪主要的印象

簡單敘述作者跟該地的關係後,可以用形容詞或名詞把對主題的感覺表達出來。

例 The library is a peaceful and quiet place.

→ The library is a place of peace and quiet.

這間圖書館是個寧靜無聲的地方。

以下提供一篇描寫朋友住處的段落,題目為 My Dream Room (我夢想的房間)。開頭第 1 句到第 3 句簡單敘述背景資料,說明作者與 Sharon 的關係和這個房間的地點。第 4 句提出主要印象,也間接指出作者想要描寫這個地方的原因是「我夢想要住在跟 Sharon 房間一樣舒適的地方」。

C範例⊃

Sharon is my classmate who used to live in the same dormitory with me. Recently, she found a nice place off campus and moved out of the crowded school dormitory. Her room is in a new apartment which is located in the center of the town. I've dreamed of living in such a comfortable place like Sharon's.

Sharon 是以前和我同寢室的同學。最近，她在校外找到一個好住所，搬出擁擠的學校宿舍。她的房間位在市中心的一棟新公寓裡。我夢想要住在跟 Sharon 房間一樣舒適的地方。

❸ 照空間順序或重要性順序來描寫

有順序的描寫就像戲劇或電影中流暢的鏡頭，帶領讀者有條理地觀察描寫文中的人、地、事、物。在描寫地方時，可依空間順序由遠到近、從左到右或從外到內，也可從最重要的物件描寫起，然後再逐漸擴展到較不重要的物件。以描寫祖父母溫馨的家為例，就可採由遠到近的空間順序，先描寫房子外面的風景，再描寫房子內部，最後描述最喜歡的房間，而這三個部分都要呈現出溫馨的印象。此文也可依重要性順序 (order of importance)，從印象最深刻或最溫馨的地方開始描寫，如祖母幫大家準備點心的廚房，接著是祖父泡茶給大家喝的前院，最後是大家聚在一起聊天的客廳，依序加以描寫。此外，描述地方的寫作常用介系詞 (片語) 來表現空間位置。

例 There is a bookcase **on the left-hand side of** the room. **On top of** the bookcase is a CD player. **Next to** the bookcase are two chairs.　房間的左手邊有一個書架。書架上是一臺 CD 播放器。書架旁是兩張椅子。

Tip

指出空間位置的介系詞 (片語) 常用的有：at、above、around、across、along、between、below、beside、beneath、behind、in、inside、near、next to、under、on the right-hand/left-hand side、on the right/left of、to/on one's right/left、in back of、in front of、in the middle of、in the center of、on top of 等。

❹ 描寫要生動傳神

空間位置交代清楚後，也要注意細節的描述，否則就像上面的例子，只是在陳述家具的位置，並未表達出對這個地方的印象，這樣就只會是一篇生硬的敘述文罷了。

1. 描寫地方時，可利用五種感官來告訴讀者看到什麼？聞到什麼？聽到什麼？味道如何？觸感如何？以下列舉一些利用不同感官，描寫對祖父母鄉間老家印象的例句：

例 Around the house, Grandpa plants roses of various colors: white, pink, and red.
在屋子周圍，爺爺種了許多顏色的玫瑰：白色、粉色和紅色。(視覺)

例 A swarm of bees are buzzing among the flowers.
一群蜜蜂正在花叢中嗡嗡叫著。(聽覺)

例 There is a sweet smell of the roses in the air.
空氣中有玫瑰花甜甜的香味。(嗅覺)

例 The papayas Grandpa plants are sweet and juicy.
爺爺種的木瓜甜又多汁。(味覺)

例 Grandpa's hands have become rough from working in the garden.
爺爺的手因為在花園裡工作而變粗了。(觸覺)

2. 利用精確的文字描述，可將❸中的例子改寫如下：

例 There is a big wooden bookcase on the left-hand side of the living room. It is filled with old books, women's fashion magazines, and Mozart CDs. On top of the bookcase is a brand new CD player playing classical music. Next to the bookcase are two chairs of pine wood. 　客廳的左手邊有一個木製大書架。上面擺滿了舊書、女性時尚雜誌和莫札特的 CD。書架上是一臺全新的 CD 播放器，正播著古典音樂。書架旁有兩張松木椅。

3. 善用比喻法來描寫地方。

例 The basement is as dark as night. 　這間地下室像夜晚一樣漆黑。(明喻)

例 Disneyland is a paradise for children. 迪士尼樂園是孩子的天堂。(暗喻)

例 My new house costs me an arm and a leg. 我的新房子所費不貲。(誇飾法)

例 This city never sleeps. 這是個不夜城。(擬人法)

描寫地方的寫作步驟：

1. 腦力激盪所有跟這個地方有關的資訊，歸類想寫的細節，並刪除無關的內容，然後才開始書寫。

> **Tip**
>
> 為了得到更多描寫的靈感，可以自問以下的問題：
> Where is the place?/What does the place look like?/What happens in the place?/What do I think of the place?/What does the place mean to me?

2. 於主題句中告訴讀者這是什麼地方，並簡短描述這個地方。

3. 於支持句中描寫此地的特色，善用五種感官和比喻法，並使用精確的文字。

4. 描寫地方時，為了表達出空間位置，常用 surround、locate、situate、place 等動詞，且這些動詞多為被動語態。

例 My grandparents' house is surrounded by trees. 我祖父母的房子四面環樹。

例 The Internet café is located/situated in the busiest area of the town.
這家網咖位於鎮上最繁忙的區域。

5. 描述空間位置時，可用不同的句型來表達同樣的意思。

例 There is a bed in the center of the bedroom.

→ In the center of the bedroom is a bed.

→ A bed is in the center of the bedroom. 臥室中間有一張床。

6. 於結論再次重述此地，並簡單摘要所描寫的細節，以加深讀者印象。

〔範文〕

主題：Neiwan—A Village of White Tung Blossoms　內灣——白色桐花之鄉

1. 腦力激盪：將所有想得到跟內灣有關的細節先寫下來，然後將細節分類，
再刪除多餘的資訊。

1. an attractive Hakka village　有魅力的客家村莊

2. most villagers used to earn their living by cutting down trees or farming
大部分的村民以前靠伐木或務農維生

3. ~~it costs about NT$20 to go from Zhudong to Neiwan by train~~
~~搭火車從竹東到內灣約臺幣 20 元~~

4. in the Zhudong area, the eastern part of Hsinchu County
位於新竹縣東部的竹東地區

5. ~~Hakka is not easy to learn　客家話不好學~~

6. coal was mined there　在那裡挖煤礦

7. the government decided to restore Neiwan　政府決定修復內灣

8. the Hakka Tung Blossom Festival　客家桐花祭

9. Hakka pounded tea and wild ginger flower flavored rice dumplings
客家擂茶和野薑花粽

10. Neiwan Theater　內灣戲院

1. ① an attractive Hakka village

2. ② most villagers used to earn their living by cutting down trees or farming

4. ① in the Zhudong area, the eastern part of Hsinchu County

6. ② coal was mined there

7. ② the government decided to restore Neiwan

8. ③ the Hakka Tung Blossom Festival

9. ③ Hakka pounded tea and wild ginger flower flavored rice dumplings

10. ③ Neiwan Theater

2. 寫出大綱

主題句： Neiwan is an attractive Hakka village.　內灣是個有魅力的客家莊。

支持細節： ① location　位置

② local history　當地的歷史

③ tourist attractions and local specialties　觀光景點及當地特產

3. 寫出段落

主題句 (1)

支持句 (2-10)

Neiwan is an attractive Hakka village in the Zhudong area, located in the eastern part of Hsinchu County. During the Japanese colonial era, most villagers used to earn their living by cutting down trees or farming. Later, coal was mined there, and Neiwan soon became a prosperous coal mining area. However, Neiwan lost its economic importance and the population dropped because of the restrictions on mining. In 2000, the government started a project to restore Neiwan to its former glory. With the efforts of both government officials and local residents, Neiwan has become a very popular tourist spot since then. Every April and May, Neiwan holds the Hakka Tung Blossom Festival, when visitors can appreciate the natural beauty of the tung blossoms. In addition, Neiwan is famous for Hakka snacks, such as Hakka pounded tea and wild ginger flower flavored rice dumplings. Last but not least, the Neiwan Theater is worth visiting. Built in 1950, it has now been turned into a restaurant in which visitors can watch old movies as they enjoy meals there.

結論句 (11)

Without doubt, if you want to take a one-day trip, Neiwan is certainly a good choice.

位於新竹縣東部竹東地區的內灣是個有魅力的客家莊。日治時期,大部分村民是靠伐木與務農維生。後來,當地發現煤礦,內灣迅速成為繁華的煤礦區。然而,由於採礦的限制,內灣失去其經濟重要性,人口也減少。在 2000 年時,政府開始重現內灣風華的修復計畫。在政府官員與當地居民的共同努力下,內灣自此成為一個熱門的觀光景點。每年的 4 和 5 月,內灣舉辦客家桐花季,讓觀光客欣賞桐花的自然美景。此外,內灣以客家點心著名,譬如客家擂茶和野薑花粽。最後但同樣重要的是,內灣戲院是值得一遊的地方。建於 1950 年,現在成為觀光客在享用餐點的同時能看懷舊電影的餐廳。無疑地,如果你想要來個一日遊,內灣絕對是個好選擇。

NOTE

以「我曾到過最難忘的地方」為題，寫一段描寫文。依照上面的例子，先腦力激盪出關於其位置、觀光景點或當地特色等細節，然後寫出大綱，善用五種感官和比喻法，並使用精確的文字，寫出包含主題句、支持句及結論句的完整段落。

題目： The Most Unforgettable Place I Have Visited

1. 腦力激盪

→

2. 寫出大綱

主題句：_____

支持細節：_____

3. 寫出段落

_____

_____

_____

_____

_____

_____

以「我想去旅行的地方」為題，寫一段描寫文。依照上面的例子，先腦力激盪出關於其位置、觀光景點或當地特色等細節，然後寫出大綱，善用五種感官和比喻法，並使用精確的文字，寫出包含主題句、支持句及結論句的完整段落。

題目：The Place I Want to Take a Trip

1. 腦力激盪

→

2. 寫出大綱

主題句：＿＿＿＿＿＿＿＿＿＿＿＿＿＿＿＿＿＿＿＿＿＿

支持細節：＿＿＿＿＿＿＿＿＿＿＿＿＿＿＿＿＿＿＿＿＿

3. 寫出段落

＿＿＿＿＿＿＿＿＿＿＿＿＿＿＿＿＿＿＿＿＿＿＿＿＿＿＿

＿＿＿＿＿＿＿＿＿＿＿＿＿＿＿＿＿＿＿＿＿＿＿＿＿＿＿

＿＿＿＿＿＿＿＿＿＿＿＿＿＿＿＿＿＿＿＿＿＿＿＿＿＿＿

＿＿＿＿＿＿＿＿＿＿＿＿＿＿＿＿＿＿＿＿＿＿＿＿＿＿＿

＿＿＿＿＿＿＿＿＿＿＿＿＿＿＿＿＿＿＿＿＿＿＿＿＿＿＿

＿＿＿＿＿＿＿＿＿＿＿＿＿＿＿＿＿＿＿＿＿＿＿＿＿＿＿

```
_____
_____
_____
_____
_____
```

7-3 描寫物品

對物品的描述亦屬描寫文,好的描述必須讓讀者彷彿親眼看見這項物品,讓他們看到你所看到和感覺到的。因此,描述物品的描寫文得注意以下細節:

1. 最好選擇自己有強烈感受的物品來描述,可以是非常喜歡或厭惡的。

2. 所有細節的描述都必須跟主題有關。

3. 描寫時可提供讀者五種感官的感受。

4. 細節的描寫順序必須合乎邏輯,可
   按照方位或重要性來描寫。

Tip
在寫描述物品的文章時,可問自己:
What does it look, sound, smell, taste
or feel like? 或 How do I feel about it?

5. 善用比喻法,並使用精確的文字。以下為部分常用來描述物品的形容詞:

opinion 意見	splendid (極好的)、wonderful (很棒的)、suitable (適合的)、unusual (不尋常的)、valuable (有價值的)、awful (糟糕的)、worthless (無價值的)、common (常見的)
sound 聽覺	loud (大聲的)、thunderous (雷鳴般的)、deafening (震耳欲聾的)、noisy (吵鬧的)、soft (輕聲的)、quiet (安靜的)、silent (寂靜的)
taste 味覺	sour (酸的)、sweet (甜的)、bitter (苦的)、spicy (辣的)、salty (鹹的)、tasty (美味的)、delicious (美味的)、yummy ((口語) 美味的)
touch 觸覺	hard (硬的)、soft (軟的)、silky (絲滑的)、smooth (平滑的)、polished (擦亮的)、rough (粗糙的)

smell 嗅覺	burnt (燒焦的)、smelly (難聞的)、perfumed (芳香的)、aromatic (芳香的)、fragrant (芳香的)、odorless (無味的)
size 尺寸	heavy (重的)、light (輕的)、tiny (極小的)、slim (苗條的)、lean (清瘦的)、enormous (巨大的)、huge (巨大的)、vast (巨大的)、gigantic (巨大的)
temperature 溫度	freezing (極冷的)、icy (結冰的)、frosty (結霜的)、 frozen (凍結的)、chilly (寒冷的)、burning (發熱的)、suffocating (悶熱的)、blazing (炎熱的)
color 顏色	yellowish (發黃的)、dark-green (深綠色的)、light-blue (淡藍色的)、ruby (深紅色的)、tan (曬黑的)、silver (銀色的)、golden (金色的)、colorless (無色的)、transparent (透明的)
shape 形狀	round (圓的)、circular (圓的)、square (方的)、triangular (三角形的)、oval (橢圓形的)、wavy (波浪形的)、straight (直的)、crooked (彎曲的)、linear (直線的)、domed (圓頂的)、vertical (垂直的)
material 材質	glass (玻璃)、wooden (木製的)、cloth (布)、concrete (混凝土)、fabric (紡織品)、cotton (棉)、plastic (塑膠)、leather (皮革)、china (瓷器)、metal (金屬)、steel (鋼)、stone (石頭)

Tip

在描寫物品時，如需用到一個以上的形容詞時，其前後順序如下：
數量 ➡ 意見 ➡ 尺寸 ➡ 溫度 ➡ 狀態 ➡ 形狀 ➡ 顏色 ➡ 來源 ➡ 材質 ➡ 功能
例 a beautiful red silk dress　一件漂亮的紅色絲綢禮服

描寫物品的寫作步驟：

1. 腦力激盪跟此物品有關的所有細節，想出可以用來形容此物品的詞彙，並刪除無關的細節。

2. 於主題句中寫出對此物品的總體印象。

3. 按照邏輯的順序來描寫，如：由左到右、由內到外、順時針方向等順序，也可依照細節的重要性從輕到重來描述。

4. 結論需要再次強調為何描述該物件。

Tip

重要的寫作關鍵得一直強調：無論是描寫人物、地方或物品，都要善用五種感官和比喻法來描寫，並使用精確的文字。

〔範文〕

主題： The Most Valuable Thing I Have 我所擁有最珍貴的東西

1. 腦力激盪： 將所有想得到跟該物品有關的細節都先寫下來，然後將細節分類。

2. 寫出大綱

1. damaged plastic band 破損的塑膠錶帶
2. silver case 銀色錶殼
3. the first watch that I received from my parents 我父母送我的第一支手錶
4. neither water nor scratch resistant 不防水也不防刮
5. a gift for my tenth birthday 我 10 歲的生日禮物
6. feature Mickey Mouse in full color on its white face
   白色的錶面以色彩繽紛的米老鼠為主角
7. special hour and minute hands 特別的時針和分針
8. date function 日期功能
9. battery-operated 電池驅動的
10. used for seven years 用了 7 年

1. ① damaged plastic band
2. ① silver case
3. ③ the first watch that I received from my parents
4. ② neither water nor scratch resistant
5. ③ a gift for my tenth birthday

6. ① feature Mickey Mouse in full color on its white face

7. ① special hour and minute hands

8. ② date function

9. ② battery-operated

10. ③ used for seven years

主題句： The most valuable thing I have is an old automatic watch.

我所擁有最珍貴的東西是一支舊的自動錶。

支持細節： ① its appearance　它的外觀

② its function　它的功能

③ its value　它的價值

3. 寫出段落

主題句 (1)

支持句 (2-6)

結論句 (7)

　　The most valuable thing I have is an old automatic watch with a damaged plastic band. It is the first watch that I received from my parents as a gift for my tenth birthday. The watch has a silver case and features Mickey Mouse in full color on its white face. The cutest things are that his little arms act as the hour and minute hands. The date function is located at the 3:00 spot. It is battery-operated. Though it's not licensed by Disney and neither water nor scratch resistant, it is the watch that has been keeping me company and telling me the time for the past seven years. The cartoon watch is definitely the thing that I cherish most.

　　我所擁有最珍貴的東西是一支有著破損塑膠錶帶的舊自動錶。那是我父母親送給我的 10 歲生日禮物。這支手錶有銀色的錶框，白色的錶面以色彩繽紛的米老鼠為主角。最可愛的是，米老鼠的兩隻小手臂正好做為時針和分針。在 3 點鐘的位置有顯示日期，是電池驅動的。雖然它並非迪士尼授權，甚至也不防水和防刮，但這支手錶在過去 7 年陪伴著我，讓我知道時間。這支卡通錶絕對是我最珍貴的東西。

以「我的學校制服」為題，寫一段描寫文。仿照上面的例子，先腦力激盪出關於其外觀、功能或價值等資訊，然後寫出大綱，善用五種感官和比喻法，並使用精確的文字，寫出包含主題句、支持句及結論句的完整段落。

題目：My School Uniform

1. 腦力激盪

➡

2. 寫出大綱

主題句：_____

支持細節：_____

_____

_____

3. 寫出段落

_____

_____

_____

_____

_____

_____

_____

_____

_____

_____

_____

_____

_____

_____

_____

_____

練習寫寫看 F

以「我最喜愛的食物」為題，寫一段描寫文。仿照上面的例子，先腦力激盪出關於其外觀、功能或價值等資訊，然後寫出大綱，善用五種感官和比喻法，並使用精確的文字，寫出包含主題句、支持句及結論句的完整段落。

題目： My Favorite Food

1. 腦力激盪

2. 寫出大綱

主題句：＿＿＿＿＿＿＿＿＿＿＿＿＿＿＿＿＿＿＿＿＿＿

支持細節：＿＿＿＿＿＿＿＿＿＿＿＿＿＿＿＿＿＿＿＿

＿＿＿＿＿＿＿＿＿＿＿＿＿＿＿＿＿＿＿＿

＿＿＿＿＿＿＿＿＿＿＿＿＿＿＿＿＿＿＿＿

3. 寫出段落

＿＿＿＿＿＿＿＿＿＿＿＿＿＿＿＿＿＿＿＿＿＿＿＿＿＿

＿＿＿＿＿＿＿＿＿＿＿＿＿＿＿＿＿＿＿＿＿＿＿＿＿＿

＿＿＿＿＿＿＿＿＿＿＿＿＿＿＿＿＿＿＿＿＿＿＿＿＿＿

＿＿＿＿＿＿＿＿＿＿＿＿＿＿＿＿＿＿＿＿＿＿＿＿＿＿

＿＿＿＿＿＿＿＿＿＿＿＿＿＿＿＿＿＿＿＿＿＿＿＿＿＿

＿＿＿＿＿＿＿＿＿＿＿＿＿＿＿＿＿＿＿＿＿＿＿＿＿＿

＿＿＿＿＿＿＿＿＿＿＿＿＿＿＿＿＿＿＿＿＿＿＿＿＿＿

＿＿＿＿＿＿＿＿＿＿＿＿＿＿＿＿＿＿＿＿＿＿＿＿＿＿

＿＿＿＿＿＿＿＿＿＿＿＿＿＿＿＿＿＿＿＿＿＿＿＿＿＿

＿＿＿＿＿＿＿＿＿＿＿＿＿＿＿＿＿＿＿＿＿＿＿＿＿＿

＿＿＿＿＿＿＿＿＿＿＿＿＿＿＿＿＿＿＿＿＿＿＿＿＿＿

Tip

在寫作完成後，可以根據下表來檢核已完成的文章是否為一篇好的描寫文，核對的清單如下：

Check to see if . . .?	Yes	No
1. there are any sentence(s) that are not related to the person, the place or the object 有任何跟人物、地方或物品無關的句子		
2. there are still some details about the person, the place or the object that can be added into the description 有一些可以加到描述文中的人物、地方或物品細節		
3. all the adjectives and expressions are appropriate 所有的形容詞和措辭都是適當的		
4. there are good and proper transitions 有好且正確的轉折詞		
5. the main idea is clear 主旨是明確的		
6. the conclusion restates the feeling the person, the place or the object brings 結論重述人物、地方或物品所帶來的感受		
7. there are no spelling or grammatical mistakes 沒有拼字或文法錯誤		
8. readers are able to make a mental picture of the person, the place or the object 讀者們能夠對人物、地方或物品有清楚的心理意象		

Unit 8　看圖寫作 (Picture Writing)

看圖寫作的定義

看圖寫作也就是看圖說故事，運用想像力將圖片轉換成有內容的文字。一般來說，看圖寫作是屬於「敘述＋描寫」(narrative + descriptive writing) 的文體。根據圖片描述主角(人、事、物)、時間、地點、場景，以及故事的背景、內容、經歷、見解、意義或影響。所以看圖寫作和人、事、物是息息相關的，生動的內容和細節是故事吸引人的重要元素。完整、合邏輯的發展能使故事精彩，而有吸引力，具啟發性的結局能使故事完整，進而引起讀者共鳴。

看圖寫作的類型

看圖寫作可分為單圖 (single picture) 和連環圖 (multiple pictures) 兩種。

單圖：只有一幅圖畫。

連環圖：至少兩幅圖，一般以三幅或四幅圖最常見，又分為兩種：完整連環圖會完整呈現圖片，故事結尾是封閉式結局 (closed ending)；而開放連環圖的最後一張圖片會是問號 (?)，故事結尾是開放式結局 (open ending)，留給作者自己想像發揮。

8-1 看圖寫作的架構

❶ 文章架構和內容

1. 文章結構

跟一般作文一樣，看圖寫作也必須要有起承轉合。一般來說，應該有三個段落。第一段為前言 (introduction)，第二段為過程 (body)，第三段為結論

(conclusion)。每一段都有主題句、支持細節和結論句,才能使每一段的文意清楚完整,而細節的部分不論是時間順序或過程等發展,一定要符合圖意並合乎邏輯。

2. 角色定位

決定以第一人稱或第三人稱敘述,以及給角色命名。

3. 順敘法或倒敘法

連環圖的看圖寫作一般多用順敘法來寫,根據圖片情節發生的順序來敘述故事,比較難用倒敘法來描寫。而單圖的看圖寫作可以用順敘法或倒敘法來寫。用倒敘法來寫時,是把圖片當作結局,先說明故事的結局,以及從此事件中所學到的教訓或領悟,再從頭寫故事發生的經過。

4. 內容情節 (plot) 的發展

前言 (introduction):描述人物 (who)、地點 (where)、時間 (when)、事件 (what/how) 和原因 (why)。

過程 (body):在心裡默問 who、when、where、what、why、how 等問題,並根據圖片的內容,運用想像力和創造力安排故事情節的呈現,如衝突 (conflict)、高潮 (climax)、過程 (process) 等,必須考量故事情節邏輯性以及合理性的發展。

結論 (conclusion):說明或強調想表現的主旨、感想、教訓或啟示等。

Tip

情節的發展必須通順且文意連貫。如果能有不落俗套的內容或驚奇的結尾能讓讀者驚豔,但這往往是可遇不可求的,與其求神來之一筆,不如通順連貫來得更為重要。

❷ 文法

1. 句子必須合乎文法，才能清楚表達文意。要達到這個目標，最好使用自己熟悉、有把握的句型，若句型能有變化更好。

2. 看圖作文一般是敘述曾經發生過的事情，所以建議時態應以過去式為主，而在圖片之前發生的事情則用過去完成式 (had + p.p.)。

例 My teacher **said** that one **would** never get anywhere if he or she **did not** work hard.　我的老師說如果不認真工作的話，人是無法有所成就的。

例 My mother **yelled** at me and **asked** me where I **had been** all night.
我媽媽大聲罵我，問我整晚去哪裡了。

3. 除了簡單句之外，善用對等連接詞來形成複合句 (compound sentence)，或用從屬連接詞來寫複雜句 (complex sentence) 等。但文章中並非句子都越長越好，應視整體內容而定。句子的結構要多變化，並交替使用長短句，這樣文章才不會單調乏味，如「我完成報告，去睡覺。」有以下不同的寫法：

例 I finished my report. I went to sleep. (簡單句)

例 I finished my report, and I went to sleep. (複合句)

例 After I finished my report, I went to sleep. (複雜句)

4. 運用適當的轉折詞來使文意更加明確。以下舉兩個例句來做比較，下一句比前一句的文意更加清楚，敘述也更為生動。

例 We got lost in the mountains, and it began to rain.
我們在山裡迷路，而且開始下雨了。

例 We got lost in the mountains. **What's worse**, it began to rain.
我們在山裡迷路。更糟的是，開始下雨了。
(加上轉折詞。)

❸ 用字遣詞

1. 除了文法觀念外，詞彙也是表達的基礎，所以平常必須多累積英文詞彙。字詞用法正確有助於清楚表達文意，用得精準更能使文章精彩。盡量使用自己有把握的詞彙，並避免過於艱澀的字詞，以免弄巧成拙。不同的動詞可以用來表達不同的情緒和反應，如：say (說)、murmur (喃喃自語)、whisper (耳語)、shout (大聲叫)、roar (怒吼) 等。

2. 根據圖片內容的需要可以描述人物外貌、情緒反應或感受，也可描述地點、天氣、氛圍來使讀者有身歷其境的感覺。記得善用五官感受 (視覺、聽覺、嗅覺、味覺、觸覺) 來做具體的描述，讓讀者更能感同身受。

3. 善用形容詞和副詞來使表達更為傳神。不同的字詞給人的印象和感覺是截然不同的，如：a slender girl (一個苗條的女孩) vs. a paper-thin girl (一個骨瘦如柴的女孩)。

以下是大考中心看圖寫作的評分標準：

	優	可
內容	主題清楚切題，並有具體、完整的相關細節支持。	主題不夠清楚或突顯，部分相關發展不全。
組織	重點分明，有開頭、發展、結尾，前後連貫，轉承語使用得當。	重點安排不妥，前後發展比例與轉承語使用欠妥。
文法、句構	全文幾乎無文法、格式、標點錯誤，文句結構富變化。	文法、格式、標點錯誤少，且未影響文意之表達。
字彙、拼字	用字精確、得宜，且幾乎無拼字、大小寫錯誤。	字詞單調、重複，用字偶有不當，少許拼字錯誤，但不影響文意之表達。

8-2 單圖的看圖寫作

所有的寫作不外乎就是寫作內容 (言之有物) 和寫作技巧 (表達精彩)，看 (look) → 想 (think) → 寫 (write) 是看圖作文的三步驟，單圖的寫作步驟為：

看　圖　〉　設定人物場景　〉　圖的定位決定　〉　故事內容

仔細觀察圖片後，根據圖片設想人物和場景。單圖的看圖寫作因為只有一個畫面，並無呈現情節的變化，所以接著必須給圖一個定位，可以把這張圖當作故事的起點、中間的過程或是結論。也就是說，這張圖可以視為是連環圖寫作的第一、第二、第三或是最後一張圖。接著構思故事的主題，這張圖片是描寫地方、敘述經驗、敘述某人的事蹟或是說明事件的發生經過等，同時也可以表達自己對圖片內容的意見和評論等，最後構想合理的情節發展。如此一來，便可寫出一個情節架構完整的故事。

以下的範例會根據下方的圖片，分別以圖片為起點、過程和結果來寫一個段落。

〔範例 1〕

以第 127 頁的圖片為故事起點：人物場景為 Peter 第一次領薪水，以第三人稱敘述第一次領到薪水的興奮心情，接著談及如何運用這筆錢，最後說明結論。

> Today was the payday. Peter was so excited because it was the first time he received the salary. He thought, "From now on, I have regular salary. How wonderful it is to have money of my own! I can manage the money all by myself."
>
> 今天是領薪日。Peter 非常興奮，因為這是他第一次領薪水。他想，「從現在開始，我有固定的收入了。能有自己的錢，真是太棒了！我可以自己決定錢的用途。」

〔範例 2〕

以第 127 頁的圖片為中間過程：除了圖片的敘述外，還得構思故事的開頭好能引導寫出中間的過程。可以敘述在找到工作之前，自己或家人的想法，或是一直找不到工作的原因、試過哪些工作、後來怎麼找到工作、工作的內容等，最後敘述感想或未來努力的目標。

> After Peter graduated from college, he decided to get a job instead of going to graduate school. Luckily, he found a job as a software engineer. Today was the first time he got the salary. He remembered that his coworkers stood up to welcome him on the first day he went to the office. This made him feel warm. During the first month in the company, he learned a lot from them. He wanted to buy soft drinks for them to show his gratitude to them.
>
> 在大學畢業後，Peter 決定去找工作，而不是去讀研究所。幸運地，他找到當軟體工程師的工作。今天是他第一次領薪水。他記得自己第一天到辦公室時，同事們起身歡迎他，讓他感到很窩心。在這間公司的第一個月，他從他們身上學到很多。他想要買飲料給他們來表達自己對他們的感激。

C範例 3D

以第 127 頁的圖片為結論：人物場景為 Peter 得到獎金或加薪，內文必須說明是什麼獎金或為什麼加薪，重點在於敘述如何贏得獎金、過程、感想或經驗分享。

Half a year ago, the manager announced that there would be a bonus for whoever could present a new business plan. To win this bonus, Peter collected, studied, and analyzed a lot of information. Besides, he consulted some experienced people in this field. He buried himself in the report. The harder he worked, the more involved he was in the work. When Peter won the bonus, he realized that hard work would pay off.

　　半年前，經理宣布提出新商業計畫的人可以得到獎金。為了贏得獎金，Peter 收集、研究和分析很多資料。此外，他請教一些在這領域經驗豐富的前輩。他全心寫這一份報告。他越是努力，就越投入工作。當 Peter 領到獎金時，他體認到努力一定會有收穫。

C範例 4D

首先必須解讀圖片的意思：路上塞車，車子前進速度緩慢。這張圖片比較適合做為文章的主體／過程，因為從圖片看到的是「在往…的路上」，所以可

以說明出發前的決定、行程準備和安排、出門後遇到的事，最後是心得和感想。接著想出合乎圖片文意的英文句子，以下為各段可以寫的內容：

緒論 (Introduction)： 說明出遊目的、地點、人物和事前的準備等。

(1) We were on the way to . . . 我們要去…

(2) We were going to visit a friend/my grandparents . . .

我們要去拜訪朋友 / 祖父母…

(3) We were going to a sightseeing-spot/the Sun Moon Lake . . .

我們要去一個景點 / 日月潭…

(4) We wanted to escape the hustle and bustle of the city.

我們想要避開城市的喧囂

(5) We made travel plans and preparations. 我們做旅遊計畫和準備。

(6) My father had the car checked. 我爸爸檢查車子。

(7) My mother prepared water, fruit, and some snacks.

我媽媽準備水、水果和點心。

(8) We brought umbrellas and coats, just in case.

我們帶了雨具和外套，以防萬一。

本文 (Body)： 在路上發生什麼事？

(1) We were caught in the traffic jam. 我們被困在車陣中。

(2) The highway was crowded, and all the cars moved very slowly.

公路壅塞，車子移動緩慢。

(3) There were times when cars could hardly move. 有時候車子幾乎不動。

(4) We were chatting and humming songs. 我們聊天和哼歌。

(5) My brother and I talked about what happened at school and even shared

secrets. 我和哥哥聊學校發生的事，甚至還分享祕密。

(6) Sometimes, we played with our smartphones. 有時候我們玩智慧型手機。

(7) We became impatient.

我們失去耐性。

(8) It was said that a truck loaded with vegetables hit a car. The vegetables were

scattered everywhere.

據說是一輛滿載蔬菜的卡車撞上一部小客車，蔬菜散落四處。

(9) The accident led to another two accidents. Everything was in chaos.

這個意外又引起另外兩起車禍。一切都很混亂。

(10) All the traffic finally came to a complete stop.　最後交通完全動彈不得。

(11) All we heard was the siren of the police cars and ambulances.

我們聽到的只有警車和救護車的警鈴聲。

(12) We were scared and nervous, but we could do nothing.

我們既害怕又緊張，但我們無法做什麼。

結論 (Conclusion)：敘述對事件或行程的感想。

(1) We didn't get home until midnight. An expected one-day trip turned out to

be a torture.　我們半夜才回到家。期待的一日之旅卻變成折磨。

(2) It was the longest day in my life.　那是我人生中最漫長的一天。

(3) My father decided to return home and had a good rest.

我爸爸決定回家，好好休息。

(4) It was a tiring, unlucky, and unforgettable day.

那是個累人、倒楣又難忘的一天。

根據第 130 頁和第 131 頁所討論的情境和句子，加上適當的詞彙和轉折詞，寫一篇英文作文 (至少 120 個單詞)。

根據圖片寫一篇英文作文 (至少 120 個單詞)。

根據圖片寫一篇英文作文 (至少 120 個單詞)。

_____

_____

_____

_____

_____

_____

_____

_____

_____

_____

_____

_____

_____

_____

_____

8-3 連環圖的看圖寫作

連環圖的順序基本上就是故事發展的順序，而完整連環圖的情節發展和結局已經由圖片決定。但不論是完整連環圖還是開放連環圖都必須先看過每一張圖片，再來思考如何銜接故事情節，讓文章能夠通順連貫。

完整連環圖：

看每一張圖 ▷ 設定人物場景 ▷ 故事大綱 ▷ 故事情節串連

開放連環圖：

看每一張圖 ▷ 設定人物場景 ▷ 故事大綱 ▷ 決定故事結局 ▷ 故事情節串連

看過連續圖的圖片後，就開始進行腦力激盪，意即想像所有可能的情節，並思考如何串連故事情節。以下加以詳述：

1. **運用想像力**：想像力越豐富，內容就會越充實。不論是單圖還是連環圖，根據「看」的結果，盡量想像所有布局和情節。設想可能的主角、人物間的關係、發生的過程、表達的主旨，也就是相關的 who、when、where、what、how 和 why。注意，開放連環圖的結局更要運用想像力來構思結局。

2. **架構情節**：從圖片所「看」到的意思可能大同小異，但圖片和圖片之間的「圖外」之意則因人而異，也是決定看圖寫作是否精彩的關鍵。決定情節發展之前，根據構想的開始和結論，把可能的情節發展一一列出。不論是單圖或連環圖，都可以發揮無限的想像力，但必須在圖片情境涵蓋範圍內，通順且合理的串連前、後圖片的情節。相較之下，連環圖的情節發展是固定的，想像空間較受限，結局也幾乎確定。注意，結局必須能呼應前面發展的結果，才會是一篇好文章。

3. **人稱的設定**：可以設定一個適合的對象，如同學、朋友親戚、家人等，也可以給主角一個名字，甚至可以用第一人稱「我」來描述，使故事更具說服力。

（範例 1）

❶  ❷

❸  ❹

思考從圖片上得到的線索，分析於下：

圖片 1：

(1) Mary has been in a relationship with John for years.

　　Mary 跟 John 交往好幾年了。

(2) He invited her to a fancy restaurant and planned to have a candle-lit dinner.

　　他請她到高級餐廳，並計畫共進燭光晚餐。

(3) Mary was excited and dressed up.　Mary 很興奮，並盛裝打扮。

圖片 2：

(1) Mary went to the restaurant on time.　Mary 準時抵達餐廳。

(2) An hour had passed, but John didn't appear.

一個小時過去了，但 John 沒有出現。

(3) She was worried about him.　她擔心他。

(4) She kept looking at her watch.　她一直看手錶。

(5) She had been waiting for more than an hour before he finally showed up.

在他終於現身前，她已經等了一個多小時。

圖片 3：

(1) John felt sorry and tried to explain.　John 感到很抱歉，試著解釋。

(2) He sent her a bunch of flowers.　他送她一束花。

(3) Mary lost her temper in spite of the flowers and his apology.

儘管有花和道歉，Mary 還是生氣了。

圖片 4：

(1) John decided to propose to her.　John 決定跟她求婚。

(2) John took out a ring from his pocket and kneeled down.

John 從口袋拿出一只戒指，單膝跪下。

(3) Mary forgave him and accepted his proposal.　Mary 原諒他，並答應求婚。

寫出文章

Mary had a date with her boyfriend John on a Saturday evening. They planned to have a candle-lit dinner and then watched a movie. Mary dressed up and arrived at the fancy restaurant on time. She was excited and couldn't wait to see her boyfriend. Ten minutes passed, but he didn't appear. She thought, "He must be stuck in heavy traffic." Ten more minutes passed, and she began to worry about him. She kept waiting for another half an hour. Not even receiving a call, she became impatient. More than an hour had passed before her boyfriend finally showed up. To her surprise, her boyfriend presented her with a bunch of flowers. She lost her temper in spite of the flowers and his apology. Suddenly, John took out a ring from his pocket, kneeled down, and proposed to her. Her anger turned into shyness right away. She accepted the ring and agreed to become his wife. This is the story my mother repeatedly told me and my sister of how she agreed to marry my father.

Mary 和男友 John 在一個周六晚上有個約會。他們計畫共進燭光晚餐，然後看場電影。Mary 盛裝打扮，並準時抵達高級餐廳。她很興奮，等不及見到男友。過了十分鐘，但他沒有出現。她想，「他一定是塞在車陣中了。」又過了十分鐘，她開始擔心他。她又繼續等了半小時。因為一通電話也沒有，她開始感到不耐煩。一個多小時過後，男友終於帶著一束花現身了。儘管有花和道歉，她還是生氣了。突然，John 從口袋拿出一只戒指、單膝跪下，並向她求婚，她的怒氣瞬間轉變為嬌羞。她接受戒指，願意嫁他為妻。這就是我媽媽反覆告訴我跟妹妹，她願意嫁給爸爸的故事。

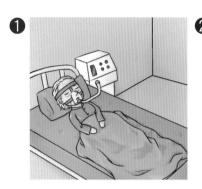  

思考從圖片上得到的線索，分析於下：

圖片1：

(1) An old lady has been on the respirator for months in the hospital.

老婦人在醫院裡戴著呼吸器好幾個月了。

(2) It seems nobody visits her.　似乎沒有人來探望她。

(3) She is unconscious, depending on the respirator to live on.

她沒有知覺，得靠呼吸器活著。

圖片2：

(1) The doctor is on his rounds.　醫生正在巡房。

(2) The doctor worries about the patient.　醫生很擔心這個病人。

(3) The doctor tries to help, but there's nothing he can do about it.

醫生很想幫忙，但他對此也無能為力。

圖片3：

(1) What do you think about the patient and her family?

你對病人與其家人的看法為何？

(2) What can the doctor do?　醫生可以做什麼？

(3) What does the doctor think?　醫生的想法是什麼？

(4) How about unplugging the respirator?　拔掉呼吸器如何？

(5) What can the patient's family do?　病人的家屬能做什麼？

(6) Should mercy killing be legalized? 安樂死應該合法嗎？

寫出文章

The old woman had been on the respirator for months in the hospital. It seemed nobody visited her. The doctor didn't know much about her. He felt sorry because there was nothing he could do about it. Perhaps watching her life being "sustained" in this way made her family feel sad. The medical truth was that this patient existed without being alive. One night, when the doctor was on his daily rounds, he heard hisses and clicks from the respirator. Suddenly, he had an urge to disconnect the old lady's respirator. However, with his hand shaking in the air, he couldn't do it. The doctor thought that if he were in this patient's situation, he would prefer to have his respirator disconnected. To him, living in a vegetative state seemed to be more than death. All in all, death is never easy.

這個老婦人在醫院裡戴著呼吸器好幾個月了，似乎沒有人來探望她。醫生對她所知不多，他感到抱歉，因為他對此也無能為力，也許看到她以這樣的方式延續生命會讓她的家人感到難過。醫學上的真相是這個病人僅僅存在而非活著。有一天晚上，當醫生在巡房時，他聽到呼吸器嘶嘶的吸氣聲。他突然有一股衝動想拔掉那老婦人的呼吸器。然而，他的手發抖著，他無法這麼做。醫生想如果他是這位病人的狀態，他寧願自己的呼吸器被拔掉。對他來說，以植物人的狀態活著比死了更糟。總而言之，死亡從不簡單。

練習寫寫看 D

根據連環圖寫一篇英文作文 (至少 120 個單詞)。

_____

_____

_____

_____

_____

_____

_____

_____

_____

_____

_____

根據連環圖寫一篇英文作文 (至少 120 個單詞)。

① ② ③ ④

_____

_____

_____

_____

_____

_____

_____

_____

_____

_____

_____

_____

根據連環圖寫一篇英文作文 (至少 120 個單詞)。

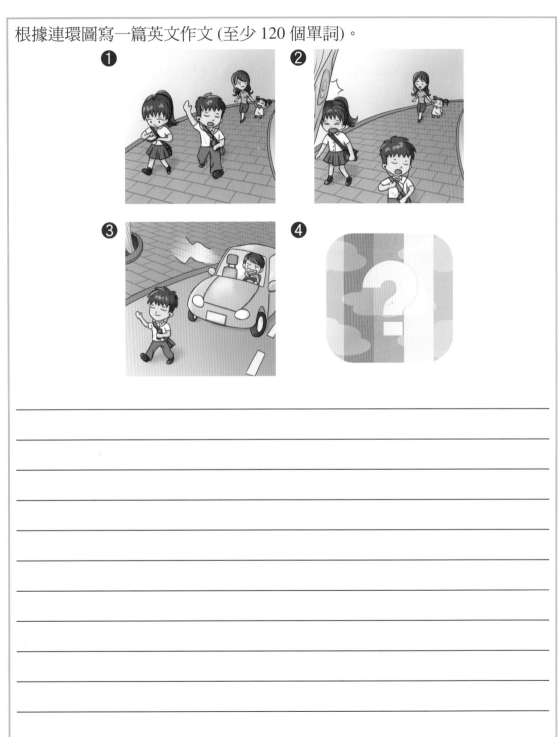

Unit
8
看圖寫作

Unit 9 說明文 (Expository)

何謂說明文？顧名思義，說明文就是用來說明事、物、現象、定義、理由、過程、因果關係，或是評論、想法、意見、比較、分類等，不論是主觀意見還是客觀判斷都屬於說明文的範疇。說明文的目的在於讓讀者了解，進而掌握、研究和應用有關的事物或現象，而說明的方法會根據主題和資料的不同而有所差異。

9-1 說明理由和評論

說明理由和評論 (giving reasons and making comments) 幾乎是所有說明文都會用到的技巧。首先，事出必有因：一件事情的發生、一個現象的存在等一定有其原因。再來說明理由和評論：對一件事、 一個案件或一個人表達自己的感受或意見，說服某人某個事實、某種觀點、確認一件事的真實性、可行性等，都必須有足夠的理由來支持論點。

根據主觀意見、客觀判斷等多方面提出理由和評論的依據：

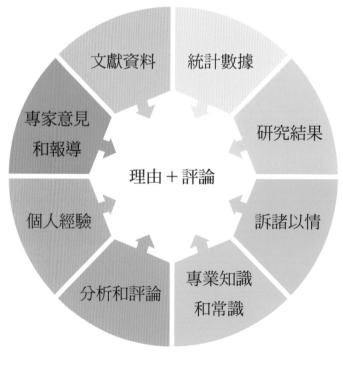

如何提出理由和寫出評論？首先從你所聽到、看到、知道的做整理和歸納，先想想如下列的問題：

1. 自己或一般人對這個故事、事件或問題的看法。

2. 列出這個故事、事件或問題的正反面意見或優缺點。

3. 自己贊成或反對哪些觀點。

4. 對個人或社會有何影響或啟發。

5. 再來整理歸納自己的答案和意見，並寫成摘要 → 段落 → 文章。

可參考以下的寫作步驟：

1. 在介紹或引言 (introduction) 的部分清楚提出需要解釋的情況和問題。

2. 接著在支持段 (supporting paragraph(s)) 中提出支持的想法和理由。

3. 提供細節和例子，將其發展成具體、有內容的段落。

4. 提出的理由和評論要有邏輯順序，如時間、空間、重要性、難易度等，要合理安排、循序漸進。

5. 結論 (conclusion) 總結主要觀點或重申理由。

善用轉折詞可以更清楚表達文意，有關理由或評論的轉折詞參考如下：

首先 / 第一	first、first of all、to begin with
最後	lastly、at last、finally、in the end、in conclusion
舉例	for example、for instance、take . . . for example
除此之外	besides、in addition、furthermore、moreover
最好 / 最重要的是	best of all、most important of all、above all
更糟的是	what's worse、to make matters worse、worst still
更好的是	what's better、better still
換句話說	in other words、that is (to say)
總之	after all、to sum up、in short、in a word

一般來說	generally、roughly speaking、in general
一般相信 / 認為 / 據報導	it is believed/thought/considered/reported that
根據	based on、according to
依我看	in my opinion、from my point of view
因此	therefore、hence、consequently、in this way、thus、as a result、accordingly

（範例 1）

針對下列評論或意見，寫出三個理由：

意見：Children should not watch too much TV.　小孩不應該看太多電視。

理由 1：Fast-paced cartoons have a negative effect on little children's attention.
　　　　快節奏的卡通對幼童的注意力有不良影響。(事實)

理由 2：Many TV programs involve sex or violence.
　　　　許多電視節目涉及性或暴力。(事實和報導)

理由 3：Watching too much TV may do harm to their eyes.
　　　　看太多電視會危害他們的眼睛。(常識和報告)

（範例 2）

根據所述事實或結果，寫出理由：

事實：School buses and taxis are painted yellow.　校車和計程車漆成黃色。

理由：Yellow is bright enough to attract people's attention.
　　　黃色夠亮可以吸引人們的注意。

事實：Stop and warning signs are often painted red.
　　　禁止和警告標誌常漆成紅色。

理由：Red is a color usually used to indicate warning or danger. When the red traffic light is on, it means, "Danger, stop!"

現象：紅色常常用來表示警告或危險。當紅燈亮時，表示「危險，停！」

〔範例 3〕

針對下列現象發表評論或看法：

現象：More and more parents would send their children to study abroad at an early age.

越來越多父母在孩子很小的時候就把他們送到國外念書。

看法：In my opinion, parents have to take many things into consideration before they make the decision. First, they have to think if their children can adapt themselves to new environments. Then, they have to know if their children are independent enough to take good care of themselves. Will their children be happy to be left alone there? Are there more advantages than disadvantages of doing so? 依我看來，父母在做這個決定之前，他們必須考量很多事情。首先，他們必須考慮孩子是否能夠適應新環境。接著，要知道他們的小孩是否夠獨立，可以照顧好自己。他們被單獨留在那裡會快樂嗎？這樣做是否優點多於缺點？

Unit

9

說明文

I 根據文意，填上適當的轉折詞。

1. Sunburn is caused by rays from the sun. These harmful rays can cause pain and swelling. _____, they may cause first-degree or second-degree burns, which can result in permanent skin damage.

2. There are many reasons why I love English class the most. _____, my English teacher is so humorous that she can make every student laugh in class. _____, she doesn't blame me for failing to answer the questions. Instead, she gives me some hints in an interesting way. _____, I can figure out the answer without feeling embarrassed. It is her encouragement that makes me learn English with great enthusiasm.

3. Do plants have feelings? _____ scientific evidence, plants can't experience pain. This is because they don't have central nervous systems and brains. Plants don't need to learn to avoid certain things. _____, this sensation (知覺) would be unnecessary.

II 針對下列評論或意見，寫出 3 個理由。

1. 意見：We must get rid of the bad habit of putting things off.

理由 1：_____

_____

理由 2：_____

_____

理由 3：_____

_____

2. 評論：There are advantages of keeping a pet.

理由 1：_____

_____

理由 2：_____

_____

理由 3：_____

_____

3. 事實：The sense of inferiority (自卑感) has a negative influence on a person.

理由 1：_____

_____

理由 2：_____

_____

理由 3：_____

_____

C 範文 1 D

閱讀下列文章，注意其結構和寫作技巧。

For coin collectors who invest money in coins, the value of a coin is determined by various factors. First, scarcity is a major determination. The rarer a coin is, the more it is worth. Note, however, that rarity has little to do with the age of a coin. Many thousand-year-old coins often sell for no more than a few dollars because there are a lot of them around, while a 1913 Liberty Head Nickel may sell for over one million U.S. dollars because there are only five in

existence. Furthermore, the demand for a particular coin will also greatly influence coin values. Some coins may command higher prices because they are more popular with collectors. For example, a 1798 dime is much rarer than a 1916 dime, but the latter sells for significantly more, simply because many more people collect early 20th century dimes than dimes from the 1700s. (102 年學測)

　　對投資在錢幣上的錢幣收藏家而言，一枚錢幣的價值取決於許多因素。首先，稀有性是一個重要的決定因素。一枚錢幣越是稀有，它就越值錢。但是需要注意的是，稀有性與錢幣的年分沒有太大的關連。許多有千年歷史的錢幣只能賣幾塊美元而已，因為它們數量很多，然而一枚 1913 年自由女神頭像的 5 分錢幣市價超過百萬美元，因為現今只有 5 枚。此外，對於一枚特定錢幣的需求量也會大大地影響其價值。某些錢幣價值不菲正是因為它們比較受到收藏家的青睞。例如，一枚 1798 年的十分錢幣雖然比 1916 年的十分錢幣來得稀少，但是後者售價卻高出許多，因為收集 20 世紀初 10 分錢的人遠比收集 18 世紀 10 分錢的人多。

文章架構：主題 → 理由 (說明) → 舉例

主題：The value of a coin is determined by various factors.

理由：1. Scarcity is a major determination.

　　　2. The demand for a particular coin will also greatly influence coin values.

舉例說明

事實：Rarity has little to do with the age of a coin.

舉例：Many thousand-year-old coins often sell for no more than a few dollars because there are a lot of them around, while a 1913 Liberty Head Nickel may sell for over one million U.S. dollars because there are only five in existence.

事實：Some coins may command higher prices because they are more popular with collectors.

舉例：For example, a 1798 dime is much rarer than a 1916 dime, but the latter sells for significantly more, simply because many more people collect early 20th century dimes than dimes from the 1700s.

範文 2

閱讀下列文章，注意其結構和寫作技巧。

I have read an article entitled "The Teacher Who Changed My Life" by Nicholas Gage. This is one of the most unforgettable articles I have ever read. In the article, the author described in detail how his teacher Marjorie Hurd inspired him to strive to become a journalist. The part that impressed me the most was the way Ms. Hurd spurred the author, a young war refugee, to understand the power of the written word. She even helped him put his love for his mother into words. And she could turn the author's grief and pain into a passion for learning. Ms. Hurd set a good example. I have learned from the story that a truly good teacher is one that can help students realize their full potential.

我讀了一篇由 Nicholas Gage 所寫，名為「改變我一生的恩師」的文章。這是我讀過最難忘的文章之一。作者在文中詳盡描述他的老師 Marjorie Hurd 是如何激勵他努力成為一名記者。令我印象最深刻的橋段是 Hurd 老師激勵作者——一個年輕的戰爭難民——去了解文字的力量。她甚至幫他將對母親的愛轉化成文字，而且她把作者的悲傷和痛苦轉變成對學習的熱情。Hurd 老師樹立好的典範。我從這個故事中知道一位真正的好老師能夠幫助學生充分發揮他們的潛能。

主題句：I have read an article entitled "The Teacher Who Changed My Life" by Nicholas Gage.

支持細節：1. a brief summary of the story

2. the part that impresses me the most

3. what I have learned from the story

結論句：I have learned from the story that a truly good teacher is one that can help students realize their full potential.

以上面兩則範文為例，寫一段以空氣汙染為題的說理文 (至少 120 個單詞)。

_____

_____

_____

_____

_____

_____

_____

_____

_____

_____

_____

_____

_____

⊂範文 3⊃

根據大綱提示，寫一篇文章。

題目：Think Again Before Buying Bottled Water　買瓶裝水前得三思

1. 寫出大綱

主題句：Is bottled water really better?

理由：1. Bottled water is potentially health-threatening.

　　　2. Bottled water causes a large amount of solid waste.

2. 寫出文章

Many people like to drink bottled water because they think that tap water may not be safe, but is bottled water really better?

Bottled water is mostly sold in plastic bottles, and that's why it is potentially health-threatening. Processing the plastic bottles can lead to the release of harmful chemical substances into the water. The chemicals can be absorbed into the body and cause physical discomfort. Health risks can also result from poor storage of bottled water. Bacteria multiply quickly if the water is exposed to heat or direct sunlight.

In addition to the health issue, bottled water causes a large amount of solid waste. It is reported that 90% of the used bottles are not recycled and dumped in landfills.

The production process and the amount of plastic bottles must be under strict control. Also, there should be a heavy fine for not recycling plastic bottles. As a result, everyone must think again before buying bottled water.

很多人喜歡喝瓶裝水，因為他們認為自來水可能不安全，但瓶裝水真的比較好嗎？

瓶裝水大多裝在塑膠瓶裡販售，這就是為什麼會有潛在的健康威脅。製造塑膠瓶的過程導致有害化學物質釋放到水中，這些化學物質會被身體吸收，引起身體不適。瓶裝水的存放不當也會造成健康的風險。如果水置於高溫或曝曬陽光下，細菌就會快速孳生。

除了健康問題外，瓶裝水還造成大量的固體垃圾。據報導，百分之90用過的瓶子沒有回收，而是丟棄在垃圾掩埋場裡。

製造過程和塑膠瓶的數量必須嚴加控管。此外，沒有回收塑膠瓶得處以重罰。因此，每個人在買瓶裝水前得三思。

Unit

9

說明文

C 範文 4 D

根據大綱提示，寫一篇文章。

題目：Always Open, Always Convenient　超商無休，天天方便

1. 寫出大綱

主題句：What makes convenience stores in Taiwan differ from those in the rest of the world?

事實：1. First, convenience stores in Taiwan offer a variety of services.

　　　2. Second, convenience stores combine regular services with special sales promotions.

結論句：Without doubt, we are increasingly depending on convenience stores.

2. 文章細節

reasons　原因	details　細節
a variety of services 各種服務	1. daily necessities, snacks, drinks, etc. 　日常用品、點心、飲料等 2. pay bills, parking fees, taxes, etc.　繳帳單、停車費、稅金等 3. withdraw or deposit money at the ATMs installed in these stores　這些店設有 ATM，可以提款或存款 4. "pay-on-pickup" services　貨到付款服務 5. book bus and railway tickets　訂客運和火車票
marketing strategies 行銷策略	commercials, promotions, new products, etc. 廣告、促銷、新商品等
others　其他原因	not far away, polite clerks, open 24/7, etc. 距離不遠、有禮貌的店員、全天候營業等

2. 寫出文章

Taiwan has the highest density of convenience stores in the world. Sometimes, two branches of the same convenience store can be found on the same block. Even in Taiwan's quiet suburbs, there is always at least one convenience store open for business. What makes convenience stores in Taiwan differ from those in the rest of the world?

First, convenience stores in Taiwan offer a variety of services. We can buy almost all the basic commodities there such as daily necessities, snacks, and drinks. Besides, we can pay bills, parking fees, taxes, and so on. We can also withdraw or deposit money at the ATMs installed in convenience stores. Best of all, convenience stores offer "pay-on-pickup" services, thus saving us a lot of time. Booking bus and railway tickets is another important service convenience stores offer.

Second, convenience stores combine regular services with special sales promotions once in a while. In this way, many people are tempted to spend money there. Last but not least, the clerks are always polite and ready to help. Without doubt, we are increasingly depending on convenience stores.

臺灣有全世界密度最高的便利商店。有時在同一條街能發現相同品牌的兩間分店。甚至在臺灣的偏鄉，也至少會開一家便利商店。是什麼造就臺灣的便利商店跟其他國家的不同呢？

首先，臺灣的便利商店提供各種服務。我們幾乎可以買到所有基本商品，如日常用品、點心和飲料等。此外，我們也能繳帳單、停車費和稅金等。我們也可以從便利商店的自動提款機提款或存款。最棒的是，便利商店提供貨到付款服務，這樣省去我們很多時間。訂客運和火車票是便利商店提供的另一項重要的服務。

第二，便利商店結合一般服務和不定時的促銷活動。這樣一來，很多人會被吸引來那裡消費。最後，同樣重要的是，店員總是很有禮貌，隨時幫忙。無疑地，我們對便利商店的依賴程度日深。

範文 5

根據大綱提示，寫一段文章表達你對某一本書或文章的意見或評論。

題目：My Thoughts on *Anne Frank's Diary* 《安妮的日記》讀後感

1. 寫出大綱

主題句：*Anne Frank's Diary*, written by a young girl, has deeply touched my heart.

支持細節：1. a brief summary of the story

2. the part that impresses me the most

3. what I have learned from the story

2. 寫出文章

Anne Frank's Diary, written by a young girl, has deeply touched my heart. Anne Frank got the diary as her birthday present at 13, when she was still leading a normal life. However, things changed completely after the Nazis took over the country and Hitler made strict laws against the Jews. The Frank family had no choice but to hide in the Secret Annex. Anne started writing her diary as a young teenager, and she matured physically and emotionally through the two years of hiding. Even though she was confined to a small place, she still showed appreciation for being able to stay with her family and worried about those who suffered outside. Even with her last breath Anne never gave up hope. This book makes me realize that the love of human nature is present even in the darkest of times.

　　《安妮的日記》是一位年輕女孩所寫的。這本書深深感動了我。安妮・法蘭克在 13 歲拿到這本日記本做為生日禮物，當時她還過著正常的生活。然而，在納粹占領國家，希特勒針對猶太人制定嚴法後，局勢完全改變。法蘭克一家別無選擇只能躲在隱密之家，安妮開始寫她的少女日記。在這兩年的躲藏日子中，她的身心變得成熟。即使她只能待在一個小小的地方，她對可以跟家人在一起表示感恩，也擔憂外面世界受苦的人。儘管只剩最後一口氣，安妮從未放棄希望。這本書讓我了解人性之愛即使在最黑暗的時刻依然存在。

C範文 6 ⊃

根據大綱提示，寫一篇文章。

題目：The Most Unforgettable Smell　最難忘的味道

1. 寫出大綱

主題句：In my memory, the most unforgettable smell is the smell of sweat of my classmates during the senior high school athletic meet.

支持細節：1.That was the smell of the sweat of my teammates on the last athletic meet in senior high.

2. I remember the good old days and feel grateful to have so many good friends.

結論句：As sweat slides down my face, the smell never fails to remind me of the effort and perseverance of my classmates and brings a smile to my face.

2. 寫出文章

In my memory, the most unforgettable smell is the smell of the sweat of my classmates during the senior high school athletic meet. How could a bad odor fascinate me?

That was the smell that brought back my fondest memories. That was the smell of the sweat of my teammates on the last athletic meet in senior high. That smell, which was not fragrant, still was an enduring part of my memories of senior high. It made me feel all over again the happiness when we won an event and the disappointment when we lost. Whenever I smell this kind of odor, I remember the good old days and feel grateful to have so many good friends.

As time went by, we graduated and went our separate ways. When I do my exercise outdoors on hot summer days, I recall the times we were all working as a team, putting all our energy into winning the competition. As sweat slides down my face, the smell never fails to remind me of the effort and perseverance

Unit
9

說明文

of my classmates and brings a smile to my face.

　　我記憶中最難忘的味道是在高中運動會時同學們汗水的味道。難聞的味道怎麼會吸引我呢？

　　那是帶我回到最美好回憶的味道，是高中最後一次運動會同學汗水的味道。一點也不香的氣味卻永遠留在我的記憶中。它讓我重溫我們勝利的喜悅和失敗的落寞。每當我聞到這個味道，我就會記得那段往日的美好時光，並感激有這麼多好朋友。

　　隨著時間飛逝，我們畢業、分道揚鑣。當我在炎炎夏日做戶外運動時，我常想起我們這個團隊為了能贏得比賽而全力以赴。當汗滴下臉頰時，這個氣味讓我想起同學們的努力和毅力，讓我忍不住微笑。(改寫自 100 年指考範文)

練習寫寫看 C

根據題目，各寫一篇英文作文 (至少 120 個單詞)。

1. 題目：Saying "No" to Drugs

_____

_____

_____

_____

_____

_____

_____

_____

_____

2. 題目：The Person Who Influences Me the Most

_____

_____

_____

_____

_____

_____

_____

_____

_____

_____

9-2 舉例說明

本寫作單元主要介紹以「舉例說明」的方式來支持主題句或論點。以寫作目的來說，和單元 9-1 一樣，都是說服讀者相信某一個事實、觀念或論點。不同的是「舉例說明」是藉由舉例來論述。「舉例說明」是很常用的寫作技巧，適用於各種文體，而且恰當的舉例能夠讓文章更具說服力、更生動和更加有趣。

❶ 舉例的作用

1. 說明或解釋一個觀念、名詞或狀況。

例 "Colors" can be used to describe how a person feels or what kind of person he or she is. For example, "he goes red" means he feels embarrassed. "He is green" means he is inexperienced. 「顏色」可以用來描述一個人的感覺或他 / 她是哪一種人。例如「He goes red.」表示他覺得很尷尬。「He is

green.」意指他沒有經驗。(舉例說明顏色可以用來描述感覺或特質。)

2. 提供事實來解釋籠統的觀念。

例 Science is not just for the laboratory, but also for daily life. For example, citrus peel can be used to clean up the stains left by markers or correction fluid.

科學不僅僅在實驗室有用，在日常生活中也有用。比如說，柑橘果皮可以用來去除馬克筆或立可白造成的汙漬。

(舉例說明科學在日常生活的實用性。)

3. 透過舉例使抽象的概念具體化。

例 Friendship needs care. Making friends can be a lot like making soup. You can't leave it alone, just as you can't leave soup on the stove unattended. Friendship, like soup, needs your time and attention.

友誼需要呵護。交朋友很像燉煮一道湯品。你不可以棄之不顧，就像你不能將擱在爐上煮的湯置之不理。友誼就像湯，需要你的時間與關注。

(舉例說明友誼需要呵護。)

4. 提供相關細節說明。

例 More and more people are taking part in volunteer work. For example, they take scout groups on camping trips, clean up town parks, and pick up litter along hiking trails. 越來越多的人參與義工工作。例如，他們帶童子軍去露營、打掃鎮上的公園以及沿著登山步道撿垃圾。

(舉例說明義工工作細節。)

5. 補充說明，並進一步提供明確和特定的方法或效果。

例 Exercise is good for health. For example, jogging can make people's heart stronger. Some say that they become more energetic. 運動對健康有益。例如，慢跑能使心臟更有力。有些人說自己變得更有活力。

(明確說明運動的益處。)

❷ 如何舉例

舉例最重要的是「恰當」，提供充分佐證主題的資料，且要明確具體，不可含糊其詞、籠統，文章才能具有說服力。佐證資料的來源如下：

1. 事實根據。

2. 引用名人和偉人的故事、寓言、神話故事等。

3. 研究和報導：書、期刊、專刊、統計、報章雜誌和新聞等報導。

4. 引用格言和引言。

5. 個人經驗和觀察。

修正以下的例子，使其更符合主旨。

例 Bob is very stingy. He once refused to lend NT$3,000 to me.

Bob 非常小氣。他曾經拒絕借我 3 千塊錢。

(→ 「曾經不借錢給我」不能支持 Bob 很小氣這個論點。)

→ Bob is very stingy. He has never donated or lent money to anyone. Nor has he treated his friends.

Bob 很小氣。他不曾捐錢或借錢給任何人，也從不請朋友。

例 Failure is the mother of success. That is, a person has to fail first before he or she can be successful.

失敗為成功之母。也就是說，一個人在成功之前必須先失敗。

(→ 並未解釋「失敗為成功之母」的概念。)

→ Failure is the mother of success. Lincoln, for example, faced many defeats throughout his life. He lost eight elections and failed in business. But he didn't give up. Finally, he became one of the greatest American presidents.

「失敗為成功之母。」以林肯為例，他一生面臨多次失敗。選舉失利 8 次、經商失敗。但他沒有放棄。最後，他成為美國最偉大的總統之一。

（範例 1）

題目：Honesty is the best policy.　誠實為上策。

例子 1：When George Washington was a child, he cut down his father's favorite tree. He made a confession when his father asked who did it. To his surprise, his father didn't blame him. Instead, he praised him for his honesty.

當喬治・華盛頓還是個小孩時，他砍倒爸爸最鍾愛的樹。當爸爸質問是誰做的時，他坦承不諱。令他意外的是，爸爸並未責罵他，反而稱讚他的誠實。

例子 2：Lying may do harm to us. Take the fable "Crying Wolf" as an example. The shepherd boy kept telling lies. As a result, he lost most of his sheep. What's worse, he was no longer trusted.

說謊可能會害到我們。以寓言故事《狼來了》為例。牧羊少年一直撒謊。結果，他損失了大批羊群。更糟的是，他再也不被信任。

（範例 2）

題目：Women have the power to change the world.
　　　女性有能力改變世界。

例子：Mother Teresa devoted her life to helping the sick and the poor. She established centers for the blind, aged, and disabled. What's more, she even started an open-air school for slum children. In 1979, she received the Nobel Peace Prize for her humanitarian work.

德蕾莎修女奉獻一生幫助貧病之人。她設立收容盲人、老人和殘障者的機構。此外，她甚至為貧民窟兒童建立一所露天學校。在 1979 年，她因其人道行動獲頒諾貝爾和平獎。

❸ 舉例的寫作原則

1. 時間順序：用順敘法或倒敘法來舉例皆可。

〔範例〕

舉柯達公司的歷史為例，隨著時間從全盛時期到破產的過程。

The camera industry is changing very fast. Take Kodak, for example. In 1998, Kodak had 170,000 employees and sold 85% of photo paper worldwide. However, with the emergence of digital cameras, Kodak's business model disappeared rapidly. Then, people had cellphones with cameras, which made it easy for them to take pictures anytime, anywhere. As a result, the company filed for bankruptcy in 2012.

相機產業改變迅速。以柯達公司為例，在 1998 年，柯達有 17 萬員工，並供應全世界百分之 85 的相紙。然而，隨著數位相機問世，柯達的商業模式迅速消失。然後，人們有照相功能的手機，讓他們隨時隨地都可以輕鬆拍照。因此，這家公司在 2012 年時聲請破產。

2. 空間距離：從前後左右或上下方位來舉例。

〔範例〕

從遠到近來描述建築物。

This building is sure to catch your eye. First, the outside walls of the tall building are painted in black and white stripes. In front of the door is a giant statue of a general riding on a horse. On entering, you will find a big garden with a wide variety of flowers.

這個建築物一定能吸引你的目光。首先，這棟高樓的外牆漆著黑白條紋。大門前是一座將軍騎在馬上的巨型雕像。一進門就可以看到一個花卉種類繁多的大花園。

3. 重要性：從最重要到最不重要，或從最不重要到最重要來舉例。

〔範例〕

閱讀下面文章後，列出所舉的例子。

> Artificial intelligence is sure to influence many industries. In the United States, some young lawyers already don't get jobs. Because of IBM Watson, people can get legal advice within seconds with 90% accuracy compared with 70% accuracy when done by humans. Watson can help diagnose cancer four times more accurate than human doctors. Facebook has a pattern recognition software that can recognize faces better than humans. In 2030, computers will become more intelligent than humans.
>
> 人工智慧確實影響到許多產業。在美國，有些年輕律師已經找不到工作。因為 IBM 的人工智慧系統華生，可以讓人們在數秒內得到具有百分之 90 正確率的法律建議，而由人提供的法律建議只有百分之 70 的正確性。比起人類醫生，華生能夠 4 倍精準地診斷出癌症。臉書有比人的辨識能力更強的臉部辨識軟體。在 2030 年，電腦將會比人類更聰明。

主題句：Artificial intelligence is sure to influence many industries.

例子 1：In the United States, some young lawyers already don't get jobs.

例子 2：Watson can help diagnose cancer four times more accurate than human doctors.

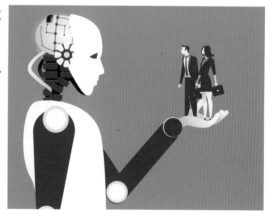

例子 3：Facebook has a pattern recognition software that can recognize faces better than humans.

❹ 轉折詞

安排次序的過程中，運用轉折詞可使文章的層次分明。

舉例	for example、for instance、such as、take . . . as an example、take . . . , for example、especially/specifically/particularly (特別是)
舉第一個例子	to begin with、for one thing、first、firstly、first of all
舉更多例子	next、second、secondly、take . . . as another example、more importantly (更重要的)、most importantly/most important of all/best of all/worst of all (最重要 / 最好 / 最糟的是)、besides/also/moreover/in addition/furthermore (此外)、last/lastly/finally
相反的例子	however、while (而)、unlike、but、on the contrary
其他	instead/instead of、likewise/in the same way/similarly (同樣地)

NOTE

I 根據上下文填入適當的轉折詞。

1. Cultures differ from country to country. _____, most Americans show affection by kissing and hugging, _____ most Asians are not used to such physical contact. Most of them greet each other by smiling, nodding their heads or shaking hands.

2. As far as I am concerned, senior high school is more fun than junior high school. _____, most teachers consider high school students "young adults." _____, high school students often make decisions on their own. _____, these students can choose from a wide range of school clubs. _____, they can make new friends and meet people with similar interests at the clubs.

3. Going to Bali was the most relaxing vacation that I have ever had. _____, I slept away half the morning without the disturbance of my alarm clock. _____, all I did was chill out. With soothing music, I lay on the chaise longue (躺椅) and enjoyed the gentle breeze. _____, I turned off my cellphone so that I wouldn't get any calls from work.

II 根據題目，舉出 3 個例子。

1. 題目：Beauty standards vary from culture to culture.

例子 **1**：_____

_____

例子 **2**：_____

_____

例子 **3**：_____

_____

2. 題目：Obesity can pose a serious threat to one's health.

例子 **1**：＿＿＿＿＿＿＿＿＿＿＿＿＿＿＿＿＿＿＿＿＿＿＿
＿＿＿＿＿＿＿＿＿＿＿＿＿＿＿＿＿＿＿＿＿＿＿

例子 **2**：＿＿＿＿＿＿＿＿＿＿＿＿＿＿＿＿＿＿＿＿＿＿＿
＿＿＿＿＿＿＿＿＿＿＿＿＿＿＿＿＿＿＿＿＿＿＿

例子 **3**：＿＿＿＿＿＿＿＿＿＿＿＿＿＿＿＿＿＿＿＿＿＿＿
＿＿＿＿＿＿＿＿＿＿＿＿＿＿＿＿＿＿＿＿＿＿＿

❺ 舉例文章的結構

Introduction 主題段	說明主題和主旨
Supporting paragraph(s) 支持段（一段或多段）	提供一個或多個例子，如果只有一段，可包括多個例子； 如果是多段，每一段分別談及不同的例子。
Concluding paragraph 結論段	摘要或簡單重申主旨，表達結果和結論。

Unit
9
說
明
文

⊂範文 1⊃

根據舉例文章的結構，寫一段探討自身壞習慣的文章。

主題句：I used to have many bad habits.

支持細節：1. Watching TV until midnight was one of them.

2. Another bad habit of mine was always putting off what I had to do.

結論句：I came to realize that if I didn't get rid of my bad habits, I would have to
pay for them sooner or later.

    I used to have many bad habits. Watching TV until midnight was one of them. Last year, on the day of the final exam, I overslept as usual because I watched TV until midnight. I had to go to school by taxi. On the way, I kept

asking the driver to drive faster. Luckily, I entered the classroom just in time. From then on, I made it a rule to go to bed before eleven o'clock. Another bad habit of mine was always putting off what I had to do. One day, my math teacher got mad since I didn't finish my homework again. I asked for her forgiveness and promised never to make the same mistake. I came to realize that if I didn't get rid of my bad habits, I would have to pay for them sooner or later.

　　我曾經有許多壞習慣。看電視看到半夜是其中之一。去年期末考那天，因為看電視看到半夜，我跟往常一樣睡過頭。我必須搭計程車去上學，一路上我不斷請司機開快一點。幸運地，我及時趕上考試。從那時起，我養成 11 點前就上床睡覺的習慣。另外一個壞習慣是拖延我該做的事情。有一天，數學老師大發雷霆，因為我又沒完成作業。我請求她的原諒，並且保證不再重蹈覆轍。我終於明白如果不改掉壞習慣，自己遲早會付出代價。

範文 2

寫一段文章，舉例說明學生如何表達對社會的關心。

　　There are many ways students can show concern for the society. For example, they can surf the Internet, read newspapers or watch news to know what has happened to the society. After knowing the social problems, they can then present their ideas to help improve the society. They can also take part in the community service clubs. On weekends or holidays, they can go to the hospitals or homeless shelters to take care of the sick and the old. Besides, they can donate their pocket money to help people in need. By getting involved, they will make society better.

　　學生有很多方式可以表達對社會的關心。比如說可以上網，看報紙或新聞來知道社會上發生什麼事。在知道社會問題後，他們才能提出自己的看法來改善社會。他們也可以參加社區服務社團，在週末或假日去醫院、遊民收容所照顧病人和老人。此外，他們也可以把零用錢捐給有需要的人。透過參與，他們讓社會變得更好。

168

根據舉例文章的結構寫一篇文章。

題目：The Most Unforgettable Movie I Have Ever Seen　我看過最難忘的電影

主題句：The movie *Titanic* is the most unforgettable one for many reasons.

支持細節：1. The story is based on a real incident.

2. There are many touching scenes about romance and true love.

3. The contrasts between selfishness and sacrifice present human nature and the real meaning of life.

4. The theme song "My Heart Will Go On" is pleasing to the ear.

結論句：All in all, the movie *Titanic* is the most unforgettable one I've ever seen.

To me, the movie *Titanic* is the most unforgettable one for many reasons. First, the story is based on a real incident. The ship was the largest one ever built at that time. However, it sank on its maiden voyage with great loss of lives.

Second, there are many touching scenes about romance and true love. For example, Jack said "You jump, I jump." to keep Rose from jumping into the sea. When the ship sank, he fell into the freezing water. He kept talking to Rose to encourage her to live until he was frozen to death. There was also a scene of an old couple lying on the bed hand in hand, waiting to die together.

Third, the contrast between the selfishness and sacrifice also present human nature and the real meaning of life. Knowing that there were not enough life jackets and life boats, some people chose to sacrifice themselves to help others while some only thought about themselves.

Last but not least, the theme song "My Heart Will Go On" is pleasing to the ear. Every time I hear the song, I can't help thinking of the touching scenes of the movie. The song will certainly go on for a long time and make the movie even more touching. All in all, the movie *Titanic* is the most unforgettable one I've ever seen.

Unit 9 說明文

對我來說，《鐵達尼號》令人難忘的原因很多。首先，這個故事是根據真人實事改編的。這艘船是當時最大的船。然而，它卻在首航沉船、造成慘重的傷亡。

第二，戲裡有許多感人的浪漫愛情場景。比如 Jack 為了阻止女主角 Rose 跳船，說：「你跳、我也跳。」當船沉了，他跌入冰冷的海水中，他不斷跟 Rose 說話，鼓勵她活下去，直到自己被凍死。還有一幕是一對老夫婦手牽著手躺在床上，一起等死。

第三，自私和犧牲的對比也呈現出人性和生命真正的意義。當知道沒有足夠的救生衣和救生艇時，有些人選擇犧牲自己去救其他人，而有些人卻只想到自己。

最後，同樣重要的是，主題曲 "My Heart Will Go On" 優美動聽。每當聽到這首歌，我就會想起電影畫面。這首歌一定會繼續流傳，讓這部電影更加感人。總之，《鐵達尼號》是我看過最難忘的電影。

NOTE

根據題目，寫出一篇舉例文章 (至少 120 個單詞)。

題目：Learning to Say No

_____

_____

_____

_____

_____

_____

_____

_____

_____

_____

_____

_____

_____

_____

_____

Unit

9

說明文

9-3 因果文

因果文 (cause and effect) 的目的在於解釋一個事件或情況的原因及影響，常見的主題如：水汙染的原因、花太多時間上網的影響等；有時也可能是一個事件造成另一事件的發生，而此結果又會導致另一事件發生的連鎖反應，如：蜜蜂絕跡會造成全球糧食大量短缺，進而導致人類的滅亡。以下為幾個因果文主題的例子：

例 What are the causes and effects of bullying? 霸凌的因果為何？

例 What are the effects of peer pressure? 同儕壓力的影響為何？

例 What are the causes and effects of the popularity of fast food restaurants?
速食餐廳受歡迎的因果為何？

例 What are the effects of online music downloading on the music industry?
線上音樂下載對音樂產業有何影響？

> **Tip**
>
> 事件發生的原因以及所造成的影響往往是多重的，但無論是原因或影響，都只要挑選
> 最重要的兩、三項來寫即可。

❶ 因果文的組織架構

根據主題，因果文可利用三種組織圖來進行腦力激盪：

1. 多原因導致一種結果：以 The Causes of Bee Decline (蜜蜂減少的原因) 為例：

主題句	
支持細節	原因 **1**：lack of flowers　花朵缺少
	原因 **2**：the use of chemicals　使用化學農藥
	原因 **3**：climate change　氣候變遷
結論句	

2. 單一原因導致多種結果：以 The Effects of Using Cellphones in Class (上課使用手機的影響) 為例：

主題句	
支持細節	影響 **1**：The users will be distracted.　使用者會分心。
	影響 **2**：Other students may be disturbed. 其他學生可能受到干擾。
	影響 **3**：The users' eyesight can be damaged. 使用者的視力會受損。
結論句	

3. 連鎖反應：同時探討主題的原因和影響，以 The Causes and Effects of Procrastination (拖延的因果) 為例：

原因		主題		影響
1. lack of motivation 　缺乏動機	→		→	1. poor grades 　成績低落
2. fear of failure 　害怕失敗	→	Procrastination 拖延	→	2. health problems 　健康問題
3. perfectionism 　完美主義	→		→	3. anxiety　焦慮

❷ 表因果關係的轉折詞

使用適當的轉折詞能讓文章更流暢，讀者更易理解文意。按詞性分類如下：

	因為 (表原因)	因此 (表結果)
連接詞	as、for、since、because	so
介系詞	due to、owing to、thanks to、because of、on account of、as a result of、in view of、in consequence of、as a consequence of	
副詞		thus、hence、therefore、as a result、for this reason、accordingly、consequently、in consequence、as a consequence

例 Samuel was caught in the rain yesterday, **so** he is sick today.

Samuel 昨天淋雨，因此他今天生病了。

➡ Samuel was caught in the rain yesterday; **thus**, he is sick today.

➡ Samuel is sick today **because** he was caught in the rain yesterday.

Samuel 今天生病了，因為他昨天淋雨。

例 Betty didn't finish the project on time, **so** she was fired.

Betty 沒有準時完成計畫，所以她被開除了。

→ Betty didn't finish the project on time; **in consequence**, she was fired.

→ Betty didn't finish the project on time; **for this reason**, she was fired.

→ **Since** Betty didn't finish the project on time, she was fired.

因為 Betty 沒有準時完成計畫，她被開除了。

I

1. 以 The Causes of Becoming Overweight (體重過重的原因) 為題，腦力激盪並填入以下組織圖：

主題句		
支持細節	原因 1：	
	原因 2：	
	原因 3：	
結論句		

2. 以 The Effects of Becoming Overweight (體重過重的影響) 為題，腦力激盪並填入以下組織圖：

主題句		
支持細節	影響 1：	
	影響 2：	
	影響 3：	
結論句		

3. 以 The Causes and Effects of Cyberbullying (網路霸凌的原因和影響) 為題，
   腦力激盪並填入以下組織圖：

原因		主題		影響
1.	→	Cyberbullying 網路霸凌	→	1.
2.	→		→	2.
3.	→		→	3.

Ⅱ 在下列各題的空格中填入適當表因果關係的轉折詞。

1. Sandy was late for school _____ she got up late.

2. Kevin had a stomachache _____ the pressure of work.

3. It rained heavily; _____, the football game was canceled.

4. Ben was sick in bed, _____ he didn't show up yesterday.

5. There has been a power failure. _____, the amusement park is not open
   today.

❸ 因果文的寫作步驟

1. 在腦力激盪出所有可能的原因或結果之後，刪除不相關的資訊，留下最相
   關的即可。一篇好的因果文是在有限的文章篇幅中，提出最相關的原因或
   結果，有時一項就足夠。

2. 在主題句中預告文章將包含幾個原因或結果，也可告訴讀者文章中要說明
   的最重要一項原因或結果，常用的主題句如下：

例 There are . . . <u>causes of/reasons for/effects of</u> _____.
   …的<u>原因</u> / <u>影響</u>有…個

例 There are . . . main <u>reasons why</u> _____.　為什麼…的主要原因有…

例 _____ has <u>great/harmful/destructive</u> effects on _____.
   …對…有<u>很大的</u> / <u>有害的</u> / <u>破壞性的</u>影響

例 One main cause/effect of _____ is . . .　…的主要原因 / 影響是…

Tip

在因果文中，經常使用表示「導致」或「起因於」的動詞。

導致：cause、lead to、result in、bring about、give rise to

起因於：result from、arise from、stem from、root in、be caused by

3. 除了可使用表達因果的轉折詞來加強段落中細節之間的關係之外，也可用表添加或次序的轉折詞來連接原因或結果，讓段落看起來更有秩序。

表添加的轉折詞	besides、in addition、additionally、moreover、furthermore
表次序的轉折詞	first/firstly、second/secondly、third/thirdly、next、then、finally、last but not least

4. 因果文通常用以下兩種方法結尾：

簡潔有力地複述之前討論的因果：此方法可使讀者在最短的時間內，掌握全文的要旨，並在最後仍能對文章的組織一目瞭然。必須注意的是，用字遣詞上不宜與前文過度重複，需要稍有變化。

呼籲讀者：在結尾時，可將所陳述的因果稍作整理，並提出有力的見解，對讀者提出呼籲，使讀者能對所討論的主題重新檢視其看法。

《範文》

主題：The Causes of Global Warming　全球暖化的原因

1. 腦力激盪：將所有可能造成全球暖化的原因都寫下來，刪除較不相關的細節，留下最重要的原因。

1. cars 汽車	1. ① cars
2. airplanes 飛機	2. ① airplanes
3. factories 工廠	3. ① factories
4. electricity 電	4. ① electricity
~~5. mining 挖礦~~	6. ② eating meat
6. eating meat 吃肉	7. ③ fertilizer use
7. fertilizer use 施肥	
~~8. buying local food~~ 買當地的食物	

2. 寫出大綱

主題句：Greenhouse gases, such as carbon dioxide, methane, and nitrogen oxide, are the primary causes of global warming.

支持細節：

原因 1：carbon dioxide

原因 2：methane

原因 3：nitrogen oxide

結論句：If we don't take action soon, our planet will be too warm to be a habitable place.

3. 寫出段落

主題句 (1)

支持句 (2-7)

¹Greenhouse gases, such as carbon dioxide, methane, and nitrogen oxide, are the primary causes of global warming. ²Cars, airplanes, and factories burn fuels, such as oil, gas, and coal, and this results in the discharge of huge amounts of carbon dioxide into the atmosphere. ³Worse still, the electricity that people use has caused an increase in the emission of carbon dioxide as well because it takes fossil fuels to generate power. ⁴Another

greenhouse gas is methane. ⁵The more meat people eat, the more animals need to be raised. ⁶This further brings about the rise of methane, for animals like pigs, cows, and sheep emit methane. ⁷Finally, each time farmers add fertilizer to soil, nitrogen oxide escapes into the atmosphere.

結論句 (8-9)

⁸These greenhouse gases trap heat in the atmosphere and don't allow them to escape into space, thus causing our planet to heat up. ⁹If we don't take action soon, our planet will be too warm to be a habitable place.

溫室氣體，如二氧化碳、沼氣和氧化氮，是全球暖化主要原因。汽車、飛機和工廠燃燒石油、瓦斯和煤等燃料，這導致大量二氧化碳排入大氣。更糟的是，人們用電也會增加二氧化碳的排放量，因為需要石化燃料來發電。另一種溫室氣體是沼氣。人們吃越多肉，就得養殖越多動物。因為像豬、牛和羊等動物會排放沼氣，這進一步增加沼氣的含量。最後，每當農人對土壤施肥時，氧化氮就會飄進大氣中。

這些溫室氣體會將熱氣困在大氣層，無法排入太空，因此造成地球越來越熱。如果我們不快點採取行動的話，地球將會熱到無法居住。

Tip

好的因果文應注意下列幾點：

1. 主題句應清楚說明討論的是原因 (cause) 或是影響 (effect)。
2. 細節順序安排的方法有：按時間順序、按重要性以及按種類。
3. 使用適當的轉折詞，讓文意通順。
4. 專注於相關與直接的原因或影響，捨棄相關性較低的。

以 The Effects of Climate Change (氣候變遷的影響) 為題,寫一段因果文。仿照上面的例子,先腦力激盪出氣候變遷可能造成的影響,然後寫出大綱和包含主題句、支持句和結論句的完整段落。

1. 腦力激盪

2. 寫出大綱

主題句: _____

支持細節:

影響 1: _____

影響 2: _____

影響 3: _____

3. 寫出段落

_____

_____

_____

_____

_____

_____

_____

_____

_____

9-4 定義文

本單元介紹定義文(giving definition)。「定義」就是解釋、詮釋，說明一個字、一個詞、一件事、一個現象、一個觀念或是一種想法等。雖然是在說明一個詞語的意義，但不僅僅是轉述字典所列出的解釋或一般認知的意思，有些詞語是具體、有明確特定的定義，例如解釋「桌子」、「汽車」等，可以具體說明其材質、大小、功能等等，每個人的定義大致相同，而且定義也不太隨著時間而改變。但有些詞語是抽象的，如「幸福」、「愛」、「成功」等，會因為每個人所處環境和經驗的不同，感受和意義也會有所不同。

定義的範疇

基本上包含許多層面，可以從 5W1H 來解釋：

What：解釋「是什麼」、「做什麼」或「有什麼作用」等。

Who：相關或影響的人。

When 和 Where：相關的時間和地點。

Why：解釋原因、說明理由或目的等。

How：解釋「功能」、「組織」或「如何進行」等。

❶ 定義的方法

1. 連結熟悉、相關或類似的東西說明，使定義更容易被了解。

2. 和相對的東西做比較、對比，可以使定義更明確。

例 Unlike ordinary people you know, a friend will show concern for you. Fair-weather friends surely keep away from you when you are in trouble. However, a real friend is always with you. 不同於你認識的一般人，朋友會關心你。當你有麻煩時，酒肉朋友一定會遠離你。然而，真正的朋友會陪在你身邊。

(同時解釋真正的朋友和酒肉朋友的差異，可以突顯出朋友的定義。)

3. 用事實、訊息、舉例、個人經驗或軼事等來解釋。

4. 從概括的大範圍縮小進入特定或單一的範圍，如定義「小學」，先說是一

個地方 (大範圍)，然後再解釋是什麼樣的地方。若要定義抽象的概念，先說明那是一種什麼樣的感覺、想法、態度等，接著再說明細節，如：「愛」的定義是一種強烈的喜歡或興趣，接著可以說明對象 (人或物品)。

例 "An elementary school" is a place where children between the ages of 6 and 12 are taught to receive primary education.

「小學」是年齡介於 6 到 12 歲的小孩接受基礎教育的地方。

例 "Love" is a strong affection for a person arising out of kinship or interpersonal relationships or a great interest in something.　「愛」是一種一個人從親屬或人際關係中所產生的強烈情感，或是對某事物的高度興趣。

具體和抽象定義的差異：

具體	抽象
外觀：形狀、大小、顏色、味道、材質	沒有實體，是一種感覺和想法
分析：功能、組織、成分、用途	主觀認定：重要或在乎的元素
客觀認知，定義差異不大	主觀認定，定義會因人而異
定義固定，不容易隨著時間改變	定義可能隨著時間改變

（範例）

題目：The Definition of "House" and "Home"　「房子」與「家」的定義

具體 (house)	住的地方 強調「地方」 外觀、內部裝潢和設備
抽象 (home)	不只是住的地方 強調「感覺」和「情感」 身心的庇護所 愛是家最重要的元素

"House" and "home" both refer to places where people live. However, there is a difference between them. "House" focuses on "the place," while "home" emphasizes "the feeling." We may describe a house as a three-story building or an apartment, what material it is used and how it is decorated. But when we talk about "home," it is more than a place where we live. It is a shelter not only for our bodies but for our minds. "Love" is the most important factor of a "home." Whenever we feel bad, we can seek comfort at home. Everyone in the family will do his or her best to take care of each other and share their happiness as well as sorrow. Without love, a home is merely a house where loneliness is all that can be found.

　　「房子」和「家」都是指人們居住的地方。然而,兩者卻有所不同。「房子」著重於「地方」,而「家」則著重於「情感」。我們可能描述房子是一棟 3 層樓的建築物或一間公寓,用了什麼材質和如何裝潢。但當我們談到「家」,這不只是居住的地方。它是身體也是心靈的住所。「愛」是一個「家」最重要的因素。每當我們感到難過,我們向家裡尋求慰藉。家中的每一分子都應該盡其所能互相照顧,一同分享快樂與傷悲。少了愛,一個家就變成只剩孤單的房子。

先根據字典或百科全書定義以下名詞,再加以舉例說明。

題目 1:A Museum　一間博物館

定義:A building or a place where works of art are displayed.
　　　藝術品陳列的地方或建築物。

舉例:The Louvre Museum in Paris, the British Museum in London and the Metropolitan Museum of Art in New York are among the most famous museums.　巴黎的羅浮宮、倫敦的大英博物館和紐約的大都會博物館是博物館中最知名的。

題目 2：A Walking Dictionary　一本活字典

定義：A dictionary is a book that gives a list of words in alphabetical order and explains what they mean. So, a walking dictionary means a person who knows about everything.　字典是一本將字彙依照字母順序排列，並解釋其涵義的書。所以活字典意指一個無所不知的人。

舉例：Our math teacher is a walking dictionary. Whatever questions we ask, she can always give us answers.　我們的數學老師是本活字典。不管我們問什麼問題，她都能給我們答案。

練習寫寫看 H

根據你的想法，寫出下列名詞的 3 種定義。

1. 題目：Success

定義 1：＿＿＿＿＿＿＿＿＿＿＿＿＿＿＿＿＿＿＿＿＿＿＿

定義 2：＿＿＿＿＿＿＿＿＿＿＿＿＿＿＿＿＿＿＿＿＿＿＿

定義 3：＿＿＿＿＿＿＿＿＿＿＿＿＿＿＿＿＿＿＿＿＿＿＿

2. 題目：A True Friend

定義 1：＿＿＿＿＿＿＿＿＿＿＿＿＿＿＿＿＿＿＿＿＿＿＿

定義 2：＿＿＿＿＿＿＿＿＿＿＿＿＿＿＿＿＿＿＿＿＿＿＿

定義 3：＿＿＿＿＿＿＿＿＿＿＿＿＿＿＿＿＿＿＿＿＿＿＿

3. 題目：Growing Up

定義 1：＿＿＿＿＿＿＿＿＿＿＿＿＿＿＿＿＿＿＿＿＿＿＿

定義 2：＿＿＿＿＿＿＿＿＿＿＿＿＿＿＿＿＿＿＿＿＿＿＿

定義 3：＿＿＿＿＿＿＿＿＿＿＿＿＿＿＿＿＿＿＿＿＿＿＿

❷ 定義文的結構

定義文的結構為：主題段：提出主題 (描述其定義) → 支持段：支持細節 (引申意義、舉例印證) → 結論段：結論 (再次強調主題或理論根據)。

⊂範例 1⊃

> An area code is a section of a telephone number which generally represents the geographical area that the phone receiving the call is based in. It is the two or three digits just before the local number. If the number being called is not in the same area as the number making the call, an area code should be dialed.
>
> 區域號碼是電話號碼的一部分，代表接受電話那方的地理區域。區域號碼是在電話號碼前加上兩位或三位數字。如果打電話和接電話的號碼不在同一區域，就得加上區域號碼。

本段定義文的結構包括：

1. What is an area code? 什麼是區域號碼？

   An area code is a section of a telephone number which generally represents the geographical area that the phone receiving the call is based in.

2. How is an area code formed? 區域號碼是如何組成的？

   It is the two or three digits just before the local number.

3. When should an area code be used? 什麼時候要用區域號碼？

   If the number being called is not in the same area as the number making the call, an area code should be dialed.

⊂範例 2⊃

> There are two kinds of heroes: heroes who carry out difficult missions in the face of great danger, and heroes who do good deeds in everyday life. The latter live an ordinary life like us, but they make a difference in the lives of others.

Heroes are selfless people who perform extraordinary acts. The mark of heroes is not necessarily the result of their action, but the reason they are willing to do for others. Even if they fail, their determination lives on for others to follow. The glory lies not in the achievement, but in the sacrifice.

英雄有兩種：一種是在面對極大危險時執行困難的任務，另一種是在日常生活中行善。後者就像我們一般過著平凡的生活，但他們卻對他人的生活有極大的影響。

英雄是做出不平凡行為的無私之人。英雄的特徵未必是他們行動的結果，而是他們願意去做的理由。即使他們失敗了，他們的決心繼續存在讓其他人得以效法。這種榮耀不在於成就，而是在於犧牲。

本段定義文的結構包括：

1. What are the two kinds of heroes?　哪兩種英雄？

Heroes who carry out difficult missions in the face of great danger, and heroes who do good deeds in everyday life.

2. How are heroes different from ordinary people?　英雄如何和一般人不同？

Heroes are selfless people who perform extraordinary acts.

3. Why are they honored and remembered?　為何他們被瞻仰和緬懷？

The glory lies not in the achievement, but in the sacrifice.

C範例 3D

題目：The Paralympics　殘障奧運會

The Paralympics are an international sports event held every four years for athletes with disabilities. This sports event will be held after the Olympic Games in the same city. The Paralympics were organized for the first time in Rome in 1960. They emphasize the participants' athletic achievements instead of their physical disabilities. The games have grown in size gradually. The number of

athletes participating in the Paralympics has increased from 400 athletes from 23 countries in 1960 to 4342 athletes from 159 countries in 2016.

　　殘障奧運會是為殘障選手們每 4 年舉辦一次的國際運動賽事。這項運動賽事會在奧運後於同一個城市舉辦。1960 年，首次在羅馬舉辦殘障奧運會。比賽強調參賽者的運動成就，而非其身體缺陷。賽事規模逐漸擴大。參加殘障奧運的選手從 1960 年的 23 國 400 人增加到 2016 年的 159 國 4342 人。

❸ 常用於定義文的轉折詞

解釋	that is、that is to say、to put it another way、in other words
表示相似性	like、in the same way、similarly、as、just as
表示差異性、對比和比較	unlike、on the contrary、however、while、nevertheless、by/in comparison、by/in contrast
更進一步說明	besides、in addition (to)、moreover、furthermore、what's more、to make matters worse/better
舉例	such as、for example/instance、take . . . as an example

根據文意，填入適當的轉折詞。

1. Some people say "Necessity is the mother of invention." _____, if something is needed, then it will be invented.

2. Making friends can be like making soup. It requires many different ingredients to develop a close friendship. _____, trust and similar interests are very important. _____, constant care is also needed.

3. A saying goes, "Out of sight, out of mind." _____, if we don't see someone for a while, we may stop thinking about him or her. _____, this is not always the case. _____, true friendship lasts forever. No matter how far away a true friend is, he or she will always be on our minds.

❹ 定義文的寫作

〔範文 1〕

題目：Tai Chi Chuan　太極拳

Tai Chi Chuan is a type of ancient Chinese martial art. People practice Tai Chi mainly for its health benefits. This centuries-old Chinese mind-body exercise is now gaining popularity in the United States.

The most familiar aspect of Tai Chi Chuan is the hand form, which is a series of slow-flowing movements with poetic names like "dragon stirring up the wind" and "wave hands like clouds." These movements, forming an exercise system, allow one to effortlessly experience the vital life force, or the Qi energy, in one's body.

Tai Chi Chuan is not only a physical but also a mental exercise. Psychologically, this exercise may increase communication between the body and the mind and enable one to deal with other people more effectively. It reduces stress and creates calmness and confidence. Relaxation and a feeling of joy are among the first noticeable differences in a Tai Chi student.

太極拳是一種古老的中國武術。人們練習太極拳主要是因為其健康利益。這項中國悠久的身心合一運動如今在美國越趨流行。

太極拳最為人所熟悉的莫過於掌勢。這個掌勢是一系列名稱頗具詩意的徐緩動作，像是「乘龍御風」和「雲手」。這些動作構成一套運動體系，使一個人能夠毫不費力地感受到體內重要的生命動力，或「氣」的能量。

太極拳不只包括身體鍛鍊，還涵蓋心靈修養。在心靈層面上，這項運動能增進身心間的交流，讓一個人能更有效地與他人應對。它能減少壓力並產生平靜與自信。放鬆與喜悅感是太極拳學習者最初能感受到的顯著差異。

(104 年學測)

範文 2

題目：Growing Up

1. 腦力激盪

先腦力激盪想出所有可能的定義，如長大的意義、時期、各方面的改變、自身的經驗、態度和感覺、觀察他人的改變等。

2. 寫出大綱

主題句：Generally speaking, when a person turns seventeen, he or she is considered not a child anymore.

支持段

主題句：How was I aware that I was no longer a kid?

支持細節：1. be independent

2. make one's own decisions

3. be sensible and reasonable

4. be treated as a grown-up

結論段

主題句：Little by little, I come to realize that a grown-up means being mature, responsible, and reasonable.

支持細節：1. keep a balance between study and play

2. show concern for others

3. 寫出文章

Generally speaking, when a person turns seventeen, he or she is considered not a child anymore. In other words, that person has reached maturity and become a grown-up. He or she can no longer enjoy the benefit of being a child such as doing something silly or having his or her own way.

How was I aware that I was no longer a kid? On the first day of going to senior high school, I was waiting for my father to drive me to school. After a while, my father asked me, "What are you waiting for? It's time. Go now or you'll be late. Don't ride your bike too fast." "Won't you drive me to school?" I said. "Well, you have grown up. You have to be independent and do what you have to do." When I asked my parents what club I should join, they answered, "That's your business. You have to start making your own decision." When I complained, they told me to be sensible. When I got angry, they told me to be reasonable. They no longer make plans for me. Instead, they begin to ask my opinions.

Little by little, I come to realize that a grown-up means being mature, responsible, and reasonable. Grown-ups must try to keep a balance between study and play. Grown-ups must show concern not only for their family members and friends but for others and the society as well. I'm glad that I am on my way to maturity.

一般來說，當一個人 17 歲時就會被認為已經不是小孩了。換句話說，他／她已經長大成熟、是大人了。他／她不再享受當小孩的好處，如：做蠢事或任性而為。

如何體會到自己不再是個孩子？第一天上高中時，我正在等爸爸載我去上學。等了好一會兒，爸爸問我：「你在等什麼？時間到了，趕快去，不然會遲到。騎腳踏車別騎太快。」我說：「您不載我去學校嗎？」「你

已經長大了，必須要獨立，做你應該做的事。」當我問爸媽自己該加入什麼社團時，他們回答：「那是你的事，你必須開始自己做決定」。當我抱怨的時候，他們告訴我要講道理。當我生氣時，他們叫我要理智，他們不再幫我制定計畫，相反地，他們開始詢問我的看法。

漸漸地，我體會到長大就表示著成熟、負責和理智。大人必須學著在讀書和玩樂間取得平衡。大人必須關懷家人朋友外，也需要關心他人與社會。我很開心自己正在變成熟了。

練習寫寫看 J

I 根據題目，寫出一段定義文。

1. 題目：A Fan

_____

_____

_____

_____

_____

_____

2. 題目：A Genius

_____

_____

_____

_____

_____

_____

II 根據題目，寫一篇定義文 (至少 120 個單字)。

題目：Happiness

_____

_____

_____

_____

_____

_____

_____

_____

_____

9-5 程序文

程序文是以「How to . . .」為主題的文章，不同的是程序文會說明和指導每一步的進行。典型的程序文如：食譜、實驗步驟、活動流程、用法指南或操作手冊等。一篇好的程序文應該包含清楚的指示、順序和步驟的說明，讓讀者可以掌握重點。

❶ 程序文的內容

程序文可能是簡單的順序敘述或是複雜的過程解說，結構上可能是段落文章或是好幾頁的過程說明。無論簡單或複雜，基本上必須包含下列項目：

1. 主題：一開始必須先說明要達成什麼目標、敘述情境和提出大綱。

2. 如果是以步驟介紹，一般用祈使句，因為一般對象是讀者「你」。

3. 列舉各步驟並加以描述。

4. 舉例說明。

5. 步驟依照時間、地方、困難度、重要性等順序作安排。

6. 可運用於介紹或提出步驟的句子，如：

Here are ways to . . .　這些是…的方法。

There are some steps you can follow.　有些你可以遵守的步驟。

The following are the steps for . . .　…的步驟如下。

The steps (you have to take) are as follows:　(你應該採取的) 步驟如下：

❷ 適當的轉折詞

用適當的轉折詞，使各個步驟順序清楚，分類如下：

表示一連串步驟	first、first of all、to begin with、second、then、after that、next、the next step、third、last、finally、the last step、last of all
表示更多步驟或步驟間的連接	on one hand . . . on the other hand、besides、in addition (to)、moreover、what's more、furthermore
表示時間	when、as、while、during、as soon as、before、after、not . . . until、at the same time、meanwhile
表示加強或提醒	more importantly、most important of all、remember to . . .、be sure to、last but not least

❸ 程序文的結構和寫作

段落寫作：主題句 + 支持句 (過程、步驟) + 結論句

文章寫作：主題段 (主題句介紹主題、背景、目標) + 支持段 (一段或數段分
　　　　　條列舉) + 結論段 (簡單說明成果、補充說明、提供建議或意見)

⊂ 範例 1 ⊃

以下是試味員品嘗冰淇淋的步驟。

　　Before tasting a sample, use your eyes first. If the ice cream doesn't look attractive, skip it. Then, use a gold spoon instead of one made of wood, plastic or other metals. This is because regular spoons leave an aftertaste that can dull the taste buds. In addition, the temperature of the ice cream may influence the taster's taste buds. If the ice cream is too cold, it will numb the taste buds.

Another thing to remember is never to swallow any ice cream. Take only a small bite of the ice cream, swishes it around in the mouth to introduce it to each of your taste buds, lightly licks your lips, and then gently breathe in so as to bring the smell up through the back of your mouth to your nose. With each step, size up whether the ice cream conveys the ideal balance between dairy sweetness and the flavor of the added ingredients. Last of all, no matter what the ice cream tastes like, spit it out, since a full stomach makes for a dull palate.

在品嘗樣品之前，先用眼睛觀察。如果冰淇淋看起來不吸引人，就會略過不品嘗。接著用金湯匙，而非由木頭、塑膠或其他金屬製成的湯匙。這是因為一般的湯匙會留下讓味蕾變遲鈍的餘味。此外，冰淇淋的溫度也會影響試味員的味蕾。如果冰淇淋太冰，它會讓味蕾麻木。

要記得不能吞下任何冰淇淋。只嘗一小口，讓它迅速在口中散布，接觸每一個味蕾，輕輕舔一下嘴唇，然後和緩地吸氣，讓氣味從嘴巴後面經由鼻咽散發上來。隨著每個步驟，仔細評估冰淇淋是否在乳製品的甜味與其他配料的風味間達到理想平衡。最後，不論冰淇淋嘗起來味道如何，把它吐掉，因為太撐的胃會造成遲鈍的味覺。

（範例 2）

以下是沙拉的製作步驟，根據這些過程寫一段程序文。

題目：How to Make a Delicious Salad　如何製作美味的沙拉

Salad is one of my family's favorite dishes. It is not difficult at all to make a delicious and healthy salad. First, choose the vegetables. I usually use lettuce, broccoli, onions, and cucumber. Then, wash the vegetables. Next, chop the vegetables into bite-sized pieces and then put them all into a big bowl. I also like

to add fruit such as tomatoes or sliced apples, along with some walnuts or almonds. Finally, I add my favorite salad dressing and toss all the ingredients together. In less than an hour, the salad is ready to serve.

沙拉是我們家喜歡的菜色之一。製作美味健康的沙拉一點都不難。第一，選擇蔬菜。我通常用萵苣、綠花椰菜、洋蔥和黃瓜。接著把蔬菜洗乾淨。下一步就是把蔬菜切成可以入口的大小，然後放入大碗。我也喜歡加上水果，如番茄或切片的蘋果，以及些許核桃或杏仁等。最後加入我喜歡的沙拉醬，混合所有的食材。不到一個小時，沙拉就可以上桌了。

範文 1

以下是一篇關於 First Aid for Burns (燒燙傷急救) 的程序文，主題段為引言，支持段說明處理的步驟，結論段說明結果或意見。

There are times we may be careless to hurt ourselves. For example, we may accidentally get burned because of hot water or fire. In this case, we must know what to do to help ourselves or others.

The first step we must take is to cool the injured area in cool running water for at least twenty minutes. Then, remove the damaged clothing carefully. Next, soak the injured area in cool water for at least twenty minutes. The fourth step is to cover the burn gently with a clean blanket. Finally, call an ambulance and send the injured person to the hospital if necessary.

If first aid is properly done, the injured person can recover quickly from burns. We'd better keep these steps in mind in case they are needed.

有些時候我們可能會不小心傷到自己，比如說因為熱水或是火而意外燙傷。在這種情況下，我們必須知道如何自救或救他人。

第一步我們必須採取的步驟是讓受傷部位至少沖 20 分鐘的冷水。然後，小心移除破損的衣物，接著再把燙傷部位浸泡在冷水中至少 20 分鐘。

第四步是用乾淨的毯子輕輕蓋在傷口上。最後，有需要的話，叫救護車將傷者送醫。

　　如果急救得當，傷者的燒燙傷可以快速復原。我們最好記住這些步驟，以備不時之需。

範文 2

以下是一篇關於 How to Prepare for a Job Interview (如何準備工作面試) 的程序文，主題段為引言，支持段說明面試前做相關準備的重要性以及面試時的整體表現 (服裝和態度)，結論段為再次簡單說明。

　　A job interview is an event everyone will face at some time in life. Being well prepared is sure to increase your chance of having a successful outcome of the interview.

　　Before the job interview, the first step is to do the research. Collecting as much related information as possible will ensure you to have a better understanding about the company. Furthermore, you are more likely to be aware of what will be the focus of the interview. Clearly, an interviewer is unlikely to hire a person who knows nothing about the company.

　　During the job interview, what you wear and how you act are important. Be sure to dress properly for the interview. It would be better to dress formally because an interview is an important occasion. If you dress too casually, it may suggest that you don't take the interview seriously. During the interview, you should be positive, confident, and honest. If you don't know the answer, be honest about it. Just make a brief apology and promise to the interviewers that you will try to find the answer.

　　To sum up, the keys to a successful job interview are making adequate preparation, having a positive attitude, and making a good impression. Even if

you don't succeed at the first time, the interview itself is a valuable lesson.

工作面試是每個人一生中都可能面對的場合。準備充分一定能夠增加面試成功的機會。

在工作面試前,第一步是做研究。盡可能地收集相關資訊能夠確保你對這個公司有充分的了解。此外,你更能知道面試的重點是什麼。顯然地,面試者不可能雇用一個對該公司一無所知的人。

工作面試時,你的穿著和行為很重要。面試一定要穿著得體。最好穿著正式,因為面試是個重要的場合。如果穿著太隨便,可能會被認為你不在乎這個面試。面試中,你應該樂觀、有信心和誠實。如果你不知道答案,就誠實以告。只需要道歉,並承諾面試官會去找答案。

總之,工作面試成功的祕訣是做好充足的準備、保持正面的態度和留下好印象。即使你第一次沒有成功,這個面試本身就是一堂寶貴的經驗。

I 下列文章敘述如何製作爆米花，請填上適當的轉折詞。

　　Popcorn is a delicious snack. However, it is reported that microwave popcorn may contain harmful substances that may cause health problems. Therefore, it is better for you to pop your own popcorn. In fact, it is very easy. The steps are _____.

　　_____, prepare a large high pot, four tablespoons of vegetable oil, and a small handful of organic popcorn kernels. _____ the kernels start popping, shake the pot to let the un-popped kernels fall to the bottom. _____ the popping slows down, remove the pot from the stove. _____, pour the popcorn into a bowl and season it with a small amount of butter, sugar or salt.

　　Following these steps, you can enjoy the healthy and yummy popcorn.

II 根據題目，寫一篇程序文 (至少 120 個單詞)。

題目：How to Plan a Party

_____

_____

_____

_____

_____

_____

_____

_____

_____

_____

Unit
9
說明文

9-6 比較與對比

比較與對比 (comparison and contrast) 是在比較兩項 (以上) 的人物、地點、事物或想法的相同相異之處。比較文 (compare) 是找出兩個 (以上) 主題的相同之處，而對比文 (contrast) 則是要找出兩個 (以上) 主題的相異之處。在寫作時，運用比較和對比的技巧可幫助讀者更加瞭解人、事、物之間的關係。

❶ 比較與對比文的組織架構

在寫比較與對比文時，最常用來腦力激盪的結構圖為文氏圖 (Venn diagram) 和表格 (table)，以下加以介紹：

文氏圖：用來思考比較兩個項目之間的相同或相異之處。

項目 A：**Traditional Learning**　　項目 B：**Online Learning**

1. less flexible
   較無彈性
2. passive learning
   被動學習
3. more interaction
   較多互動

provide knowledge
提供知識

1. more flexible
   較有彈性
2. active learning
   主動學習
3. less interaction
   較少互動

表格：用表格的方式，依照分析的特色來比較兩個項目，例：

	Traditional Learning	**Online Learning**
特色 1：flexibility	less	more
特色 2：learning	passive	active
特色 3：interaction	more	less

Tip

用表格進行腦力激盪的方式，其實跟安排細節的整合式寫作法 (the block method) 相同，只是腦力激盪時應將所有想得到的特色都列舉出來，再加以篩選。請看第 201 頁會介紹整合式寫作法。

➋ 比較與對比的詞彙

使用適當的詞彙，能讓文章更流暢，讀者更容易理解文意。列舉於下：

表示相同處	表示相異處
have something in common (有相同的…)、resemble (像)、equal (與…相等)、similarity (相似處)、alike、identical (一模一樣)、similar to (與…相似)、the same as (與…相同)、similarly (類似地)、likewise、in the same way (同樣地)、by the same token (同樣地)、also、too、just as、like	have nothing in common (沒有相同的…)、differ (in) (在…方面不同)、difference (相異處)、different from (與…不同)、however、otherwise、nevertheless、conversely (相反地)、in/by contrast、on the contrary、on the other hand、instead、although、but、yet、while、whereas、unlike、in spite of、despite、as opposed to (相對於…)

例 Friendship, **like** soup, needs your time and attention.
友誼，像湯一樣，需要你的時間和關注。

例 Rabbits, **unlike** other animals, touch the ground with their back feet first when they are running.　跟其他動物不同，兔子在跑步時，後腳先著地。

例 **Likewise**, animal imagery can be found in many English expressions, and it has given color to this language.　同樣地，在許多英文用語中可以找到動物的意象，這使得這個語言更加有趣。

例 Miyazaki's films consist of characters that are very **different from** the ones in typical Hollywood animations.
宮崎駿的電影包含許多跟典型好萊塢動畫不同的角色。

另外，表示比較可用 compare A with B (比較 A 和 B)、compared with (與…比較)、in comparison with (與…比較) 等，例：

例 Before you decide where to live, you had better **compare** the school dorm **with**

off-campus housing.

決定住在哪裡之前，你最好比較學校宿舍及校外住所。

例 **In comparison with** the school dorm, off-campus housing is usually more expensive. 與學校宿舍相比，校外住所通常比較貴。

I

1. 以 Living in a City vs. Living in a Country (城市生活 vs. 鄉村生活) 為題，
   腦力激盪並填入以下文氏圖。

   項目 A：**Living in a City**　　　項目 B：**Living in a Country**

   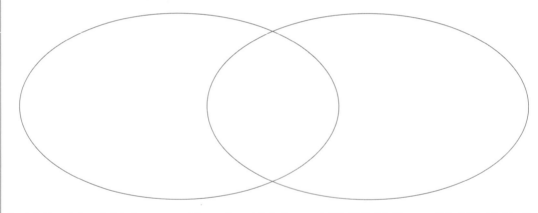

2. 以 Positive Thinkers vs. Negative Thinkers (正面思考者 vs. 負面思考者) 為
   題，腦力激盪並填入以下表格。

	Positive Thinkers	**Negative Thinkers**
特色 1：feeling		
特色 2：state of mind		
特色 3：expectations		
特色 4：health		

II 請填入適當的詞彙。

1. Henry is _____ his brother in appearance. It's hard to tell the difference in their looks.

2. The food in the restaurant is delicious. _____, the service is excellent.

3. Tina, _____ her diligent sister, is very lazy.

4. _____ her old age, Ms. Hanks still looks young.

5. _____ the two cameras look similar, one is more expensive than the other.

6. Bright colors usually make people feel happy, _____ dark ones make them feel sad.

7. I agree with George. My opinion is exactly _____ his.

8. Spoken language is usually _____ written language. The latter is more formal.

❸ 比較與對比文的寫作架構

1. 收集資料，分析相同或相異之處，利用文氏圖或表格將細節分類。

2. 開始寫比較與對比的段落時，須以能清楚點出比較或對比的主題句開頭。

例 There are **similarities/differences** between A and B.
A 與 B 有相同 / 相異之處。

例 Even though A **is similar to** B, they are **not identical**.
儘管 A 與 B 相似，但他們不盡相同。

例 A and B **differ in** three ways.　A 與 B 在 3 個方面有所不同。

3. 安排文章主體 (body) 的細節，常見的方式有整合式 (塊狀) 寫作法 (the block method) 和逐條式 (點狀) 寫作法 (the point-by-point method)，說明於下：

整合式 (塊狀) 寫作法 ：以談論的主題為主，先描述項目 A，並把要談的特色全部列出，再描述項目 B，並列出相對應的特色。

逐條式 (點狀) 寫作法 ：這種方法是以比較的要點為主，逐項討論 A、B 兩
個項目之間的相異點。

以下以比較 Ms. Li 和 Ms. Wang 兩位教師的教學態度、教學方法及師生關係
的差異為例：

整合式 (塊狀) 寫作法	逐條式 (點狀) 寫作法
項目 A：Ms. Li	特色 1：teaching attitude
特色 1：teaching attitude	項目 A：Ms. Li
特色 2：teaching method	項目 B：Ms. Wang
特色 3：teacher-student relationship	特色 2：teaching method
項目 B：Ms. Wang	項目 A：Ms. Li
特色 1：teaching attitude	項目 B：Ms. Wang
特色 2：teaching method	特色 3：teacher-student relationship
特色 3：teacher-student relationship	項目 A：Ms. Li
	項目 B：Ms. Wang

Tip

進行比較與對比文的寫作時，應注意以下事項：

1. 寫作前應先決定文章走向為比較或對比，切忌在同段落同時比較和對比兩個事物。

2. 一旦選定整合式或逐條式的寫作方法就不可任意更換。

3. 描述兩個比較或對照的事物時，應注意篇幅應該相當，不應偏重某一事物。

以下試比較 Living in a School Dormitory vs. Living at Home (住宿舍 vs. 住家裡) 的差異性。

整合式 (塊狀) 寫作法	逐條式 (點狀) 寫作法
項目 A：＿＿＿＿＿＿＿＿	特色 1：＿＿＿＿＿＿＿＿
特色 1：＿＿＿＿＿＿＿＿	項目 A：＿＿＿＿＿＿＿＿
特色 2：＿＿＿＿＿＿＿＿	項目 B：＿＿＿＿＿＿＿＿
項目 B：＿＿＿＿＿＿＿＿	特色 2：＿＿＿＿＿＿＿＿
特色 1：＿＿＿＿＿＿＿＿	項目 A：＿＿＿＿＿＿＿＿
特色 2：＿＿＿＿＿＿＿＿	項目 B：＿＿＿＿＿＿＿＿

❹ 比較與對比文的寫作步驟

（範文 1）

以下以 The Differences Between British English and American English (英語與美語的差異) 為題，寫一段對比文。先腦力激盪兩者的差異，然後寫出文章架構，使用逐條式 (點狀) 寫作法組織細節，寫出包含主題句、支持句及結論句的一段文章。

1. 腦力激盪

	British English	American English
特色 1：grammar	use present perfect tense 用現在完成式	use simple past tense 用過去簡單式
特色 2：spelling	"-our," "-tre"	"-or," "-ter"
特色 3：vocabulary	flat, lift, ground floor 公寓、電梯、一樓	apartment, elevator, first floor　公寓、電梯、一樓

Unit
9
說明文

2. 寫出大綱

主題句：Besides pronunciation, there are a few differences between British

English and American English.

除了發音之外，英語與美語之間有些微的差異。

文章架構：逐條式 (點狀) 寫作法

特色 1：**grammar**	特色 2：**vocabulary**	特色 3：**spelling**
項目 A：British English	項目 A：British English	項目 A：British English
項目 B：American English	項目 B：American English	項目 B：American English

3. 寫出文章

Besides pronunciation, there are a few differences between British English and American English. When it comes to grammar, speakers of British English tend to use present perfect tense more, while Americans use the simple past tense. For example, British people may say, "Sorry, but I've broken your computer." Americans may say, "Sorry, but I broke your computer." As for spelling, British English and American English also have different rules. For instance, an extra "u" is found in some British words like colour, humour, and labour. Another example is "-tre" in British English such as "theatre" and "centre," but "-ter" in American English like "theater" and "center." The most notable difference between British English and American English is probably vocabulary. For example, a "flat" in British English is replaced by an "apartment" in American English. In Britain, you need to take a "lift" to the "ground" floor. Yet, in America, you take an "elevator" to the "first" floor. Though Britons and Americans have no difficulty communicating with each other, as an English learner, you need to pay attention to these differences.

除了發音之外，英語與美語之間有些微的差異。當說到文法時，英語人士更傾向用現在完成式，美語人士則用過去簡單式。譬如，英國人可能說：「對不起，但我已經弄壞你的電腦。」美國人可能說：「對不起，但我弄壞你的電腦。」至於拼音，英語與美語也有不同的法則。例如，有些英語單字會發現多一個的「u」，像是：colour、humour 和 labour。另一個例子是英語的「-tre」，如 theatre 和 centre；在美語是 theater 和 center。英語與美語間最顯著的差異或許是單字。譬如，英語的公寓「flat」，在美語中變成「apartment」。在英國，你會搭電梯「lift」去一樓「the ground floor」。然而，在美國，你會搭電梯「elevator」去一樓「the first floor」。雖然英國人和美國人溝通無礙，身為一位英文學習者，你必須注意這些差異性。

〔範文 2〕

以 The Differences Between City Life and Country Life (城市生活與鄉村生活的差異) 為題，先腦力激盪可能的差異，然後寫出文章架構，使用整合式 (塊狀) 寫作法組織細節，寫出一篇對比文。

1. 腦力激盪

	City Life	Country Life
特色 1：convenience	public transportation, more stores, museums	difficult to buy daily necessities
特色 2：job opportunities	more	fewer
特色 3：environment	hustle and bustle	clean, quiet, and peaceful
特色 4：pace of life	fast	slow

2. 文章架構

項目 A：City Life	項目 B：Country Life
特色 1：convenience	特色 1：convenience
特色 2：job opportunities	特色 2：job opportunities
特色 3：environment	特色 3：environment
特色 4：pace of life	特色 4：pace of life

3. 寫出文章

There are differences between city life and country life. First, one living in a city can enjoy all the convenience, such as public transportation, shopping malls, museums, and exhibitions. Since there are many stores and companies in a city, people can get a job easily. However, the hustle and bustle of a city often makes its residents feel stressed, which can affect their health. In addition, the pace of city life is quite fast. This also contributes to city people's health problems.

Life in a country, on the contrary, is less convenient. One may need to walk or drive a long way to buy daily necessities. With few stores and companies, there is a lack of job opportunities in a country. Nevertheless, the countryside is clean, quiet, and peaceful. The slow pace of country life makes people feel relaxed.

All in all, there are advantages and disadvantages of living in a city or in a country, and the choice of where to live depends on one's personal needs.

城市生活與鄉村生活是有所不同的。首先，住在城市的人可以享受所有便利設施，譬如大眾運輸、購物商場、博物館和展覽。由於城市裡有許多商家和公司，人們能夠容易找到工作。然而，城市的喧囂忙碌常使得其居民備感壓力，這會影響到他們的健康。此外，城市生活步調相當快，這也會造成城市居民的健康問題。

相較之下，鄉村的生活較不方便。得走一段路或開好遠的車去買日常用品。因為商家和公司不多，鄉村缺少工作機會。然而，鄉村是乾淨、安靜且平和的。鄉村生活的慢步調讓人們感到放鬆。

　　總而言之，住在城市或鄉村都各有其優缺點，而住在哪裡的選擇則取決於個人所需。

練習寫寫看 N

根據腦力激盪和文章架構，使用逐條式(點狀)寫作法來組織細節，寫一篇對比文(至少 120 個單詞)。

題目：The Differences Between College Graduates and High School Graduates

1. 腦力激盪

	College Graduates	**High School Graduates**
特色 1：age	around 22	around 18
特色 2：attitudes towards graduation	under pressure	enthusiastic

2. 文章架構

特色 1：**age**	特色 2：**attitudes towards graduation**
項目 A：College Graduates	項目 A：College Graduates
項目 B：High School Graduates	項目 B：High School Graduates

3. 寫出文章

_____

_____

_____

_____

_____

_____

_____

_____

_____

_____

_____

9-7 分類文

分類文 (classification) 是作者將人、事、物、想法等按照其共同特質分門別類。段落的主題一般出現在第一句，文中通常包括各類別的實例以及說明。

❶ 分類文的寫作要點

想要寫一篇好的分類文，應注意以下要點：

1. 需要選擇一個範圍夠大，並可以分類的主題，然後根據主題找出能分類的項目，如鞋子可依樣式 (styles)、功用 (functions)、材質 (textures) 等來分類，例：

樣式 (styles)：

功用 (functions)：

分類主題 shoes divided by functions (不同功用的鞋子)		
種類 1 sports shoes (運動鞋)	**種類 2** formal and casual shoes (正式與休閒鞋)	**種類 3** dance shoes (舞鞋)

材質 (textures)：

分類主題 shoes divided by textures (不同材質的鞋子)				
種類 1 shoes made of leather (皮鞋)	**種類 2** shoes made of textiles (紡織布料鞋)	**種類 3** shoes made of synthetics (合成皮鞋)	**種類 4** shoes made of rubber (橡膠鞋)	**種類 5** shoes made of foam (泡沫塑膠鞋)

2. 分類必須要根據單一原則，如欲將主題縮小為運動鞋，則應於文章開頭指明文章內容是關於運動鞋的分類，如運動鞋可根據其功用分成跑步鞋、登山鞋、溯溪鞋等，此文就不宜加入涼鞋等其他類別的鞋。

3. 每一類都應有清楚的說明或舉例，各類的舉例數目和篇幅也應差不多。

4. 分類文常用的轉折詞，列舉於下：

表示次序的轉折詞	第一：first(ly)、in the first place、to begin with、to start with、in the beginning
	第二：second(ly)、in the second place、next、then
	最後：finally、last(ly)、last but not least
表示說明的轉折詞	that is (to say)、in other words、namely
表示舉例的轉折詞	for example、for instance、as an example

I 以 Types of Learners (學習者的種類) 為題，根據學習類型分成 3 種類別。

分類主題
learners divided by learning styles

↓ ↓ ↓

種類 1	種類 2	種類 3
_____	_____	_____

II 填入適當的轉折詞。

to begin with   for example   lastly   second

    According to different learning styles, learners can be classified into three main types: learning by hearing, seeing, and doing. ¹_____, learners who learn by hearing (auditory learners) would rather listen to their learning materials than read them. They basically depend on listening to either teachers or other forms of audio instructions to learn new things. ²_____, learners who learn by seeing (visual learners) learn best through graphics, demonstrations, and written texts. They rely on visual aids to learn effectively. ³_____, they may use pictures, videos or diagrams to help them process the information. ⁴_____, for learners who learn by doing (physical learners), physically performing a process is the way to learn. They process information through "hands-on" experience. For this kind of students, learning by doing is the easiest way for them to learn.

❷ 分類文的寫作步驟

1. 收集好資料後，決定分類原則，刪除不符合此原則的細節，可利用能清楚表示分類原則及類別的圖形。

> **Tip**
> 分類文的圖表不限於本課介紹的形式，只要能表示分類原則及類別的圖形均可，類別的數目可依實際情形來做增減。

2. 撰寫分類文的主題句時，可包含表示分類的動詞或動詞片語，如：classify、be classified into、group、be grouped into、sort、be sorted into、divide、be divided into、separate、be separated into、categorize、be categorized into 等。也可以包含表達種類的名詞，如：type、kind、part、group、variety、class、division、category 等。

例 We can **classify** energy resources **into** two types—renewable and non-renewable.

我們可將能源分為兩類：可再生與不可再生的。

例 All countries in the world can **be categorized/classified/divided/grouped/sorted into** one of the three categories: developed countries, developing countries, and underdeveloped countries. 世界上所有的國家可分成以下 3 種類別之一：已開發國家、開發中國家和未開發國家。

例 There are four **types** of clubs in my school, namely academic clubs, sports, recreation, and voluntary groups.

我學校的社團分為 4 種：也就是學術、運動、休閒與服務社團。

3. 分類文的主體應注意：各種類描述先後應按照主題句中出現的順序。描述或舉例說明時，得留意每個種類所占的篇幅，亦即舉例的數目應盡量相同。

4. 文章的末段應提供一個結論句，先以表示結論的轉折詞開頭，再將全文內容概括說明一次。

Unit

9

說明文

I 為下列兩段分類文分別寫出適當的主題句。

1. _____

First, for those who have suffered verbal abuse, it is highly possible that they have low self-esteem. Some of them may even have gone through an identity crisis. Moreover, verbal abuse often leaves scars in the minds of its victims. Sometimes, these scars are so deep that some victims may suffer from post-traumatic stress disorder, which may lead to an increased risk of suicide. Last, a few victims end up imposing their own pain on other people. They do so mainly because this is the only way of expression that they know.

2. _____

Of the above three methods, regular exercise is the healthiest. Whether you go to a gym, work out at home or take part in an exercise class, it not only keeps you in good shape but also helps you stay healthy. The second best way to lose weight is through calorie control. By carefully calculating and limiting the calories you eat every day, you can reach your ideal weight without affecting your health. Lastly, having a gastric bypass surgery (胃繞道手術) is also an effective way to get rid of excess weight. Most of the people who have undergone this operation can lose 65% of their excess weight in the first year after surgery.

II 根據第一大題的練習題 (2.)，寫出關於減重 (weight loss) 的結論句。

_____

_____

_____

_____

《範例》

題目：The Three Main Types of Volcanoes　3 種主要的火山類型

1. 腦力激盪

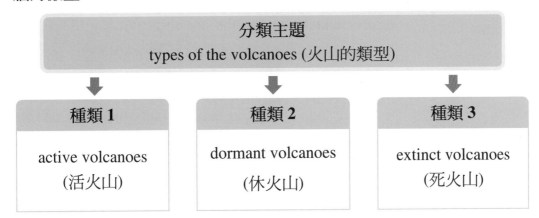

分類主題
types of the volcanoes (火山的類型)

種類 1	種類 2	種類 3
active volcanoes (活火山)	dormant volcanoes (休火山)	extinct volcanoes (死火山)

2. 寫出大綱

主題句：Scientists have categorized volcanoes into three main categories: active, dormant, and extinct.

支持細節：

1. an example of an active volcano

2. an example of a dormant volcano

3. an example of an extinct volcano

結論句：In short, the above classification is primarily based on a volcano's eruptive pattern.

3. 寫出段落

主題段 (1) ➤ ¹Scientists have categorized volcanoes into three main categories: active, dormant, and extinct.

支持段 (2-10) ➤ ²An active volcano is erupting now or may erupt again in the near future. ³One example of an active volcano

is Mount Merapi in Indonesia. [4]It erupted in 2018, choking the sky with thick black smoke. [5]A dormant volcano is a volcano that hasn't erupted for a long time, but for which there is the possibility of future eruption. [6]For example, Mount Changbai in China is a dormant volcano that erupted in 1903. [7]It had remained inactive for more than 100 years. [8]An extinct volcano is one that erupted thousands of years ago, and it has no likelihood of eruption. [9]Mount Kilimanjaro in Tanzania had its major eruption about 100,000 years ago, and it had no possibility of erupting again. [10]Thus, it is categorized into the group of extinct volcanoes.

結論段 (11)

[11]In short, the above classification is mainly based on a volcano's eruptive pattern.

科學家將火山主要分成三類：活火山、休火山和死火山。

活火山是現在噴發或近期會噴發的火山。印尼的梅拉比火山為活火山的例子之一。它於 2018 年噴發，天空黑煙密布。休火山是許久未噴發，但未來仍有可能噴發。例如，中國的長白山是休火山，在 1903 年曾噴發過。它有 100 多年沒有活動了。死火山是數千年前曾噴發，而且不可能再噴發的火山。例如，坦尚尼亞的吉力馬札羅山在 10 萬年前曾經噴發，而且沒有再噴發的可能性。因此，它被歸類成死火山。

簡言之，上述分類法主要依據火山噴發的形式來分類。

以 Types of Energy Resources (能源的種類) 為題，先腦力激盪出能源的類別，並以「We can classify energy resources into two types—renewable and non-renewable.」為主題句，寫出一篇分類文 (至少 120 個單詞)。

1. 腦力激盪

分類主題
types of energy resources

種類 1	種類 2
_____	_____

2. 寫出文章

_____

_____

_____

_____

_____

_____

_____

_____

_____

_____

_____

_____

_____

以 Categories of Bullying (霸凌) 為題，先腦力激盪出霸凌的類別，並以「Bullying, upsetting or hurting another person repeatedly, falls into four categories, namely physical bullying, verbal bullying, relational bullying, and cyberbullying.」為主題句，寫出一篇分類文 (至少 120 個單詞)。

1. 腦力激盪

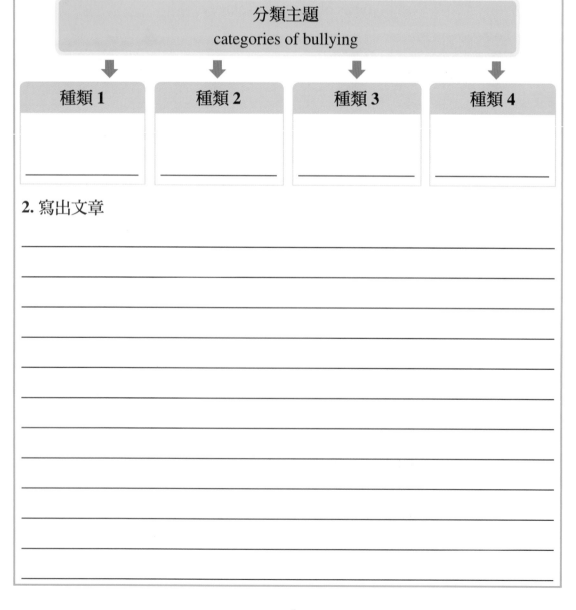

分類主題
categories of bullying

種類 1	種類 2	種類 3	種類 4
_____	_____	_____	_____

2. 寫出文章

_____

_____

_____

_____

_____

_____

_____

_____

_____

_____

_____

_____

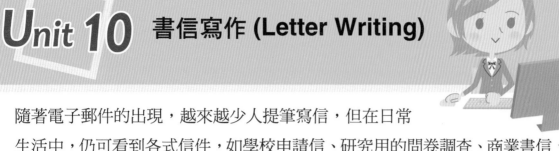

Unit 10 書信寫作 (Letter Writing)

隨著電子郵件的出現,越來越少人提筆寫信,但在日常生活中,仍可看到各式信件,如學校申請信、研究用的問卷調查、商業書信、道歉信、感謝信、安慰信或是詢問信等,都相當常見,只是形式上從書面變成電子郵件。

10-1 書信和信封的寫作格式

一般書信分成正式與非正式兩類,在寫作格式上有所不同,以下分別介紹:

❶ 正式書信的寫作格式

舉凡學校申請信、商業書信、求職信等都屬於正式信件 (a formal letter)。正式信件對版面以及用字遣詞的要求都較為嚴謹。以下列出書寫正式書信的 7 項基本要求:

1. 起首 (heading):把寄件人的地址、連絡電話、商標或電子郵件信箱等寫在信件上方並靠左對齊。

2. 日期 (date):起首的資料寫完後,直接於下行寫上日期,同樣靠左對齊。最好避免使用全是數字的簡式寫法,因為容易造成混淆。

> **Tip**
> 日期的寫法可略分為美式及英式寫法:
> 美式寫法:月 / 日 / 年,如 October 8th, 2019
> 英式寫法:日 / 月 / 年,如 8th October, 2019

3. 信內地址 (inside address):
   日期下方空兩行並靠左對齊寫下收件人的姓名、頭銜以及住址。

4. 收件人稱謂 (salutation):如果知道收件人姓名,可在收件人姓名、地址後空兩行寫下,後面加冒號,但不要寫出對方的名字。若不知道對方姓名,可寫 Dear Sir:、Dear Madam:、Dear Sir or Madam:、Ladies and Gentlemen: 或 To whom it may concern:。

5. 本文 (body)：正式信件的用字遣詞必須正式，應避免口語英文。

6. 結尾敬語 (complimentary close)：結尾敬語寫在本文的下兩行，靠左對齊，後面加逗號，如：Respectfully,、Sincerely,、Sincerely yours,、Yours truly,、Truly yours,、Best regards, 等。

7. 簽名 (signature)：結尾敬語下空兩行寫下寄件人姓名 (親筆簽名以及打字簽名)。

一般而言，書信的對齊格式可分為以下 3 種：

1. 齊頭式 (full-block form)：齊頭式為最常見的正式信件格式，其書寫一律由左方開始，靠左對齊，因此信件左方呈現一垂直線狀，不過右方可能參差不齊。本章節的正式書信皆採用此格式。

2. 半齊頭式 (semi-block/indented form)：日期、結尾敬語、簽名等置中對齊，其餘部分，包括收件人姓名、稱謂、主旨等靠左對齊；正文部分每段均首縮約五個字母。本章節的非正式書信皆採用此格式。

3. 改良齊平式 (modified-block form)：日期、結尾敬語、簽名等置中對齊，正文與其餘部分則靠左對齊，其中正文不需內縮。

Tip
齊頭式是最常用的信件格式，也最不容易出錯，建議使用此格式。

（範例）

以下是一封正式的求職信，由 Susan Lin 寫給 World Trading Company。

8F., No. 100, Sec. 3, Datong Rd.,
Neipu Township, Pingtung County 91244 ｝起首 (heading)

May 10, 2019 ← 日期 (date)

```
Mr. Marley
General Manager
World Trading Company          } 信內地址 (inside address)
10F., No. 258, Sec. 2, Bade Rd.,
Zhongshan Dist., Taipei City 10492


Dear Mr. Marley: ← 收件人稱謂 (salutation)


本文 (body)


Sincerely, ← 結尾敬語 (complimentary close)


Susan Lin ← 親筆簽名 (handwritten signature)
Susan Lin ← 打字簽名 (typed signature)
```

❷ 非正式書信的寫作格式

相較於正式信件，非正式信件 (an informal letter) 在格式和內容上都比較自由，請見右圖。以下列出書寫非正式書信的 6 項基本要求：

1. **起首**：在非正式信件中常省略起首。

2. **日期**：在第一行居中寫下日期。

3. **收件人稱謂**：對於長輩或較不熟識的朋友要先加上稱謂，後面加逗號，如 Dear Mr. Chen,；至於晚輩或是較親近的朋友則可直呼名字，如 Dear Amy,。

```
                              日期 (date)


         收件人稱謂 (salutation)
         本文 (body)


            結尾敬語 (complimentary close)
                    簽名 (signature)
```

4. **本文**：可在進入信的主題前加一些問候語、詢問健康等。

5. **結尾敬語**：結尾敬語寫在本文的下兩行，後面加逗號，常用的結尾敬語有：Sincerely, 、Sincerely yours, 、Yours truly, 、Best regards, 、Best wishes, 、Love, 、Your friend, 、All the best, 、Your son/daughter, 等。

6. **簽名**：以親筆簽名為佳，並對齊上方的結尾敬語。

〔範例〕

以下是一封 Susan 寫給她朋友 Andrew 的信。

Oct. 20, 2019 ← 日期 (date)
Dear Andrew, ← 收件人稱謂 (salutation)
本文 (body)
Best wishes, ← 結尾敬語 (complimentary close)
Susan ← 親筆簽名 (handwritten signature)

❸ 信封的撰寫格式

以下為西式信封的撰寫格式：

1. 寄件人的姓名和地址應寫在信封左上角，而收件人的姓名和地址則應寫在信封中間。

2. 跟中文的寫法不同，英文地址的寫法是由最小的單位門牌號碼開始寫起，依次為弄、巷、段、街/路、鄉/鎮/區、市/縣/州/省、郵遞區號、國名等。

> **Tip**
>
> 常見的地址單位以及其縮寫：
>
> | 樓 Floor (F.) | 號 Number (No.) | 巷 Lane (Ln.) |
> |---|---|---|
> | 弄 Alley (Aly.) | 街 Street (St.) | 路 Road (Rd.) |
> | 大道 Boulevard (Blvd.) | 大街 Avenue (Ave.) | 段 Section (Sec.) |
> | 村 Village | 鄉 Township | 鎮 Town |
> | 區 District (Dist.) | 縣 County | 市 City |

3. 郵票貼於右上角，且郵寄的方式有：航空信 (Via Airmail)、快遞 (Express)、限時專送 (Special Delivery)、掛號 (Registered) 等。

《範 例》

以下是一封 Susan 寫信給她朋友 Andrew 的信封。

Susan Lin

8F., No. 100, Sec. 3, Datong Rd.,

Neipu Township, Pingtung County 91244

} 寄件人地址
(the sender's address)

Mr. Andrew Wang

6F., NO. 50, Ln. 42, Minxiang St.,

Yonghe District, New Taipei City 23454

} 收件人地址
(the recipient's address)

練習寫寫看 A

Ⅰ 在下列空格填入至少 3 個正確的收件人稱謂和結尾敬語。

	收件人稱謂	結尾敬語
正式信件		
非正式信件		

II 請以你的地址作為寄件人地址填好信封，收件人為一家公司或一所學校。

根據書信目的不同，內容的重點也會不一樣，以下分別說明邀請函、感謝信、道歉信、忠告信以及抱怨信的寫法。

10-2 邀請函

邀請的原因種類很多，如邀請參加某一個活動、宴會、典禮、聚會、餐敘等，此時可以用書信格式或卡片格式撰寫邀請函 (an invitation letter)。無論是正式還是非正式，邀請函一定要提供足夠的訊息讓收件人可以決定是否參與這個活動。寫邀請函時必須注意下列事項：

1. 邀請函若以卡片格式書寫，通常會開門見山地告知邀請人邀請的目的，並直接以 "You are cordially invited to _____ (活動主題)" 做為第一句；若要強調主辦人，則可以用 "_____ (邀請人或主辦活動人的姓名) request the honor of your presence for _____ (邀請原因)" 做為第一句。

2. 一般的邀請函通常以書信格式來書寫，且會根據與被邀者的關係和活動的正式與否來決定邀請函的體例為正式或非正式。

3. 邀請函的內容應包括：

What：活動目的、餐點內容等。

Who：主辦人、受邀者。

When：什麼時間舉辦、什麼時候需要回覆。

Where：在哪裡舉辦 (有時會附上簡易地圖或交通方式)。

How：舉辦方式、聯絡方式。

4. 其他相關的規定或建議，如應穿著正式或非正式服裝、是否準備禮物等。

5. 全文內容最後可表示期盼對方能夠參與，並提供聯絡資訊或電話。也可註明 RSVP，表示 please reply，請受邀者回覆是否參加活動。

（範例）

以下為畢業派對的正式邀請函。

邀請參加的 活動名稱 (1)	¹You are cordially invited to the graduation party
活動內容 (2-6)	²**Who:** Every member of Class 308 ³**When:** May 30, 6:30 p.m. ⁴**Where:** Happy KTV (No. 150, Xin 1st Rd., Xinyi Dist., Keelung City) ⁵**Why:** To celebrate the graduation ⁶**What:** Singing and celebrating with food and drink supplied by the KTV
回覆方式 (7)	⁷RSVP by May 25, to Paul at 0988-000-000.
其他的建議或規定 (8-9)	⁸The attendees have to prepare a small gift. ⁹The host will draw names for the gift exchange at the end of the party.

Unit
10
書信寫作

誠摯邀請你參加畢業派對

對象：308 班全體成員

時間：5 月 30 日晚上 6 點 30 分

地點：快樂 KTV (基隆市信義區信一路 150 號)

原因：慶祝畢業

活動內容：唱歌慶祝、KTV 用餐

5 月 25 日前以電話 (0988-000-000) 回覆 Paul。

參加者需準備小禮物。

派對結束時，主辦人會抽名字來交換禮物。

寫一封正式的同學會邀請函給你的國中同學 (Class 314 of 2017)。

_____

Who: _____

When: _____

Where: _____

Why: _____

_____

_____

需要表達感謝的場合很多,例如收到禮物、受到邀請、得到幫助或獲得有用的建議等。寫感謝信 (a thank-you letter) 時必須注意下列事項:

1. 信中一開始就直接表示感謝。以下為表示感謝的常見用法:

Thank you for your <u>kindness</u>/<u>help</u>/<u>hospitality</u> . . . 謝謝你的<u>好意</u> / <u>協助</u> / <u>招待</u>…

I would like to express my <u>thanks</u>/<u>appreciation</u>/<u>gratitude</u> to . . . (for . . .)

(為…) 我要對…表達感謝

It was very <u>kind</u>/<u>thoughtful</u> of you to give me . . . 你真體貼,給了我…

How <u>nice</u>/<u>thoughtful</u> of you to . . . 你真好 / 體貼…

I (greatly) appreciate your . . . 我 (非常) 感謝你的…

It was a(n) <u>pleasure</u>/<u>honor</u> for me to . . . 我很樂意 / 榮幸…

2. 簡短生動地敘述要表達感謝的事情。

3. 說明受惠的過程。

4. 結尾可再次表達感謝,並誠摯地祝福對方。

> **Tip**
> 感謝信的風格、語氣和用字的正式與否,可視與對方的親近程度而定。

範例

以下為 Ariel 寫給圖書管理員 Ruth 先生的感謝信。

October 5, 2019

Dear Mr. Ruth,

簡略道謝 (1-2) → ¹Thank you for taking the time and trouble to help me find the books and information I needed for my report. ²Without your help, I wouldn't have been able to hand it in on time.

自己遇到的問題 (3-5)

³I used to go to the library to borrow novels. ⁴This was the first time I went to the library for a class. ⁵I never thought that I would have a hard time finding what I wanted.

最後再次感謝對方的協助 (6-9)

⁶You taught me how to make good use of the library. ⁷I have learned more than I expected. ⁸Thank you for your patience and help. ⁹Best of all, I'm glad that we become friends.

Best wishes,

Ariel

2019 年 10 月 5 日

親愛的 Ruth 先生：

　　謝謝您花時間，並竭力幫我找到報告所需的書籍和資料。沒有您的幫忙，我就無法準時交報告。

　　我以前會到圖書館借小說。這是我第一次為了課程上圖書館。沒想到這麼難找到我所需要的資料。

　　您教我如何善用圖書館。我學到了超乎自己原先所預期的。感謝您的耐心和協助。最棒的是，很高興我們成為朋友。

最好的祝福，

Ariel

練習寫寫看 C

Carol 姑姑送一支智慧型手機做為你的生日禮物，寫一封感謝信來答謝她。

_____

_____

_____

_____

_____

_____

_____

_____

_____

_____

_____

_____

_____

_____

_____

_____

Unit
10
書信寫作

10-4 道歉信

道歉信 (a letter of apology) 通常用來表達歉意和請求原諒，有時候你會傷到別人的感情、做錯事、失約、弄壞物品等，這時都應該表示歉意。寫道歉信時必須注意下列事項：

1. 信件一開始就要直接、誠摯地表達歉意。以下為表達歉意的常見用法：

I'm terribly/very sorry for . . .　我為…感到非常抱歉

Pardon me for . . .　原諒我做了…

It was all my fault.　都是我的錯。

How stupid/careless of me to . . .　我多愚蠢 / 不小心…

I owe you an apology.　我該向你道歉。

Please forgive my ignorance/rudeness.　請原諒我的無知 / 無禮。

Please don't be mad at me.　請別生我的氣。

Please accept my sincere apology.　請接受我誠摯的道歉。

2. 解釋發生的原因以及你的感覺。

3. 說明你會如何賠償或彌補對方所蒙受的傷害和損失。

4. 祈求對方的寬恕和諒解，並承諾不再犯同樣的錯誤。

5. 最後再道歉一次，強調你是多麼希望得到原諒。

> **Tip**
> 1. 道歉信應盡快寄出。
> 2. 語氣、形式和用字視發生的場合以及道歉者和接受道歉者的關係而定。
> 3. 信必須簡短、針對要點。

Jimmy 因為說話頂撞媽媽，所以寫一封信跟媽媽道歉。

Dec. 10

Dear Mom,

道歉和簡略發生的
原因 (1-4)

¹I'm sorry for what I said to you last night. ²I shouldn't have talked back to you like that. ³I don't know why I lost my temper. ⁴To be honest, I've been under a lot of stress these days.

提出如何彌補對方
(5-8)

⁵I know you and Dad care about me. ⁶I really appreciate it. ⁷I also know that you and Dad expect a lot of me. ⁸I'll study harder and try to get good grades.

再度表示歉意
(9-11)

⁹Please forgive me, Mom. ¹⁰I am very grateful to you for taking care of me. ¹¹I'll never make the same mistake again.

Your son,
Jimmy

12 月 10 日

親愛的媽媽：

很抱歉，我昨晚說了那些話。我不該那樣頂嘴。我不知道為何發脾氣。老實說，我近日壓力很大。

我知道您和爸爸很關心我。我真的非常感激。我也知道您和爸爸對我期望很高。我會更用功念書，盡力考到好成績。

媽媽，請原諒我。我很感激您的照顧。我絕不會重蹈覆轍。

您的兒子，
Jimmy

Unit

10

書信寫作

C範例 2D

對於無法答應對方的邀約或請求，亦可撰寫所謂的「致歉信」(a letter of regret)，如 Max 受邀參加同學會，他卻不克參加，即可以寫一封「致歉信」，向對方說明自己感到很遺憾以及無法與會的理由。

Aug. 18

Dear Carlos,

Thank you for the invitation. I'd like to go to the class reunion, but I won't be available on that day. It happens to be my grandpa's birthday. My uncle, aunt, and my parents plan to give my grandpa a surprise. We will visit my grandparents early in the morning and then have a lunch together. It has been one month since we visited them last time. I'm looking forward to seeing them. Please forgive me. I hope you guys and the teachers will have a great time.

Yours,
Max

8 月 18 日

親愛的 Carlos,

謝謝你的邀請。我很想參加班上的同學會，但我那天剛好沒空。那天是我爺爺的生日。我的伯父、伯母以及我爸媽計畫給爺爺一個驚喜。我們一大早就要到祖父母家，然後會一起共進午餐。我們已經一個月沒見面了。我非常希望見到他們。請原諒我。希望你們和老師們能有段愉快的時光。

你的，
Max

Helen 上禮拜向好友 Joseph 借了相機去旅行。然而，在旅行途中不小心把相機弄丟了，所以 Helen 寫一封道歉信向 Joseph 表示歉意。

_____

_____

_____

_____

_____

_____

_____

_____

_____

_____

_____

_____

_____

_____

10-5 忠告信

忠告信 (a letter of advice) 可分為兩種：尋求忠告和給予他人忠告。遇到問題時，可寫信尋問別人的建議。這類信件應注意以下事項：

1. 簡單扼要地說明自己的問題。

2. 誠摯希望對方能給予忠告，並先表示感謝。

C範例1つ

Jimmy 不知道大學應主修哪一科，寫一封信向黃老師請教。

April 10, 2019

Dear Mr. Huang,

說明這封信的來意 (1)

¹I am writing the letter to seek your advice. ²Recently, I have difficulty choosing my major in university. ³My parents want me to be a lawyer, but I am interested in mass media because I dream of becoming a director. ⁴We cannot reach an agreement and have had several arguments. ⁵I hope you can give me some advice.

說明自己遇到的問題 (2-4)

希望對方給予忠告 (5)

Yours sincerely,

Jimmy

2019 年 4 月 10 日

親愛的黃老師：

我寫這封信來尋求您的忠告。最近，我在選擇大學主修上遇到困難。我父母要我當律師，但我對大眾傳播有興趣，因為我夢想當導演。我們無法達成共識，發生過幾次口角。希望您能給我一些建議。

您誠摯的，

Jimmy

當身邊有人需要忠告時，可寫一封信協助此人面對或處理問題。寫忠告信時應注意下列事項：

1. 別人尋求你的忠告時，你應盡快回應。

2. 針對問題給予忠告，並注意不要出現批評字眼。

3. 忠告內容如有數點，可用表示次序的轉折詞來連接。

4. 如果沒有能力給予忠告，應表達遺憾，並建議對方尋求更專業的協助。

5. 最後應表達希望自己的忠告能有所幫助。

〔範例 2〕

黃老師寫一封信給 Jimmy，給他一些關於大學主修科目的忠告。

April 11, 2019

Dear Jimmy,

表達感謝對方的信任 (1-2)

¹I am very happy that you turn to me when you need help. ²Yet, I'm afraid I don't have a definite answer for you.

給對方的忠告 (3-10)

³The following is the only advice I can give you. ⁴You should ask yourself which job, being a lawyer or a director, is what you would like to do for the rest of your life? ⁵Which job can give you a sense of achievement? ⁶If you have an answer, go for it. ⁷If you are still uncertain, list the advantages and disadvantages of the two jobs. ⁸It will be easier for you to make a choice in this way. ⁹Last, you should take your parents' opinion into consideration. ¹⁰You can open your heart to them, and I believe they will support you.

希望忠告能對對方有所幫助 (11-13)

¹¹I hope my advice will be helpful to you. ¹²Good Luck! ¹³If you have made your final decision, please let me know.

Yours,
David Huang

Unit
10

書信寫作

2019 年 4 月 11 日

親愛的 Jimmy：

　　很高興你需要幫忙時向我求助。然而，我恐怕無法給你一個明確的答案。

　　以下是我唯一能給你的忠告。你應該問問自己哪一種工作，當律師還是當導演，是你這輩子想做的工作？哪一種工作能讓你有成就感？如果你有答案，就努力去爭取。若還是不確定，就分別列出這兩種工作的優缺點。這樣你會比較容易做出選擇。最後，你應該考慮你父母的意見。你可以對他們敞開心胸，我相信他們都會支持你的。

　　希望我的忠告能幫上忙。祝你好運！如果你做出最後的決定，請讓我知道。

你的，

David Huang

NOTE

---

1. 上課有時需要用智慧型手機查資料，但 Wendy 害怕無法克制自己不玩
手機遊戲，因此陷入兩難，她寫一封信向好友 Ken 尋求忠告。

_____

_____

_____

_____

_____

_____

_____

_____

_____

_____

_____

_____

_____

_____

_____

_____

_____

2. Ken 寫一封忠告信給 Wendy，並給她一些關於使用智慧型手機的建議。

_____

_____

_____

_____

_____

_____

_____

_____

_____

_____

_____

_____

_____

_____

10-6 抱怨信

生活中難免會發生讓人抱怨的事情，如朋友間的不愉快或失望的購物經驗等。此時，因為有限的溝通管道，會需要寫抱怨信 (a letter of complaint)。寫抱怨信時，須注意以下事項：

1. 用簡單明瞭的句子來描述問題以及所造成的影響，讓讀者一看就懂。

2. 內容要專注於主題，篇幅切勿太長，一般在一頁以內。

3. 明確指出事件發生的時間和地點。

4. 寫出曾經嘗試，但卻無效的處理方式。

5. 注意禮貌，即使是抱怨信也不可失禮。

6. 要求對方在合理的期限內給予回應。

7. 若為購物糾紛，最後附上收據或發票影本之類的相關證據，以資佐證。

範例

Susan Lin 寫信跟經銷商抱怨最近購買的電腦壞了，並要求退款。

March 30, 2019

Dear Sir or Madam,

事情發生的時間和地點 (1-2)

[1]On March 14, I bought a computer in one of your agencies at No.68, Gongyi Rd., Taichung City. [2]I paid NT$35,000 for a brand-new MacBook Pro, as shown on the enclosed copy of the sales slip.

陳述要抱怨的事情 (3-5)

[3]It worked well for a week, but it suddenly crashed while I was using it on March 22. [4]After that, I couldn't boot it up anymore. [5]I immediately contacted the agency where I had bought the computer, but the clerk refused to refund the money I had paid for this computer.

提出解決方案 (6-9)

[6]However, as far as I know, Apple Inc. always has the one-year refund policy. [7]I think your company should take responsibility for this situation and give me a full refund. [8]I would appreciate it if you could write or call me at (04)1233-2312 at your convenience. [9]Thank you for your assistance.

Sincerely,
Susan Lin

Unit **10**
書信寫作

2019 年 3 月 30 日

親愛的先生 / 女士：

3 月 14 日，我在貴公司位於臺中市公益路 68 號的經銷店，買了一臺電腦。我付了 3 萬 5 千元買一臺全新的 MacBook Pro，如附件的收據影本。

第一個星期運作順利，但在 3 月 22 日時，我用到一半就突然當機。之後就再也無法開機。我立刻跟買電腦的經銷商聯絡，但店員拒絕退費給我。

然而，就我所知，蘋果公司有一年保證退費的政策。我認為貴公司應該對此情況負責，並給我全額退費。如果您方便時寫信或打我的電話 (04)1233-2312，我會很感激。謝謝您的協助。

謹啟
Susan Lin

NOTE

Jane Wang 在 QQ 百貨公司買了一件圓點洋裝，然而洋裝上有污漬，她寫一封抱怨信給該百貨公司的業務經理。

_____

_____

_____

_____

_____

_____

_____

_____

_____

_____

_____

_____

_____

_____

_____

Unit

10

書信寫作

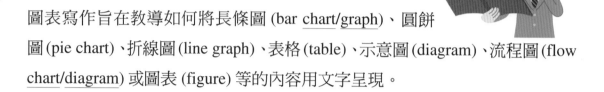

Unit 11 圖表寫作 (Chart Writing)

圖表寫作旨在教導如何將長條圖 (bar chart/graph)、圓餅圖 (pie chart)、折線圖 (line graph)、表格 (table)、示意圖 (diagram)、流程圖 (flow chart/diagram) 或圖表 (figure) 等的內容用文字呈現。

以下說明圖表寫作的注意事項：

❶ 瞭解圖表資料

1. 確認標題或主題：題目敘述或圖表標題通常會概述題型的資料，如雅思 (IELTS) 的 Writing Task 1 是用英文來說明圖表，而指考則是以中文說明。

2. 分析主要的趨勢：可以朝以下幾個方向進行分析：找出最高點 (peak/the highest point)、最低點 (bottom/the lowest point/trough)、差異處以及相同處。

Tip
1. 可以用原級來表示相同處。
2. 使用 similar、similarity、in the same way 等來表示相同處。
3. 使用 while、whereas、difference 等來表示差異處。

❷ 圖表寫作的撰寫步驟

1. 圖表的主題句：主題句是引言，基本上會先描述圖表的基本資訊。

常用詞彙	主詞：chart/graph/table/diagram/figure/illustration
	動詞：show/display/demonstrate/reveal/suggest/present (呈現出)、illustrate (說明)、give information about (提供關於⋯資訊)
常用句型	The chart shows (that) . . . 圖表顯示⋯
	According to/Based on the chart, . . . 根據圖表⋯
	As can be seen from the chart, . . . 如圖表所示⋯

⟮範例 1⟯

以 103 年指考為例,圖表說明為中文,翻譯關於圖表的說明即可。

提示:下圖呈現的是美國某高中的全體學生每天進行各種活動的時間分配。

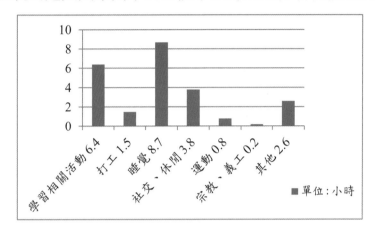

主題句:The bar chart shows how students in a high school in the United States allocate their time to different activities every day.　這個長條圖呈現出美國某高中的全體學生每天進行各種活動的時間分配。

⟮範例 2⟯

以仿雅思的 Writing Task 1 為例,需要將題目的圖表說明加以改寫。

提示:The graph below shows the average income of families and individuals in Canada from 2001 to 2010.

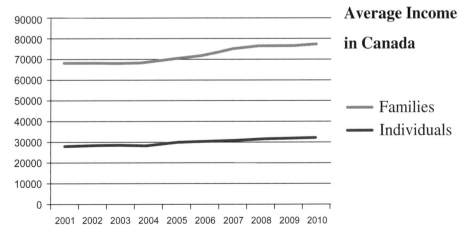

(圖片來源:https://goo.gl/o5np6w)

Unit 11 圖表寫作

主題句：As can be seen from the line graph, it illustrates, from the year 2001 to 2010, trends in the income of families and individuals on average in Canada.

如同該折線圖所示，它說明 2001 到 2010 年加拿大家庭和個人平均所得的走勢。

2. 圖表的內容：找出主要趨勢，尤其是最高點、最低點、差異處或相同處，然後依據其中的數據加以佐證。以下介紹常用於圖表的字彙、同義字和句型：

表示趨勢的常用字彙

名詞	increase/rise/growth (增加)、decrease/fall/drop/reduction/decline (減少)
動詞	increase/rise/grow (增加)、peak (達到高峰)、decrease/fall/drop/reduce/decline (減少)
形容詞	slight (些微的)、steady (穩定的)、gradual (逐漸的)、dramatic (驟然的)、sharp/steep (急遽的)、sudden (突然的)、considerable (大量的)、significant (顯著的)
副詞	slightly (些微地)、steadily (穩定地)、gradually (逐漸)、dramatically (驟然)、sharply/steeply (急遽地)、suddenly (突然)、considerably (大量地)、significantly (顯著地)、approximately (大約)
介系詞	above/over (超過)、about/around (大約)、below/under (少於)

常用字彙的同義字

組／種類	比例／部分	數量	花費	地區
group	proportion	number	cost	area
type	ratio	amount	expense	region
category	portion	quantity	expenditure	zone
class	part		spending	district

常用句型

1. 最高級句型：

例 In 1940, Columbia had **the lowest** population of the three countries, at around 25,000. 在 1940 年，哥倫比亞是 3 個國家中人口數最少的，約 25,000 人。

2. 比較級句型：

例 By the year 1970, over 40% of the population in Taiwan were children. This was **lower than** that in 1960 when it peaked at around 45%. 1970 年，臺灣有超過 40% 的人口是小孩。低於 1960 年的最高點約 45%。

Tip

根據文章的內容，可以使用下列的轉折詞連接：

1. 表示次序的轉折詞，如：first、second、last 等。

2. 表示比較、對照的轉折詞：in contrast to、by/in comparison to、on the contrary 等。

（範例）

以 103 年指考題為例。下圖呈現的是美國某高中的全體學生每天進行各種活動的時間分配。請描述該圖所呈現之特別現象。

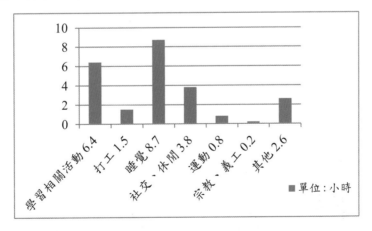

Sleeping makes up the largest proportion of the high school students' time in a day (about 8.7 hours), while they only spend 0.2 hour on religious or voluntary work. The second largest amount of time these students spend each

day is curricular activities (around 6.4 hours). Besides, 3.8 hours a day is spent on hanging out with friends and doing recreational activities. Every day they spend 0.8 hours exercising and 1.5 hours working part-time. As for the rest 2.6 hours, it can be used to do other things, such as preparing a friend's birthday gift or doing household chores, etc.

　　睡眠占去這些高中生一天最大比例的時間 (約 8.7 小時)，然而他們只花 0.2 小時從事宗教或志工工作。這些學生每天花第二多的時間在學習上 (約 6.4 小時)。此外，一天有 3.8 小時是花在社交與休閒活動。他們每天運動 0.8 小時以及打工 1.5 小時。至於剩下的 2.6 小時則被用來做其他事情，如準備朋友的生日禮物或做家事等。

3. **做出結論**：歸結前面的主要論述，做出簡單的總結或對未來的推測。通常會先用表示結論的轉折詞做為結論的開場。以 103 年指考題為例：

結論句：In short, except for sleeping time, students in this school have over eight hours of daytime which is available for them to do activities other than studies. 簡言之，除了睡覺時間外，此校的學生在白天有超過 8 小時的時間可做學習以外的事。

根據圖表，寫出主題句、曲線圖分析的支持段以及結論句。

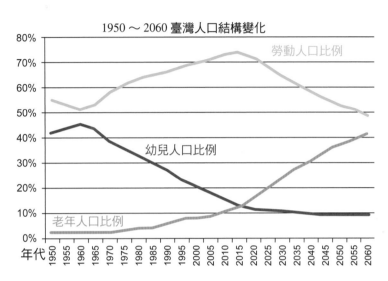

1950～2060 臺灣人口結構變化

(圖片來源：https://goo.gl/9RHgc2)

1.

主題句：＿＿＿＿＿＿＿＿＿＿＿＿＿＿＿＿＿＿＿＿＿＿＿＿＿＿＿＿

＿＿＿＿＿＿＿＿＿＿＿＿＿＿＿＿＿＿＿＿＿＿＿＿＿＿＿＿＿＿＿＿

2. 根據圖表，寫出關於臺灣人口結構變化曲線圖分析的支持段。

＿＿＿＿＿＿＿＿＿＿＿＿＿＿＿＿＿＿＿＿＿＿＿＿＿＿＿＿＿＿＿＿＿＿

＿＿＿＿＿＿＿＿＿＿＿＿＿＿＿＿＿＿＿＿＿＿＿＿＿＿＿＿＿＿＿＿＿＿

＿＿＿＿＿＿＿＿＿＿＿＿＿＿＿＿＿＿＿＿＿＿＿＿＿＿＿＿＿＿＿＿＿＿

＿＿＿＿＿＿＿＿＿＿＿＿＿＿＿＿＿＿＿＿＿＿＿＿＿＿＿＿＿＿＿＿＿＿

＿＿＿＿＿＿＿＿＿＿＿＿＿＿＿＿＿＿＿＿＿＿＿＿＿＿＿＿＿＿＿＿＿＿

＿＿＿＿＿＿＿＿＿＿＿＿＿＿＿＿＿＿＿＿＿＿＿＿＿＿＿＿＿＿＿＿＿＿

＿＿＿＿＿＿＿＿＿＿＿＿＿＿＿＿＿＿＿＿＿＿＿＿＿＿＿＿＿＿＿＿＿＿

Unit

11

圖表寫作

3.

結論句：_____

_____

_____

_____

_____

（範文）

下面的表格為分析男性與女性消費者到 QQ 超市購物的原因。

Reasons for shopping at QQ Supermarket 在 QQ 超市購物的原因	no. of men 男性人數	no. of women 女性人數
location　地點	5	12
competitive prices　有競爭力的價格	2	24
good reputation　好名聲	9	17
sufficient parking spaces　足夠的停車位	27	7
24/7 shopping　24 小時全年無休	17	0

主題段 (1)

[1]The table above shows the main reasons why the surveyed 60 men and 60 women do their shopping at QQ Supermarket.

支持段：分析圖表 (2-6)

[2]Overall, of the five reasons, namely location, competitive prices, good reputation, sufficient parking spaces, and 24/7 shopping, the major factor that leads to these men's decision is sufficient parking spaces (27), while 24 women shop at the supermarket primarily because of its competitive prices. [3]Besides, men pay

246

attention to the issues of location and prices least, while parking spaces and all-day service are women's last concern. [4]As for reputation, it is the second dominating reason for women to choose a place to buy grocery. [5]17 women inquired consider it important. [6]Although it is in third place in terms of reasons influencing men's choice, only 9 out of the 60 men notice good reputation.

結論段 (7)

[7]To sum up, it is clear that the men and the women interviewed have different preferences for the choice of supermarkets.

上面的表格顯示受訪的 60 位男性與 60 位女性為何到 QQ 超市購物的原因。

一般來說,在 5 個原因中,也就是地點、有競爭力的價格、好名聲、足夠的停車位和24小時全年無休,影響這些男性決定的主要原因是足夠的停車位(27位),然而 24 位女性到這間超市購物主要因為其有競爭力的價格。此外,男性最不在乎地點和價格,而停車位和全天營業是女性最不在乎的。至於名聲,這是女性選擇購買物品的次要原因,有 17 位女性認為名聲重要。雖然它是影響男性選擇的第三個原因,但 60 位男性中只有 9 人會注意到好名聲。

總之,受訪男性和女性顯然在選擇超市上有著不同的偏好。

圖表寫作

下面的圓餅圖顯示一般英國家庭的用電比例。根據此圖表，寫出一篇分成兩個段落的文章。在第一段中，概述該圖表所呈現的資訊。然後在第二段中，寫出自己國家或家中的用電情形。

What electricity is used for:

■ Heating rooms, heating water

■ Ovens, kettles, washing machines

■ Lighting, TVs, radios

■ Vacuum cleaners, food mixers, electric tools

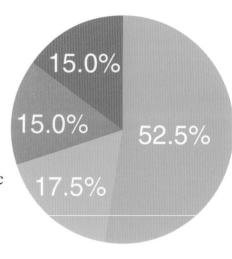

_____

_____

_____

_____

_____

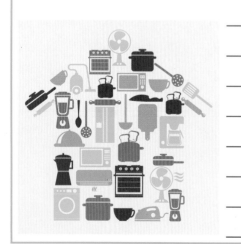

_____

_____

_____

_____

_____

_____

_____

Unit 12 議論文 (Argumentative Writing)

議論文是針對議題闡述個人的看法，並提出有利的證據來支持自己的看法，目的在於說服讀者接受作者的觀點。

議論文的主題常包含以下幾類：

1. 表達贊成或反對的觀點。

2. 分析優缺點。

3. 提供問題的解決方法。

> **Tip**
>
> 常見的議論文主題有：
> Should death penalty be abolished?　應該廢除死刑嗎？
> Should restrictions be imposed on the use of cellphones in public places?
> 在公共場所使用手機是否應該有所限制？
> Should animal testing be permitted?　是否應該允許動物實驗？
> Should we use nuclear power?　我們是否應該使用核電？

12-1 議論文的架構

想要寫一篇好的議論文，應注意以下兩個要點：

1. 搜集足夠的資料：為了讓自己的論述足以說服讀者，必須利用網站、報導、文章等來搜集各種相關且可靠的資料。更可以透過實例、數據、事實、個人經驗或專家意見等，來證明自己的論點，讓文章更具說服力。

> **Tip**
>
> 在寫議論文時，應注意下列事項：
> 1. 不論議論文的主題跟你的意見是相同或相左，最好都能先了解他人已做過的論述，以避免重複的討論，或意見陳述時的偏頗。
> 2. 議論文的寫作往往一不小心就會出現以偏概全的語氣，因此務必小心語氣，避免情緒化、偏激的字詞。

2. 基本架構：在議論文的段落中，主題句就要表達自己的意見，主體部分提出原因和例子來支持自己的觀點，結論句就換一種說法來再次強調自己的觀點。形式如下：

> **Topic Sentence**
> your opinion
>
> **Body**
> reason + example (1, 2, 3 . . .)
>
> **Concluding Sentence**
> your opinion

在議論文寫作中，可利用 OREO 結構圖，以證據來支持自己的論點，如以下範例所示：

╔範 例╗

題目：Should people have cosmetic surgery

　　　to improve their appearance?

　　　人們應該利用整形手術來改善外貌？

O **(Opinion)**	I oppose the idea of sacrificing health in order to look good. 我反對為了美貌就犧牲健康的想法。
R **(Reason)**	What's the use of being physically attractive if we have to risk our lives to enjoy it?　如果必須冒著生命危險，外表美麗又有何用？
E **(Example)**	Some people even have stomach surgery to restrict their food consumption, regardless of the possibility of fatal side effects. 有些人甚至會進行胃部手術來限制飲食，完全不顧致命副作用的可能性。
O **(Opinion)**	Even though looking good might strengthen a person's confidence, it is still unwise to go to such extremes in order to get the looks he or she wants. 儘管美貌可以讓人增加自信，但透過極端的方式來得到自己想要的長相，還是不明智的。

根據題目，將下列 (A) 至 (D) 選項分別填入 OREO 組織圖中。

題目：Should students wear school uniforms?

(A) If all the students wear the same school uniforms, it can help develop a strong group spirit.

(B) In conclusion, wearing school uniforms can make students identify with their school, so this policy should not be abandoned.

(C) I agree that students should wear school uniforms.

(D) Take myself, for example. Whenever I put on my school uniform, I start to act better in public places because I don't want to disgrace my school.

O (Opinion)	_____
R (Reason)	_____
E (Example)	_____
O (Opinion)	_____

12-2 常用的轉折詞與用語

以下介紹議論文常用的轉折詞與用語，包括下列幾種：

連接理由的轉折詞：

表次序	The first reason is . . . （第一個的原因是…） Another reason is . . . （其他的原因是…） firstly（第一） secondly（第二）
表添加	besides、moreover、furthermore、in addition、additionally、what's more（此外）

Unit

12

議論文

表達個人意見：

就我而言	as far as I am concerned as for me
我認為	I think/consider/believe/agree that . . . It is my belief that . . . in my opinion/view I am of the opinion that . . . from my point of view

陳述事實的用語：

事實上	in fact、as a matter of fact、actually、in reality
不用說	It goes without saying that . . .、needless to say
無疑地	without a doubt、undoubtedly

表示結論的轉折詞：

因此	as a result、therefore、consequently、in consequence、accordingly、 thus
這樣的話	in this way
簡言之	in short、in brief
總之	to sum up、to conclude、in conclusion

 練習寫寫看 B

請圈選出正確的轉折詞或用語。

1. The dress looks nice, but (*in my opinion/besides*), it is too expensive.

2. Young children can learn quickly; (*as far as I am concerned/what's more*), they also remember everything they have learned.

3. (*Firstly/Therefore*), I got up late. Another reason was that I didn't catch the school bus. That's why I was late for school.

4. When I was little, (*it goes without saying that/it was my belief that*) there were angels in the world.

5. Many people bet that Germany will win the World Cup. (*As for me/In this way*), the odds are in favor of Argentina.

12-3 議論文的寫作步驟

議論文的寫作步驟如下：

1. 腦力激盪：蒐集資料，支持論點的細節來源可以根據事實、個人經驗、實驗結果、統計數據、邏輯推理或報章雜誌等。刪除不相關的理由後，挑選最重要的幾項，並按重要性來書寫。

〔範例〕

題目：Students should go to school in uniform.　學生們應該穿制服上學。

Arguments (論點)：

Uniform can represent group identity.　制服能代表團體認同。

It is not necessary to spend time considering what to wear.

不用花時間考慮要穿什麼。

It helps save time and money.　有助省時間和省錢。

The schools that students attend are easily recognizable.

可輕易辨認出學生所就讀的學校。

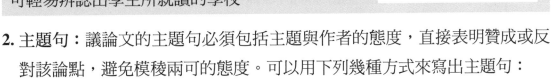

2. 主題句：議論文的主題句必須包括主題與作者的態度，直接表明贊成或反對該論點，避免模稜兩可的態度。可以用下列幾種方式來寫出主題句：

直接表達個人意見

直接表明贊成或反對該論點，甚至可以透過反對的意見來突顯自己支持的觀

Unit

12

議論文

點，如：

例 Though some teachers oppose the idea of using *Anne Frank's Diary* in the classrooms, I believe that it is a good text for teaching.　雖然有些老師反對在課堂上教《安妮的日記》，但我認為它是個很好的教材。

例 Though the social networking website, Facebook, enables millions of people to set up connections with others, I don't think it actually helps build up relationships among friends.　雖然社群網站臉書讓數百萬人能跟其他人建立關係，但我不認為它真的能幫助建立朋友間的情誼。

從客觀的角度

可以從客觀的角度來寫主題句，如：

例 Parents should give their children more freedom to do what they like to do. 父母應給孩子更多自由去做他們喜歡做的事情。

例 Glass straws, in fact, are not as eco-friendly as most people think. 事實上，玻璃吸管並非如大多數人認為的那樣環保。

3. 寫出大綱

題目：Should the book *Anne Frank's Diary* be taught in schools?

《安妮的日記》這本書應該成為學校的教材嗎？

O (Opinion)	I believe that *Anne Frank's Diary* is a good text for teaching. 我認為《安妮的日記》是個好教材。
R (Reason)	Students can learn more about the Holocaust through the book. 透過這本書，學生可知道更多關於猶太人大屠殺的事件。
E (Example)	By reading about the situation of Anne Frank and the other people in her diary, students learn about the Holocaust through an individual's voice rather than through news reports or historical records. 藉由閱讀日記裡關於安妮與其他人的遭遇，學生透過個人的聲音，而非新聞報導或歷史記錄來知道大屠殺事件。
R (Reason)	Students will not be confronted with the violence and horror of the Holocaust.　學生不會面對大屠殺的血腥與暴力。

E **(Example)**	The diary ended when Anne and her family were taken away from the Secret Annex, with no further description of the suffering of the Jews in the concentration camps.　當安妮和家人被帶離密室時這本書就結束了，並未進一步描述猶太人在集中營所受的磨難。
R **(Reason)**	The book conveys a message of hope and compassion. 這本書傳達出希望與憐憫的訊息。
E **(Example)**	Even while Anne was confined to the hiding place, she still maintained a positive attitude and expressed great sympathy for those who were suffering.　甚至當安妮被困在躲藏的地方時，她仍然保持正向的態度並同情那些正在受苦的人。
O **(Opinion)**	To sum up, *Anne Frank's Diary* is an excellent choice for teaching students about the Holocaust. 總之，《安妮的日記》是教導學生關於猶太人大屠殺的絕佳教材。

Tip

注意使用表次序 (first、second 等)、表添加 (besides、in addition 等) 或表重要性 (more important、most importantly 等) 的轉折詞來連接支持論點的理由。

4. 寫出文章

主題段 (1)

¹Though some teachers oppose the idea of using *Anne Frank's Diary* in the classrooms, I believe that it is a good text for teaching.

支持段 (2-8)

²First of all, students can learn more about the Holocaust through the book. ³By reading about the situation of Anne Frank and the other people in her diary, students learn about the Holocaust through an individual's voice rather than through news reports or historical records. ⁴At the same time, students will not be confronted with the violence and horror of the Holocaust. ⁵The diary ended when Anne and her family were taken away from

Unit
12
議論文

the Secret Annex, with no further description of the suffering of the Jews in the concentration camps. [6]Even without such terrifying details, students are still able to understand the horrifying reality that Anne experienced. [7]Most importantly, the book conveys a message of hope and compassion. [8]Even while Anne was confined to the hiding place, she still maintained a positive attitude and expressed great sympathy for those who were suffering.

結論段 (9)

[9]To sum up, *Anne Frank's Diary* is an excellent choice for teaching young people about the Holocaust.

雖然有些老師反對在課堂上教《安妮的日記》，但我認為它是個很好的教材。

首先，透過這本書，學生可知道更多關於猶太人大屠殺的事件。藉由閱讀日記裡關於安妮與其他人的遭遇，學生透過個人的聲音，而非新聞報導或歷史記錄來知道大屠殺事件。同時，學生不會面對大屠殺的血腥與暴力。當安妮和家人被帶離密室時這本書就結束了，並未進一步描述猶太人在集中營所受的磨難。儘管沒有這些令人害怕的細節，學生仍可以了解到安妮所經歷的那些恐怖的事實。更重要的是，這本書傳達出希望與憐憫的訊息。甚至當安妮被困在躲藏的地方時，她仍然保持正向的態度並同情那些正在受苦的人。

總之，《安妮的日記》是教導學生關於猶太人大屠殺的絕佳教材。

Tip

完成一篇議論文後，應檢查自己的文章是否符合下列要點：

1. 一開始就簡明扼要地表明自己的觀點。
2. 根據事實或相關資料來支持自己的論點。
3. 以說理的語氣書寫。
4. 避免使用過多的陳腔濫調。
5. 立場要明確。
6. 文章要有洞察力，不可流於說教。
7. 文章的結論要清楚地重申立場。
8. 應使用清楚、有力且直接的文字書寫。

練習寫寫看 C

I 根據題目，各列出 4 個相關的論點。

題目 1：The Benefits of Riding a Bike to School

論點：

1. _____
2. _____
3. _____
4. _____

題目 2：Involvement in School Clubs

論點：

1. _____
2. _____
3. _____
4. _____

Unit
12
議論文

Ⅲ 請勾選出適合當議論文主題句的句子。

_____ 1. The pollution in the river was caused by the chemical factory.

_____ 2. More renewable energy should be used to replace fossil fuel.

_____ 3. Taiwan's declining birth rate is a matter of considerable public concern.

_____ 4. The singer has won the Grammy Awards for three times.

_____ 5. When little children have behavior problems, I believe that their parents are to blame.

Ⅲ 根據題目，進行腦力激盪後，填入 OREO 結構圖並寫出一篇議論文 (至少 120 個單詞)。

題目：Do Social Networks Bring People Together?

腦力激盪：

O	_____ _____
R	_____ _____
E	_____ _____
R	_____ _____
E	_____ _____
O	_____ _____

寫出文章：

_____

_____

_____

_____

_____

_____

_____

_____

_____

_____

Ⅳ 根據題目，寫出一篇議論文 (至少 120 個單詞)。

題目：Should High School Students Join a School Club?

_____

_____

_____

_____

_____

_____

_____

_____

_____

_____

_____

_____

_____

Unit

12

議論文

大考翻譯 實戰題本

英語 *Make Me High* 系列

英文作文
這樣寫，
就 OK!

解答本

張淑娛、應惠蕙　編著
車昀庭　審定

三民書局

Unit 1

練習寫寫看 A

1. BCDE

解析

從英文句子的結構來說，「學英文」不是「必須天天練習」的主詞，其主詞應該是「人」，所以 (A) 句是錯的。(B) 句根據文意，用不定詞 (to V) 表示目的，主詞可以是 we 或 you；(C) 句和 (D) 句說明學英文需要什麼條件，合乎英文語法結構；(E) 句以從屬子句 (If...,) + 主要子句來表達。

2. CDE

解析

(A)(B) 句是錯的，因為桌子 (The desk) 或桌上 (On the desk) 都不可能「擁有 (has)」鉛筆。(C) 句以鉛筆為主詞，表示鉛筆是在桌上；(D) 句是把地方副詞放在句首的倒裝句型：「地方副詞 + 不及物動詞 + 主詞」；(E) 句是「there + be 動詞」的句型，表示「有…」。

3. ACD

解析

(B) 句是錯的，因為「作業是被交出去」，主詞和動詞的關係是被動的，所以得用被動語態；(E) 句是錯誤的，因為缺少動詞。

練習寫寫看 B

I

1. 主詞 : we

We will take a trip to Australia during my summer vacation.

2. 主詞 : you

You should go to bed earlier.

3. 主詞 : it

It has been raining for a week.

解析

it 可以表示天氣、距離、價值或重量。

4. 主詞 : it

It takes about half an hour to go from Taipei to Taoyuan by train.

5. 主詞 : English

English is spoken in many countries.

解析

英文是被講的，所以用被動形式。

II

1. was given; looks

2. will go

3. was stolen; felt sad

4. have lived; was born

練習寫寫看 C

1. delicious food

2. famous tourist attractions

3. the house with a garage

4. an old man with/wearing a long beard

5. the girl with/(who is) wearing jeans

6. the ability to speak English

7. a boring person

8. a beautiful charming girl

練習寫寫看 D

I

1. F

Yuanbao was a type of money.

2. C

3. F

If you have an opportunity to visit Tainan, don't forget to taste a variety of local foods.

4. C

5. F

A cellphone is so popular that it has become

something necessary in our lives.

II

1. B

If you own a car that does not run and cannot be fixed, this car is a white elephant.

2. A

There are advantages of getting into the habit of taking notes.

3. D

These inventions can change our way of life.

4. C

And I can have someone to talk to.

5. B

The poor may have to worry about their next meal, while the rich may spend tens of thousands on a handbag.

練習寫寫看 E

1. C 2. R 3. R 4. R 5. C

練習寫寫看 F

I

1. → If there is anything you don't understand, just let me know and I'll help you.

2. → As long as/If you keep working hard, you are sure to get somewhere.

3. → Don't panic when you get a flat tire on the freeway.

4. → Leo won't forgive you unless you make a sincere apology.

5. → Mary insisted on marrying Jack, even though her parents strongly objected.

6. → The fool love wealth, while/whereas the wise treasure truth.

II

1. → It had been raining heavily for days; therefore, many low-lying areas were flooded.

2. → A man can stay alive for more than a week without food. However, a man without water can hardly live for more than three days.

3. → Robert works as a volunteer in the hospital. Moreover/Furthermore, he donates money to the orphanage regularly.

4. → Jerry had a sore throat; therefore, he couldn't speak at the meeting.

III

1. → The press has a strong influence. It can bring about significant changes to the lives of ordinary people.

   → The press has a strong influence, so/because it can bring about significant changes to the lives of ordinary people.

2. → Turn to the last page, and you will find the key to the questions.

   → If you turn to the last page, you will find the key to the questions.

3. → Small islands could soon be underwater; the residents of major cities are likely to have nowhere to live by the end of the 21st century.

   → Small islands could soon be underwater, and the residents of major cities are likely to have nowhere to live by the end of the 21st century.

4. → The ice-cream taster uses a gold spoon because regular spoons leave an aftertaste that can dull the taste buds.

5. → William works two part-time jobs in order that/so he could save enough money to study abroad.

練習寫寫看 G

I

1. ;/.   2. ,/,/,/.
3. "/?/"   4. ;/,
5. ,/!   6. ,/;/,/.
7. "/?/"   8. —
9. :/,/,/,   10. ,/"/./,/ "
11. ;/—/.   12. ,/,

II

1. ,/,/,/,/,/"/,"/,"/"/,/,!/"/,/"

Unit 2

練習寫寫看 A

主題 : food

點子 :

> What's my favorite food? I like sashimi,
> noodles, and tofu. I usually have some cookies
> after dinner. By the way, some foreign dishes
> look scary.
> I think green vegetables are good for you.
> I know fast food is bad for one's health. I
> also like to eat organic food. Western food is
> different from eastern food. I went for a meal in
> a Chinese restaurant.

主題句 : A healthy diet can make a big difference.

練習寫寫看 B

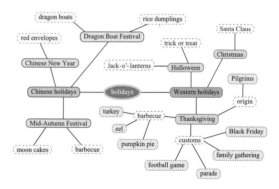

主題句 : Thanksgiving is celebrated with customs.

加長的主題句 : Thanksgiving, a Western holiday, is generally celebrated with customs, such as family gatherings, parades, and football games.

練習寫寫看 C

For:

1. in case of emergency

2. instant answers

3. effective learning tools

4. access to information

5. multimedia learning

Against:

1. distraction

2. cheating

3. inappropriate materials

4. not everyone can afford a smartphone

Unit 3

練習寫寫看 A

What kind: The **cute black** cat is eating.

How: The cute black cat is eating **hungrily**.

Where: The cute black cat is eating hungrily **in the kitchen**.

When: The cute black cat is eating hungrily in the kitchen **right now**.

Why: The cute black cat is eating hungrily in the kitchen right now **because it hasn't eaten anything for two days**.

練習寫寫看 B

1. old

2. old; angrily

3. old; angrily; the manager of the restaurant

4. old; angrily; the manager of the restaurant; posted it on the Internet

5. old; angrily; the manager of the restaurant; posted it on the Internet; the food was really terrible

練習寫寫看 C

I

1. On the hall walls, Jack saw many sports medals and some pictures of students.

2. Do you want to go to the movies or stay home?

3. I'd be glad to play basketball with you, but it must be after school.

II

1. that fell from the sky

2. one of my close friends

3. after I tore it open

4. exercising every day

5. begging to come with his mother

Unit 4

練習寫寫看 A

I

1. Based on
2. All in all
3. Therefore
4. In fact
5. that is
6. In other words
7. otherwise
8. Accordingly
9. In general
10. while
11. Despite
12. Instead

II

1. C 2. A 3. D 4. F 5. B

練習寫寫看 B

I

1. C 2. B 3. A 4. C

II

1. *As a result*, the government decided to send a unit of soldiers to help the locals.
2. *To make matters worse*, he even lied to the teacher, saying that he had left the assignment at home. *Therefore*, the teacher got very angry and punished him severely.
3. *Needless to say*, helping others is a source of happiness.
4. *Besides*, I can surf the Internet for information. *Consequently*, my cellphone has become a necessity in my life.
5. *According to studies*, blue plates can spoil a person's appetite.
6. *In addition*, through volunteer work, he gains valuable job experience. *Better still*, volunteering helps him realize what he is able to do best.

Unit 5

練習寫寫看 A

1.

There is a French proverb that says, "A stingy man is always poor." Once upon a time a stingy man hid all of his money in a hole and put a heavy stone to the top. One day, he lifted the stone but found no penny there. He cried so loudly that his neighbors came out to see what was going on. One of the neighbors told him that he didn't need to be unhappy at all since he never thought of how to do with the money.

2.

In many languages, certain animals have specific characteristics. In Chinese, for example, dogs represent loyalty, and tigers are a symbol of authority. Likewise, animal imagery can be found in many English expressions. "As busy as a bee" and "as quiet as a mouse" vividly describe a busy person and a quiet person. The imagery does give color to the language.

3.

Pineapple, baozi, and zongzi are considered good luck in Chinese culture. The pronunciation of the word for "pineapple" in Taiwanese means "prosperity or good luck will come." Naturally, it has become a symbol of wealth in Chinese culture. Thus, it is common to find pineapples placed in houses during Chinese New Year. Baozi and zongzi are another example. The pronunciation of the two words "bao zong" sounds like "a sure victory." As a result, many Chinese people give those who are going to take an exam baozi and zongzi as gifts.

4.

Jim and Della were a young couple who loved each other so much, but they were very poor. For Christmas, Della decided to buy Jim a chain for his cherished pocket watch given to him by his father. To make more money, Della had her long hair cut off and sold. Meanwhile, Jim decided to sell his watch to buy Della a beautiful set of combs for her long hair. Although disappointed to find the gift they chose became useless, they were all pleased.

練習寫寫看 B

I

1. A   2. B   3. D

II

1. Different cultures have different ways to express love for each other.
2. Today, many people believe that owning brand-name products helps to strengthen their image and increase their confidence.
3. Different colors are used for different purposes.
4. We should always tell the truth.
5. Onions can be divided into two categories: fresh onions and storage onions.

練習寫寫看 C

1. B   2. C   3. A   4. D   5. C

練習寫寫看 D

I

1.

主題句：Things often have more uses than you could ever imagine.

支持細節 1：Some common items that we use every day can seem to perform magic when you know how to use

them.

支持細節 2：You can add a sugar cube to coffee or tea to make the drink sweet.

支持細節 3：Sugar cubes can keep cookies crisp.

2.

主題句：Many patients have reported a decrease in pain after a good laugh.

支持細節 1：This reduction in pain may result from chemicals produced in the blood.

支持細節 2：Patients might feel less pain because their muscles are more relaxed.

支持細節 3：Patients are simply distracted from thinking about their pain.

II

1.

支持細節 1：The food is ready in a short time.

支持細節 2：The place is usually big and clean.

支持細節 3：It's easy to find a fast-food restaurant in most cities.

2.

支持細節 1：Quite a few young couples choose to have only one child or no child at all.

支持細節 2：Some couples can't afford to raise any child.

支持細節 3：More and more people would prefer to be single.

3.

支持細節 1：They may realize the value of money and become more economical.

支持細節 2：They could learn to make better use of time.

支持細節 3：They could gain work experiences.

4.

支持細節 1：They might develop the habit of

wasting money.

支持細節 2：Working part-time may become an excuse for neglecting their studies.

支持細節 3：Working part-time may influence their health.

練習寫寫看 E

I
1. D　2. B　3. D

II
1. B　2. D　3. A　4. C

III

1. Clearly, we have learned about the importance of honesty since we were kids.

2. Television can play an important part in childhood education as long as parents make good use of it.

3. It is not surprising that so many men and women have trouble communicating with each other.

4. As for me, being an exchange student in Japan was a truly unforgettable experience.

5. Therefore, sunburn is something we can't ignore.

練習寫寫看 F

1.

Research has proven that weather plays a part in people's moods. Warmer temperatures and exposure to sunshine can help increase positive thinking, while cold, rainy days bring anxiety. Thus, many people believe that bad weather can reduce productivity and efficiency.

However, there is a surprising link between such beliefs and the actual effect of weather on people's work performance. Through data from laboratory experiments as well as observations of a Japanese bank in real life, researchers find that weather conditions indeed influence a worker's focus. To many people's surprise, when the weather is bad, individuals tend to focus more on their work rather than thinking about activities they could engage in outside of work. Workers can be greatly distracted by photos showing outdoor activities, such as sailing on a sunny day or walking in the woods, and thus lower their productivity.

The findings conclude that workers are actually most productive when the weather is lousy—and only if nothing reminds them of good weather.

2.

It was stressful for me because this was the first week that I became a high school senior. In this week, I took tests every day and spent most of my time studying.

I was advised to prepare for the college entrance examination as soon as possible. Thus, I had to plan my study schedule. First, I made a study plan. Second, I had to review previous lessons and preview new ones. I did the review in order to move information into my long-term memory. I also did the preview, and thus I could gain a better understanding of new lessons. Besides, I changed my study habits so that I could do things more efficiently. Most of all, I exercised to stay healthy. I knew that health meant everything.

To sum up, life in the third year of senior high school is completely different from the first two years. Clearly, I should make good use of my time to face a challenging future ahead of me.

Unit 6

練習寫寫看 A

I

2. TN

I am standing at the gate of my new school. I am so nervous that my heart is pounding because today is my first day at an American high school.

3. FN

At that time, Jack was a primary school student. One day, when he was cleaning the classroom, he picked up a five-dollar bill. Without thinking, he put it in his pocket. Later, Helen, one of his best friends, told him she had lost her money with tears in her eyes. He comforted her and felt regret. He decided to wait until there was no one in the classroom. Then, he put the money in Helen's drawer.

練習寫寫看 B

1.
E → F → A → C → G → H → B → D → I

2.
C → G → E → I → A → H → F → B → D

練習寫寫看 C

1.

1. got up late on a school day
2. taxis were coming and going
3. my glasses flew off, everyone started looking at me
4. found my glasses, but they were broken
5. streets were crowded with buses
6. overslept and missed the bus
7. rushed out of the door, began to rain

8. didn't want to waste time running back home to get an umbrella, simply put my schoolbag under my jacket
9. got all wet and had to change my clothes
10. very hard for me to see anything with my face covered with muddy water
11. my bad day didn't end there
12. trying to find my glasses, a car drove through a puddle of water and splashed water all over me
13. I felt embarrassed
14. wet and dirty from head to toe, I finally arrived at school
15. my classmates saw me, they all broke out into laughter
16. suddenly, slipped and fell on the wet sidewalk

Group A:

6. overslept and missed the bus
7. rushed out of the door, began to rain
8. didn't want to waste time running back home to get an umbrella, simply put my schoolbag under my jacket

Group B:

16. suddenly, slipped and fell on the wet sidewalk
3. my glasses flew off, everyone started looking at me
13. I felt embarrassed
11. my bad day didn't end there
12. trying to find my glasses, a car drove through a puddle of water and splashed water all over me
10. very hard for me to see anything with my face covered with muddy water

4. found my glasses, but they were broken

Group C:

14. wet and dirty from head to toe, I finally arrived at school

15. my classmates saw me, they all broke out into laughter

2.

主題句：I had a very bad day yesterday

支持細節：

Group A: overslept and forgot to bring an umbrella

Group B: slipped on the sidewalk and broke my glasses

Group C: was teased by my classmates

3.

I had a very bad day yesterday. It began when I overslept and missed the bus. Then, as I rushed out of the door, it began to rain. I didn't want to waste any time running back home to get an umbrella, so I simply put my schoolbag under my jacket. Suddenly, I slipped and fell on the wet sidewalk. My glasses flew off, and everyone started looking at me. I felt very embarrassed. However, my bad day didn't end there. As I was trying to find my glasses, a car drove through a puddle of water and splashed water all over me. It was very hard for me to see anything with my face covered with muddy water. I finally found my glasses, but they were broken. Wet and dirty from head to toe, I finally arrived at school. When my classmates saw me, they all broke out into laughter. Yesterday was really not my day.

Unit 7

練習寫寫看 A

1.

1. Joe likes to wear black T-shirts and old jeans
2. Joe is interested in computers
3. Joe has straight, green hair
4. Joe's knowledge of computers is second to none
5. Joe is tall

1. ① Joe likes to wear black T-shirts and old jeans
2. ② Joe is interested in computers
3. ① Joe has straight, green hair
4. ② Joe's knowledge of computers is second to none
5. ① Joe is tall

2.

主題句：My best friend, Joe, really lives his life in his own way.

支持細節：① his looks and style

② his knowledge of computers

3.

My best friend, Joe, really lives his life in his own way. He is a tall guy with straight hair that is dyed green. He usually wears black T-shirts and a pair of old blue jeans that are torn at the knees. These clothes make him look a little sloppy, but he doesn't care. He believes that his style suits him well. Also, Joe claims that his knowledge of computers is second to none. He always begins our conversations by excitedly telling me interesting things he found on the Internet the night before.

While most of us are busy preparing for the college entrance exams, Joe has devoted himself to Internet and saved all of his money to upgrade his computer. Unwilling to be an ordinary student, Joe insists on living his life in his own way.

練習寫寫看 B

1.

| 1. teach us to see the amusing and bright side of things |
| 2. average height and a little chubby |
| 3. increase students' motivation to learn |
| 4. "take part in a contest can be fun, even though we lose it" |
| 5. a good sense of humor |
| 6. guide my classmates and I to join a math contest when I was a freshman |

| 1. ② teach us to see the amusing and bright side of things |
| 2. ① average height and a little chubby |
| 3. ② increase students' motivation to learn |
| 4. ③ "take part in a contest can be fun, even though we lose it" |
| 5. ① a good sense of humor |
| 6. ③ guide my classmates and I to join a math contest when I was a freshman |

2.

主題句：The teacher who inspires me the most is Mr. Chang, my math teacher in senior high school.

支持細節：① his looks and personality

② his teaching style

③ an unforgettable experience with him

3.

The teacher who inspires me the most is Mr. Chang, my math teacher in senior high school. Mr. Chang is of average height and a little chubby. With a good sense of humor, he always created a pleasant atmosphere in class and taught us to see the amusing and bright side of things. He knew how to increase students' motivation to learn by giving simple directions.

I still remember that Mr. Chang guided my classmates and I to join a math contest when I was a freshman. With his instruction and guidance, we all tried our best to prepare for the competition. When the day was to come, we were ready for the contest and thought that we would win a big prize. To our great disappointment, however, we didn't win any prize. Feeling discouraged, we all burst into tears. Instead of crying with us, Mr. Chang smiled, saying that taking part in a contest could be fun even though we lost it. He told us that entering a competition taught us many things, such as courage, a sense of fair play, and the spirit of teamwork. Until now, I still keep Mr. Chang's words in mind.

練習寫看 C

1.

| 1. on the east coast of Taiwan |
| 2. the Central Cross-Island Highway |
| 3. the red suspension bridge and the temples |
| 4. the Eternal Spring Shrine |
| 5. a marble canyon |
| 6. high-rising cliffs, deep river valleys, and uniquely shaped rocks |
| 7. the gorge is eroded by the Liwu River |

1. ① on the east coast of Taiwan
2. ③ the Central Cross-Island Highway
3. ③ the red suspension bridge and the temples
4. ③ the Eternal Spring Shrine
5. ② a marble canyon
6. ② high-rising cliffs, deep river valleys, and uniquely shaped rocks
7. ② the gorge is eroded by the Liwu River

2.
主題句：Last year, I took an unforgettable trip to Taroko Gorge with my family.
支持細節：① location
② the natural features
③ the man-made features

3.

Last year, I took an unforgettable trip to Taroko Gorge with my family. Taroko Gorge is one of Taiwan's main tourist attractions on the east coast of Taiwan. Eroded by the Liwu River, the gorge is a marble canyon and famous for its high-rising cliffs, deep river valleys, and uniquely shaped rocks. We saw mountains towering above the deep valleys. Following the hiking trails, my family and I went to see the red suspension bridge and the temples set in the mountains. We also visited the Eternal Spring Shrine, which is built over a waterfall and pays tribute to the people who sacrificed their lives when building the Central Cross-Island Highway. All in all, I knew that the wonderful views of Taroko Gorge would always shine brightly in my mind.

練習寫寫看 D

1.
1. a volcanic island
2. *Mamma Mia* is set in a beautiful Greek island like Santorini
3. 200 kilometers to the southeast of mainland Greece
4. go diving
5. leisurely walk on the beaches
6. in Aegean Sea
7. cave houses and rock formations
8. nice weather
9. stay in the whitewashed house

1. ① a volcanic island
2. ② *Mamma Mia* is set in a beautiful Greek island like Santorini
3. ① 200 kilometers to the southeast of mainland Greece
4. ③ go diving
5. ③ leisurely walk on the beaches
6. ① in Aegean Sea
7. ② cave houses and rock formations
8. ② nice weather
9. ③ stay in the whitewashed house

2.
主題句：The place I want to take a trip to is Santorini, a volcanic island located in the Aegean Sea.
支持細節：① location
② attractions and the reasons why I want to visit the place
③ activities I will do during my stay there

3.

The place I want to take a trip to is Santorini,

a volcanic island located in the Aegean Sea. About 200 kilometers to the southeast of mainland Greece, Santorini benefits from nice weather and is famous for its stunning scenery. Every year, it attracts a lot of tourists to this small Greek island. They can also enjoy the unusual cave houses and rock formations. Ever since I watched the film *Mamma Mia*, which is set in a beautiful Greek island like Santorini, I have been deeply attracted by the awesome scenery in the film. I hope I can visit Santorini one day. During my stay there, I will stay in the whitewashed house and leisurely walk on the beaches. Besides, I will go diving into the deep blue sea. Thrown into a fascinating and relaxing place, I believe every picture I take there will be like a fine postcard.

練習寫寫看 E

1.

1. a cotton dress shirt
2. a pleated skirt or loose-fitting pants
3. must be worn all the time except for PE class
4. a sense of school unity and spirit
5. a navy blue wool coat
6. a sense of belonging

1. ② a cotton dress shirt
2. ② a pleated skirt or loose-fitting pants
3. ① must be worn all the time except for PE class
4. ③ a sense of school unity and spirit
5. ② a navy blue wool coat
6. ③ a sense of belonging

2.

主題句：A white shirt and black skirt or pants are the clothes that students at our school are required to wear.

支持細節：① when it is worn
② how it looks and what it is made of
③ what it means to me

3.

A white shirt and black skirt or pants are the clothes that students at our school are required to wear. Except for PE class, this uniform must be worn all the time. Worn by students on a daily basis, the uniform consists of a cotton dress shirt (short-sleeved for the summer and long-sleeved for the winter) and a pleated skirt or loose-fitting pants. Some students who don't consider it fashionable enough wear more stylish tailor-made skirts or pants. In the winter, students have to wear a navy blue wool coat. To me, these uniforms help develop a sense of school unity and spirit. The school uniform can bring school together since everyone looks the same in the white shirts and black skirts or pants. Whether the uniform looks plain or fashionable, it gives me a sense of belonging and makes me proud of being a part of the school.

練習寫寫看 F

1.

1. include garlic, onion, ground pork, Italian seasoning, and tomato sauce
2. the color of tomato sauce
3. eat the pasta so fast
4. neither too crunchy nor too soft
5. fried with olive oil
6. make my mouth water
7. make me forget my manners
8. plain at first sight

1. ② include garlic, onion, ground pork, Italian seasoning, and tomato sauce
2. ① the color of tomato sauce
3. ③ eat the pasta so fast
4. ① neither too crunchy nor too soft
5. ② fried with olive oil
6. ③ make my mouth water
7. ③ make me forget my manners
8. ① plain at first sight

2.

主題句：My favorite food is my mom's spaghetti with meat sauce.

支持細節：① its appearance
　　　　　② its ingredients
　　　　　③ how much I like it and how delicious it is

3.

My favorite food is my mom's spaghetti with meat sauce. Though it looks plain at first sight, with only the color of tomato sauce, once you have a first bite, you'll want to eat some more. The meat sauce includes garlic, onion, ground pork, Italian seasoning, and tomato sauce, all fried with olive oil. The mixture of the ingredients contributes to the flavor and appearance of the delicious dish. The spaghetti is neither too crunchy nor too soft. The blend of the well-prepared spaghetti and yummy sauce always makes me forget my manners. I may eat the pasta so fast that the sauce ends up on my face and clothes. Without doubt, it is my mom's homemade spaghetti with meat sauce that makes my mouth water.

Unit 8

◉ 練習寫寫看 A

We planned to go to the Sun Moon Lake this Saturday because we wanted to escape the hustle and bustle of the city. Before embarking on our trip, we made travel plans and preparations. For example, my father had the car checked, and my mother prepared some food. We also brought umbrellas and coats, just in case.

However, as soon as we got onto the highway, we were caught in the traffic jam. The highway was crowded, and all the cars moved very slowly. There were times when cars could hardly move. With time to kill, we chatted, hummed songs, and played with the smartphones. It was said that a truck loaded with vegetables hit a car. The vegetables were scattered everywhere. What's worse, the accident led to another two accidents. Everything was in chaos. All we heard was the siren of the police cars and ambulances. We were scared and nervous, but we could do nothing.

We didn't get home until midnight. An expected one-day trip turned out to be a torture. We decided to return home and had a good rest. It was a tiring, unlucky, and unforgettable day.

◉ 練習寫寫看 B

It was a warm day in spring. The sky was blue, and the cloud was white. As usual, Mr. Lin and his wife went to the park in the community and sat on the same bench to take a rest. They enjoyed seeing the people there and talking about the good old days. It seemed that they were never tired of talking about how they met, got married,

and raised their children. That day, there were few people in the park. They saw a boy sitting under a big tree with his puppy dog and a little girl standing right in front of the drinking fountain. She seemed curious about the fountain. On the garbage can was a cat, which seemed to keep them company. Suddenly, the little girl let out a cry because the water suddenly flushed out of the fountain. That amused the old couple. It reminded them of their daughter, who did the same years ago. How time flew!

練習寫寫看 C

Mrs. White is one of the teachers I will never forget. With short wavy hair, she had a pleasant personality and always wore a smile on her face. In my memory, she looked elegant and confident all the time.

Mrs. White was a responsible and strict teacher. She asked us to stay focused in class. If a student dozed off, she would tap him or her on the shoulder and say that it is time to wake up. She had a rule: never put off until the next class what you should learn and understand in this one. Therefore, during the break, she would stay in the classroom to answer our questions and solve our problems. Besides, we were not allowed to delay handing in assignments. If a student failed to hand in the assignment, he or she would be given extra homework as a punishment.

To our amazement, Mrs. White was knowledgeable. It seemed that there was nothing she didn't know. She could talk about everything, such as science, movies, fashion, and even video games. All in all, it was an honor to be her student.

練習寫寫看 D

A high school girl was sitting with her eyes closed in one of the priority seats on the MRT. She was apparently unaware of an elderly woman standing beside her because she fell asleep. Without the girl's knowledge, another passenger had videotaped the scene and posted it on YouTube. He even claimed that the high school girl pretended not to notice the old woman. Before long, the clip had gotten tens of thousands of views. Hundreds of messages were posted, most of which were mean words.

At this point, one of the girl's teachers spoke up for her. He said that the student had had a terrible stomachache that day and that she had every right to sit on the priority seat. As a result of this incident, people began to realize the "unseen" needs of some passengers.

練習寫寫看 E

The bittersweet memory of my daughter learning to ride a bicycle still remained in my mind. The anxiety I felt about the injuries she might suffer if she fell off the bike had kept me from allowing her to learn to ride a bicycle for quite some time.

Again and again, she asked my permission. Finally, I yielded to her begging and gave in. As expected, she fell off several times, hurt her knee, and shed tears. I came to comfort her immediately. However, instead of quitting, she stood up and tried again. At last, she learned the trick and went down the curved path of the park.

She rode the bicycle happily, and she finally stopped to give me a wave. With a smile on my face, I stood still and knew that my daughter has grown up.

🖊 練習寫寫看 F

Jenny and Jared are twins, and they received new iPhones as their birthday gifts from their parents yesterday. They were thrilled to get the fancy presents. Jenny was fascinated by the multiple functions the iPhone had and thus became a phubber since she couldn't take her eyes off the screen. On the other hand, Jared had already mastered the smartphone's functions and indulged in the tracks he had downloaded from iTunes.

This morning, the twins walked to school with their iPhones. Jenny fixed her eyes on her smartphone again, while Jared was happily enjoying the top songs on the billboard. Their mother and young sister followed behind them to keep them company. All of a sudden, Jenny hit a tree trunk because she paid no attention to the road ahead. So strong was the impact that she almost passed out. Jenny's mother came to her aid immediately, blaming her for not concentrating on walking. Meanwhile, Jared was still listening to music with his eyes closed. Not noticing what was going on, he kept walking.

While crossing the road, Jared was still wearing his earphones. The volume he set was too high for him to hear other sounds. Little did he know that he had blocked the way of some cars. At that time, an angry driver honked his car horn. "Pay attention to traffic safety, dude!" shouted the man as he pointed behind. Jared was shocked to see that there was a heavy traffic jam. To his embarrassment, he apologized and walked across the street quickly.

Before long, Jared saw his family on the sidewalk and surprisingly found Jenny had a bruise on her forehead. Annoyed with the twins, their mother decided to take back their iPhones until they learned the importance of safety. Staring at each other, Jenny and Jared exchanged a knowing look. They would keep today's lesson in mind forever.

(改編自學測佳作)

Unit 9

練習寫寫看 A

I

1. What's worse/Worse still

2. First/First of all; Second; Therefore/As a result/ Hence/Thus

3. According to/Based on; Therefore/As a result/ Hence/Thus

II

1.

理由 1：As the saying goes, "Procrastination is the thief of time. Putting off things that we should do is just a waste of time.

理由 2：If we are in the habit of putting things off, we will be less likely to get things done on time.

理由 3：Once bad habits are formed, it's difficult to break them.

2.

理由 1：Keeping a pet can make a person become responsible because he or she has to take care of it.

理由 2：Pets can help people relax and lower their stress levels.

理由 3：According to the medical report, keeping pets can make the elderly live longer.

3.

理由 1：People with a sense of inferiority have no confidence in themselves.

理由 2：The sense of inferiority may turn into mental scars.

理由 3：Such people are more likely to be blamed or neglected.

練習寫寫看 B

Air pollution is getting more and more serious and threatening people's health. It is reported that the number of people with lung problems is increasing these years. Two factors are responsible for the worsening air quality: factories and an excessive number of vehicles.

Factories release large amount of harmful chemicals into the air. Factories can be found at every corner of the earth, and there is no place that has not been affected by them. On the other hand, exhaust fumes emitting from vehicles including trucks, jeeps, cars, trains, and airplanes cause enormous amount of pollution. People rely on fossil fuels to fulfill their daily basic needs of transportation. However, the overuse of fossil fuels is polluting the air and the environment. Clearly, they are the main causes of air pollution.

練習寫寫看 C

1.

We must all say "No" to drugs for a number of reasons. First, taking drugs is against the law. Those who break the law will never escape punishment. So, they may end up in prison or rehab (勒戒所). Second, taking drugs not only damages one's health but ruins one's life. Once a person is addicted to drugs, his or her physical and mental health begin to deteriorate. What's worse, since a drug addict needs a lot of money for the drugs, he or she is likely to commit crimes to get enough money.

In fact, the rates of criminal behavior, violence, and fatal accidents among drug users are much higher than those among the general population. This in turn costs the country a large amount of money every year. This is the money that could be used to benefit the public.

In a word, taking drugs is a foolish thing. If we don't say "No" to drugs now, there will be no bright future for us to say "Yes."

2.

There are many people that have had influence on me, but the one who has influenced me the most is my friend Jack. Jack is my neighbor, and he is now a college student. There are a number of reasons that I admire him.

First, he is very talented. He can play several musical instruments, including the guitar, the piano, and the drums. He likes to compose music and write songs, and he has written more than thirty songs. His songs are fun to listen to, and they have some deep meanings, too.

Second, Jack is always willing to help people. He spends most of his free time volunteering in the community. He helps children to develop an interest in music and teaches them how to play the guitar for free. Even though he spends so much time doing voluntary work, he is still able to do well academically.

Inspired by Jack, I have started learning to play the guitar. I've been even trying to compose music like he does. Also, I have decided to join a volunteer group. I want to help other people. Jack is my role model. I hope that someday I will be like him and have a positive influence on other people.

🖋 練習寫寫看 D

I

1. For instance/example; while

2. For one thing; Therefore; Besides/In addition/

Furthermore; Best of all

3. For one thing; For another; Besides/In addition/ Furthermore

II

1.

例子 1：In Samoa, a woman is not considered attractive unless she weighs more than 200 pounds.

例子 2：In Asian countries, women with fair skin are supposed more beautiful.

例子 3：In western countries, women prefer to have tanned skin and blonde hair.

2.

例子 1：Overweight people are more likely to suffer from diabetes (糖尿病) and heart disease.

例子 2：Obese people often have bad habits that make them less healthy. For example, they often eat a lot.

例子 3：According to medical research, extremely obese people die earlier than people of normal weight.

🖋 練習寫寫看 E

Life isn't always about saying yes to everything. Before we say yes, we have to think seriously about the consequences. If we promise someone to do something, we should keep the promise. Otherwise, we will lose credibility. In reality, sometimes saying no is the wise decision to make.

I remember one time that I said no to my friends. It was hard for me because I didn't use to say no to my friends. During that time, I had to practice every weekend since the school volleyball game was approaching. But one Sunday, my friends asked me to go to a birthday party with them. It was an afternoon party. That is, I would have to skip volleyball practice if I decided to go to the party. I thought about it for some time, but in the end, I said no to my friends. I told them I had to practice volleyball that day and that was something concerning the honor of my class. I was surprised that they didn't get angry. Instead, they respected my decision.

Through this experience, I learn it is not rude to say no to others when it is necessary. Sometimes, saying no is the right thing to do.

練習寫寫看 F

I

1.

原因 1：an unhealthy lifestyle

原因 2：lack of exercise

原因 3：eating disorder

2.

影響 1：health problems

影響 2：psychological problems

影響 3：social problems

3.

原因：1. for revenge

　　　2. for fun

　　　3. to boost one's ego

影響：1. low self-esteem

　　　2. depression

　　　3. suicide

II

1. because/as/since

2. because of/due to/on account of

3. therefore/thus/as a result/as a consequence/
   in consequence/consequently/for this reason

4. so

5. Therefore/Thus/As a result/
   As a consequence/In consequence/

Consequently/For this reason

練習寫寫看 G

1.

1. wildfires　野火	1. wildfires
2. ice sheet is melting 冰層融冰	2. ice sheet is melting
~~3. air pollution~~ 空氣汙染	4. floods and droughts
4. floods and droughts 水災和旱災	
~~5. animals and plants~~ ~~動物與植物~~	

2.

主題句：Climate change has already affected our planet in many serious ways.

影響 1：major wildfires

影響 2：the ice surrounding the North Pole and the South Pole has begun to melt

影響 3：great floods and droughts

3.

Climate change has already affected our planet in many serious ways. For one thing, unusually hot weather has caused major wildfires in the United States, Indonesia, and Australia. For another, the ice surrounding the North Pole and the South Pole has begun to melt, causing the earth's sea level to rise. If this continues, some big cities like London, New York, and Taipei might be underwater by the end of this century. Last, scientists think of all the recent great floods and droughts as evidence of severe climate change. Thus, it is essential that we take immediate action to deal with climate change before it is too late to save the earth.

練習寫寫看 H

1.

定義 1：Success is a feeling of pride and a sense of achievement.

定義 2：Some people think that those who make a lot of money are successful people.

定義 3：As for a student, success is about getting good grades.

2.

定義 1：A friend in need is a friend indeed. A true friend is ready to help without asking anything in return.

定義 2：A true friend shares both happiness and sorrow.

定義 3：A true friend will never betray you no matter what happens.

3.

定義 1：You have grown up because you become mature and responsible.

定義 2：Growing up means not making complaints without any reason.

定義 3：Growing up means showing concern for others.

練習寫寫看 I

1. In other words

2. For instance/example; In addition/Besides

3. That is to say; However/Nevertheless; For instance/example

練習寫寫看 J

I

1.

A fan is someone who likes something or someone very much. Take my brother, for example. He is a big fan of Taylor Swift. He not only has all of the singer's albums but also listens to her songs all the time. Besides, my brother follows her Facebook, IG, and Twitter. He even claims that he knows everything about Taylor Swift.

2.

A genius is someone who is born intelligent and learns much faster than others. Wolfgang Amadeus Mozart showed great musical ability from his earliest childhood. He learned to play keyboards when he was at the age of three. He composed music for the piano at the age of five, writing his first full symphony when he was just nine years old. He composed more than 600 works in his lifetime. He is among the most popular classical composers. Without doubt, his influence is profound on Western classical music.

II

Happiness is a feeling of being pleased and satisfied. With such a feeling, a person's mind is filled with comfort, peace, and love. This feeling has nothing to do with fame, power, wealth or social status.

Happiness is a feeling everyone can possess. It's a state of mind. Celebrities may be afraid of losing their fame and popularity. Rich people worry about their businesses going down. They may have trouble enjoying the feeling of true happiness. However, children jump for joy when they are given toys. A person has the sense of happiness when having a dinner with his or her family members. People enjoy the feeling of happiness when they see the beautiful scenery, listen to music, or receive calls from their good friends. Something simple and ordinary can be the source of true happiness.

All in all, happiness lies not in what we have but how we think. In a state of happiness, we

tend to look on the bright side, which makes us feel happier. Happiness can be contagious. Our happiness may pass on to others easily. Without doubt, happiness is what makes our lives worth living.

練習寫寫看 K

I

as follows; First (of all); When/While/As; As soon as; Last/Lastly/Finally

II

 There are times we have to hold a party such as birthdays, reunions, and other occasions for celebration. As a result, it is necessary to know how to plan a party.

 There are some steps to follow. First of all, you need to decide on who or how many you want to invite. Depending on the reason why the party is held, you may invite your family members, relatives, friends or classmates. Then, you need to decide when to hold the party. Generally speaking, weekends are better choices, since most people don't have to go to work or school.

 Next, you have to decide where to hold the party. If you decide to hold the party at a restaurant, you must be sure of the number of the attendants and make a reservation. To be efficient, you can first ask by telephone to get a rough idea. After these are settled down, you can start to send out the invitations. Some restaurants offer a free party-invitation system on their websites. In that case, you only have to type in the email addresses of your guests, and the system will send out the invitations to them automatically. Later, it will inform you about who has accepted your invitation and who hasn't.

 In fact, it is not difficult to plan a party. It only takes some time and effort to organize it.

練習寫寫看 L

I

1.

文式圖

1. convenient 2. more job opportunities 3. polluted air	places to live	1. inconvenient 2. less job opportunities 3. fresh air

2.

	Positive Thinkers	Negative Thinkers
特色 1	happy	unhappy
特色 2	optimistic, more confident	pessimistic, less confident
特色 3	the best	the worst
特色 4	lower risk of depression and heart disease	higher risk of depression and heart disease

II

1. like   2. Also
3. unlike   4. In spite of
5. Although   6. while
7. the same as   8. different from

練習寫寫看 M

整合式 (塊狀) 寫作法
項目 A：Living in a School Dormitory
特色 1：living expenses
特色 2：freedom and independence
項目 B：Living at Home
特色 1：living expenses

特色 2：freedom and independence

逐條式 (點狀) 寫作法

特色 1：living expenses
項目 A：Living in a School Dormitory
項目 B：Living at Home
特色 2：freedom and independence
項目 A：Living in a School Dormitory
項目 B：Living at Home

🖉 練習寫寫看 N

College graduates and high school graduates differ in the following ways. First, their ages are not the same. Generally speaking, college graduates are four to seven years older than high school graduates. The former are about 22, while the latter are around 18.

In addition, compared to college graduates, high school graduates tend to be more enthusiastic about graduation because it symbolizes their independence. Most parents allow high school graduates to study in other cities since they are no longer considered children. However, unlike high school graduates, college graduates need to decide whether to find a job or pursue further study. Therefore, college graduates are normally under more pressure.

So, based on these considerations, it seems that college graduates and high school graduates have little in common.

🖉 練習寫寫看 O

I

種類 1：learn by hearing (auditory learners)
種類 2：learn by seeing (visual learners)
種類 3：learn by doing (physical learners)

II

1. To begin with
2. Second
3. For example
4. Lastly

🖉 練習寫寫看 P

I

1. Verbal abuse may have the following three negative effects on the abused.
2. Regular exercise, calorie control, and surgery are three most effective ways to lose weight.

II

Without a doubt, if you are on a weight loss program, doing exercise, going on a diet or having a surgery can help you lose weight.

🖉 練習寫寫看 Q

1.
種類 1：renewable energy resources
種類 2：non-renewable energy resources
2.

We can classify energy resources into two types—renewable and non-renewable. Renewable energy resources are natural resources that cannot be used up. In other words, they can be renewed by nature within a short timescale (期限). Wind, water, and sunlight are examples of renewable energy resources. They are considered to be eco-friendly while being used to generate electricity.

Non-renewable resources, on the other hand, are in limited supplies and take a long time to form or refill. Thus, they are running out. Fossil fuels, coal, and natural gas fall into this category. Today, most of the electricity comes from power plants that burn fossil fuels, which releases greenhouse

gases and further causes global warming. In brief, the above is how energy resources are categorized.

練習寫寫看 R

1.

種類 1：physical bullying

種類 2：verbal bullying

種類 3：relational bullying

種類 4：cyberbullying

2.

Bullying, upsetting or hurting another person repeatedly, falls into four categories, namely physical bullying, verbal bullying, relational bullying, and cyberbullying.

To begin with, physical bullying involves hurting a person's body. It includes touching, kicking, hitting or pushing. The second type is verbal bullying, which has something to do with saying mean things such as teasing, calling names, insulting, and threatening, etc. Another category of bullying is relational bullying, which is designed to hurt someone's reputation or relationships. Spreading rumors about someone, embarrassing someone in public, and leaving someone out intentionally are examples of relational bullying. With the prevalence of social websites, more and more bullying occurs on the Internet. This kind of bullying is called cyberbullying. It involves imitating others, spreading rumors or excluding others online.

No matter what kind of bullying it is, it is not allowed to happen.

Unit 10

練習寫寫看 A

I

	收件人稱謂	結尾敬語
正式信件	Dear Sir: Dear Madam: To whom it may concern:	Sincerely, Sincerely yours, Respectfully,
非正式信件	Hi Jack, Dear sis, My dear friend,	Love, Your daughter, Best wishes,

II

Jack Hong

No. 101, Sec. 2, Kuang Fu Rd.,

Hsinchu City, Taiwan 30013

stamp

Ms. Amy Lin

San Min Book Co., Ltd.

2F., No. 386, Fuxing North Rd.,

Zhongshan Dist., Taipei City 10476

🖋 練習寫寫看 B

You are cordially invited to our class reunion

Who: Class 314 of 2017

When: July 3rd, 2019, 11:00 a.m.

Where: ABC café near our junior high school

Why: To meet old friends and catch up on
　　　what's new with everyone

RSVP by June 20th, 2019, to Dennis at 0933-888-666.

Come and reminisce (緬懷) with Class 314 of 2017.

🖋 練習寫寫看 C

June 25, 2019

Dear Aunt Carol,

　　How kind of you to give me a smartphone as my birthday gift! I was really excited when I received your gift. I had wanted a smartphone for a long time, but I never dreamed that I could get one so soon. Aunt Carol, thank you so much!

　　I used to envy my classmates who had smartphones. They could check information, chat, and exchange ideas online anytime. When they worked on English assignments, they could use the dictionary apps on their smartphones to look up new words. Now, I can do the same. It will help me a lot both in daily life and in my schoolwork. I promise to make good use of it.

　　It has been a long time since I visited you. I plan to pay you a visit. Will you be available next Sunday? Thank you once again for the wonderful gift.

　　　　　　　Your nephew,

　　　　　　　Nathan

🖋 練習寫寫看 D

Dec. 10, 2018

Dear Joseph,

　　Thank you for lending me your camera. I took it with me on the trip to Tokyo. I was shocked to find that the camera was gone when I arrived at the hostel I was going to stay in. I looked everywhere for it, but it was no use. I wondered if I had left the camera on the airplane. As a result, I called the lost-and-found at the airport, but they said nobody had turned in a camera. I'm so sorry about that, and I have felt bad over the past few days.

　　Joseph, let me buy you a new camera exactly the same as the one I lost. I'd like to treat you to dinner as well. Let me know your decision. Please forgive me for my carelessness and accept my apology.

　　　　　　　Regretfully,

　　　　　　　Helen

🖋 練習寫寫看 E

1.

Sep. 29, 2018

Dear Ken,

　　I need your advice. I don't know if I should bring a smartphone to school. You know I am an Internet addict. I am afraid that I cannot control myself and use the smartphone to play games in class. However, some teachers ask us to look for information by using smartphones. It seems I cannot do without it at school. What should I do? Can you give me some advice?

　　　　　　　Your friend,

　　　　　　　Wendy

2.

Sep. 30, 2018

Dear Wendy,

    I can understand you are caught in a dilemma now. This is a very tricky problem. A smartphone is indispensable as more and more teachers ask their students to look for information on the Internet, but many students cannot resist the temptation of using smartphones for fun in class. In my opinion, the question lies in you. If you are not determined to overcome your smartphone addiction, nobody can help you.

    My advice is that you clearly list your rules of smartphone usage. For example, never use your smartphone in class unless at the request of your teachers. Second, don't play mobile games all the time. Instead, you should set a time limit. Of course, you can add more rules to the list. As long as you obey the rules, you can benefit from the technology instead of allowing it to control your life.

    Hopefully, my advice can help solve your problem as soon as possible.

Your friend,

Ken

練習寫寫看 F

July 10, 2019

Dear Sir or Madam,

Yesterday I went to buy a polka-dot dress at the QQ department store in Kaohsiung City. However, when I arrived home and opened the bag, I found a stain right in the back of the dress. Then, I went back to the counter to make an exchange. To my surprise, the clerk told me that no refunds for that dress.

I really don't understand that there was no refund for that dress. First, I had the receipt with me when I went back to the store. Second, I demanded a refund instead of an exchange because that dress was out of stock. Third, I went to the store the same day I bought it.

I write this letter to request that you make up for this mistake. I would appreciate it if you could write or call me at 0986-000-000 at your convenience. I look forward to hearing from you soon.

Yours sincerely,

Jane Wang

Unit 11

練習寫寫看 A

1.

主題句：The line graph shows the population change in elders, children, and labor force from 1950 to 2060 in Taiwan.

2.

The percentage of the elderly steadily increased until 2015 when it started to have a steep rise to slightly over 40%. Though there was a slight increase from 1950 to 1960, the number of children born each year fell dramatically from above 40% to 10% since then. In 2015, there were more seniors than children for the first time in Taiwan's history. In contrast, the percentage of labor force reached a peak of around 75% in 2015. After that, it faced a steep slope, and it is expected to be lower than 50% by 2060.

3.

結論句：In conclusion, with the significant decrease of birth rate, more than 40 % of the population will be senior citizens, which results in a big drop of labor force and further slows Taiwan's economy.

練習寫寫看 B

The pie chart above shows how an average house uses electricity in the United Kingdom. More than half of the electricity is used for heating rooms and water. About eighteen percent of the electricity is consumed by ovens, kettles, and washing machines. The rest is equally divided into two parts. One is used in lighting, TVs, and radios, and the other is in the use of vacuum cleaners, food mixers, and electric tools.

Unlike the United Kingdom, Taiwan is very hot and humid. Since the climates in these two countries are totally different, how electricity is used differs as well. Dehumidifiers and air conditioners consume a large proportion of electricity in Taiwan. Other electric appliances such as TVs, refrigerators, and washing machines also consume much electricity. Besides, many families have several computers and they are used a lot in Taiwan. In this way, the electricity consumption by computers also plays a part.

Unit 12

練習寫寫看 A

O	C
R	A
E	D
O	B

練習寫寫看 B

1. in my opinion
2. what's more
3. Firstly
4. it was my belief that
5. As for me

練習寫寫看 C

I

題目 1：The Benefits of Riding a Bike to School

1. It's eco-friendly and economical.
2. Cycling is good for students' health.
3. It provides students more freedom outside of school.
4. Parents don't have to drive their children to and from school.

題目 2：Involvement in School Clubs

For:

1. It allows students to pursue their own interests.
2. Students have a chance to meet people with similar interests.
3. It helps students relieve stress.
4. Communication, cooperation, and other social skills are developed.

Against:

1. Students spend a lot of time joining school clubs.
2. They may find it difficult to strike a balance between school clubs and studies.
3. They end up getting bad grades.
4. They will waste money on school clubs and interests.

II

2, 3, 5

III

1.

O	Though social networks, such as Facebook, Twitter, etc., can enable millions of people to set up connections with their friends, I don't think it actually helps build up relationships among friends.
R	It makes people closer to someone they're far away from, but farther from someone they're close to.
E	A bunch of friends hang out together when all of them are caught up in their smartphones. They constantly check out the latest updates on Facebook instead of having a talk with their friends.
R	People sometimes post hateful messages on Facebook in the heat of anger when they have problems with their friends.
E	Their relationship might never be what it used to be.
O	Social networks make people grow further apart instead of bringing them together.

Though social networks, such as Facebook, Twitter, etc., can enable millions of people to set up connections with their friends, I don't think it actually helps build up relationships among friends. It makes people closer to someone they're far away from, but farther from someone they're close to. For example, a bunch of friends hang out together when all of them are caught up in their smartphones. They constantly check out the latest updates on Facebook instead of having a talk with their friends.

Moreover, people sometimes post hateful messages on Facebook in the heat of anger when they have problems with their friends. Even though they regret their doings at once, it is too late because the post might be viewed and possibly shared by a number of common friends. As a result, their relationship might never be what it used to be.

In short, I believe that social networks make people grow further apart instead of bringing them together.

IV

For:

Though some people argue that joining a school club takes a lot of time, it is a good idea for high school students because they have reached a stage in their lives where their own interests begin to develop.

There are many advantages of belonging to a school club. For one thing, students may discover something they are really interested in outside the regular curriculum. There are clubs for almost every kind of activity, such as photography clubs, bands, choirs, and street dance groups. There are clubs devoted to drama, broadcasting, skating, swimming, and movie studies. Of course, there are clubs for every kind of ball games.

A club is also a place where students can develop their abilities in the specific area. Take my brother, for example. After he joined the guitar club, he not only learned to play the guitar, but also gained a better appreciation for listening to music.

Last but not least, a club is a place to make new friends. Clubs and the activities give students from different classes a chance to meet and talk about their common interests.

Without doubt, joining a school club can offer students a way to pursue their own interests, improve communication skills, and develop their full potential.

Against:

Though some people claim that joining school clubs can help students pursue their own interests, I think that it is not good for them because it is time-consuming and money-consuming.

First, the disadvantage of joining school clubs is time-consuming. Since students spend a lot of time on club activities, they may not have enough time to do their homework or review lessons. They may find it difficult to strike a balance between school clubs and studies, and they end up getting bad grades.

Besides, I think joining school clubs is money-consuming. Students may have to spend money on school clubs. They also waste a lot of money on their interests because they may try many different things.

All in all, I prefer not to join school clubs because students with bad time and money management might mess up their lives and studies. As for me, I think a student's top priority is to focus on studies.

作文100隨身讀

三民英語編輯小組　彙整
三民／東大英文教材主編　車畇庭　審定

作文100，
大考英文作文的搶分祕笈！

★ 一手掌握，作文必勝：
　口袋書型式，大小適中，讓你隨時隨地都能加強作文。
★ 分類彙整，篇篇實用：
　全書共100篇作文範例，共分為3大部分：看圖寫作、
　信函寫作和主題寫作。
★ 取材廣泛，主題豐富：
　不僅蒐羅近年學測、指考及各校模擬考試作文題目，還
　提供各式主題範文。
★ 單字片語，學以致用：
　詳列重要單字片語，讓你一邊學作文，一邊累積字彙。
★ 寫作技巧，指點迷津：
　提供精闢的寫作建議，教你如何下筆，讓你考試臨場發
　揮自如。

題本與解答本不分售
14-80084G